MAYBE SHE'LL STAY

ALSO BY ROBYN LUCAS

Paper Doll Lina

MAYBE SHE'LL STAY

a novel

ROBYN LUCAS

LAKE UNION
PUBLISHING

Published by Lake Union Publishing, Seattle

www.apub.com

Amazon, the Amazon logo, and Lake Union Publishing are trademarks of Amazon.com, Inc., or its affiliates.

ISBN-13: 9781542033657 (paperback)
ISBN-13: 9781542033640 (digital)

Cover design by Adrienne Krogh
Cover illustration by Sylvia Pericles

Printed in the United States of America

For everyone who has had to live under the cloud of a narcissistic parent: you are loved.
To Charlie and Hannah, my heartbeats
&
To Jae, all the adventures with you

CHAPTER 1

It's not technically a walk of shame if you're driving back home, right?

Nancy Jewel tried to convince herself of that one last time before slipping back into her date-night dress. It'd met all her requirements the night before: short, to show off her gloriously long, tanned legs; cerulean, her favorite color, with a dark-greenish sheen that shimmered in different lighting; and perfectly tailored to her busty figure, creating the illusion of a waistline and a backside. She liked to think of it as her mermaid dress, luring men in with a swish of her hips until they gave her what she wanted. Now it was nothing more than a reminder that she'd seriously messed up.

Maybe that was her problem this morning. She'd gotten just what she'd wanted out of Keith—a gloriously passionate night—but she'd been sloppy enough to fall asleep instead of leaving shortly afterward like she always had. She'd felt all romantic after spending the weekend at his youngest sister's rustic wedding. It had been in an old barn, illuminated by candlelight and lanterns, their glow warm against the cool fall night. The never-ending champagne had sedated her sensibilities.

She had only meant to pacify Keith with a few minutes of cuddling. Instead, she had been more tired than she'd estimated and was now going to miss a coffee date with her best friend and possibly be late for her first class of the week.

Keith's house was a pin-drop silent, ultramodern monstrosity of glass and steel in a high-end suburb nestled in the farthest corner of Athens, Georgia. She'd visited only a handful of times—all late-night rendezvous—and never considered how ridiculously bright and suspiciously clean his place was until witnessing it in the late-morning sunlight. His massive bedroom took up half of the first floor, and if she'd had time or cared more, she would have poked around. Keith, on the other hand, had been gone when she'd woken moments earlier. His side of the bed cold, the crumpled pillow and sheets the only evidence he'd been there.

Nancy wondered if she should've felt something more than *meh* when she'd noticed his absence, but it was all she could muster. His purpose had been served, and now it was past time for her to leave. It wasn't like they were *dating* dating or anything, and they sure as hell weren't married—they'd already tried that seventeen years ago. Their marriage had lasted less than six months, a few weeks longer than their passion had burned, but they'd kept in touch throughout the years, eventually finding each other's beds every now and then when they weren't with other people.

This latest frienifit period with Keith had been going on since Halloween, when she'd drunk-dialed him on a whim. He'd met her for dinner the very next day. It worked for her. It seemed to work for him as well, or so she thought, unsure of what his absence meant. Was he an early-morning runner? Did he have a meeting or have to be in for work? She vaguely remembered something about him now being a CrossFit fanatic. His lean forty-five-year-old body definitely showed it, so maybe he'd left for a session. Either way, she'd text him after her class to make sure they were good.

As she stumbled onto the cold marble bathroom floor, she heard a door close, followed by footsteps and rustling. It was a little relieving knowing he'd returned. She wasn't sure why and didn't really have the desire to unpack it. She was simply glad he had and continued on with her bathroom necessities.

After several minutes, a kettle whistled, followed by a whir of crunching and grinding. The glorious rich, earthy smell of coffee followed. *Pour-over?* She hadn't quite pegged him as a pour-over type of guy, but it would be no surprise. He proudly sported a man bun and well-groomed beard. It didn't take Sherlock Holmes–level sleuthing to put two and two together when Keith had shown up to their most recent reacquaintance date in a bespoke suit, complete with matching vest and pocket square.

"Morning!" Keith said a little too happily from the bathroom doorway, two mugs of coffee in his hands.

"Um, morning." Nancy frowned at the black coffee. Only serial killers drank black coffee.

He gently shoved a mug into her hands. "I visit this small family farm in Colombia every quarter. Their fresh beans are top tier, and I roast them myself. There's a technique, you know?" Keith took a long sip of coffee, the heat leaving little foggy patches on his thin, round glasses. He slid them back up his nose as he did some weird thing with his mouth that reminded her of a fine-wine sommelier. Nancy tried everything to keep from bursting out in laughter.

He seemed to wait for her to take a sip, raising his brows slightly. "You should be here on roasting day. This place smells like heaven."

Roasting day? Nancy humored him, bringing the cup to her lips and grimacing. It tasted like dirty water and regret.

"It's bold, but if you let it stay in your mouth a little longer, you'll pick up the sweet, almost caramel hints." He took another mouthful. *"Mmm."*

"Thanks a lot. You really didn't have to. I didn't mean to stay over."

"I'm glad you did. Forgot how incredibly sexy you are in the first morning light." He caressed her cheek with his thumb and went in for a kiss with his gross coffee breath.

Definitely tastes like regret, Nancy thought. "I should probably get going." She placed her cup on the bathroom sink. Some dark-brown liquid dribbled down the side of the mug and pooled onto the white marble surface. She went to wipe it off.

"I'll get that. Don't worry," Keith said, reaching for her hand. "I, um . . . I got us some breakfast. Pancakes because you're a no-nonsense, straight-to-the-point sort of person."

"Is that what a pancake person is?" Nancy asked with discomfort at the possible larger significance. *Pancakes?*

"Well, yeah. There are three types of people in the world: waffle people, pancake people, and heathens."

Nancy laughed, hoping he'd join, but there was zero indication of humor or sarcasm in his narrow green eyes.

"No, really. Think about it. Waffle people are carefree and spontaneous. They like options and take chances. Pancake people know what they want and go after it. Decisive. Diligent." He drank more coffee. "And frankly, I don't trust people who don't like pancakes or waffles. Says a lot about their character."

Nancy couldn't believe this fully grown man before her had based his entire existence on whether people liked pancakes or waffles. Now she realized why their marriage had never worked out and why she could tolerate him in only small, random doses. She'd met her fair share of oddballs, but he might just take the cake . . . or pancake.

Keith's finger trailed down her arm to her hand, where he held it, then brought it to his lips. "Besides, I was thinking we could have breakfast and a little after-breakfast treat. I took the day off just to be here with you."

The inkling of discomfort Nancy had felt earlier sprouted into full-on panic as her fears were confirmed. Pancakes after several hookups meant one thing: a serious relationship. Keith wanted more from her.

More . . .

More of her time. More of her space. More of her patience. More of her peace of mind. More of her heart and her soul. More of her identity. More of her until she had nothing left. She'd already been through relationships—romantic, familial, and platonic—where she'd given and given and at the end didn't recognize herself. She'd already tried. First with her mom, then with her older brother, Jeff, and countless "friends," and of course with all her husbands, fiancés, and boyfriends.

More was something she would never give to anyone again. Frienifits and hookups worked best for Nancy. Zero expectations. Zero commitments. Zero drama. It was the only way she wanted to be with someone romantically. "Hey, Keith." She shrugged away from his grasp and patted his shoulder. "You're totally my favorite ex-husband, and you know how I feel about you."

"Yeah, last night was—"

"Last night." She sidestepped around him, needing to find the rest of her stuff and bounce. "Last night was nice."

A smile spread across his face. He fingered the curled sides of his groomed mustache cartoonishly. "I'm so glad we're finally on the same page. I want—"

"Keith." Nancy used her professor voice to take charge of the situation. "This is cool and all." She hurried across Keith's room, carefully stepping over the clothing and blankets strewn here and there until she found her shoes and her cell phone. She'd missed several calls: one from her best friend, Lina; one from an unfamiliar number; and one from Beckett, her department head. She double-checked the time and grumbled. Ugh, she'd missed her two meetings this morning. Lina had probably called out of concern, whereas Beckett had most likely called to gloat and remind Nancy she'd lost the bet they'd made Friday before leaving for the weekend. Twenty bucks if the other was late that Monday morning. Both had been chronically late since the beginning of the semester, but Nancy had been sure she'd win the twenty bucks, since Beckett had always been later.

Nancy pinched the bridge of her nose. This was not how her Monday was supposed to go. She was supposed to be strolling into the café to meet Lina for coffee and give her a mouthful of rich gossip, then gloating in her office as Beckett walked in with a crisp twenty-dollar bill in hand and a look of defeat. She liked her life uncomplicated and preferred the freedom that accompanied being single. There was no way she'd let Keith box her in again. She glanced over at him, annoyance at the situation growing with each breath. "Keith, I thought we had an understanding."

He held his mug close to his chest like it was his favorite toy. "I was under the impression that this was becoming more than just a few get-togethers. We've been seeing a whole hell of a lot of each other recently."

"It's only been two weeks." Nancy needed to be clear. Keith was nice enough, and their handful of hookups scratched all her itches and left her pleased, but that was all it was ever going to be. The idea of being with Keith in that way again was as uncomfortable as the five-inch stilettos she was now fastening. The thin, textured straps nipped at her ankles and bit into the tops of her feet when she stood. That was how being locked into a relationship made her feel: shackled and hobbled, like she could never truly be herself 100 percent in any relationship. Her entire life had proved that.

"I'm going to be late for class. I'll call you later, and we can talk about this, okay?" she said after a moment.

"Not this again, Nance."

"Come on. You know we do this dance every few years or so. It's what we do."

"What if I want us to do something else?"

"What if I'm fine with how we are now?"

Keith sighed. "I took you to my sister's wedding. We did wedding stuff all weekend. You were *my* Nance again. We were *us* again. I really thought—"

Nancy held up a hand. "Keith, I'm going to stop you there. I went because you asked and I didn't have plans. I told you this. I've been very up front about everything." The tension pinching Keith's face made the hair on Nancy's arms prickle with familiarity.

"You were with my sisters practically all weekend. That didn't mean anything to you?"

Nancy started toward the bedroom door to make a quick escape.

"Hold on for a sec. Can't we talk this out?" He grabbed her arm.

She shrugged away from him. "What do you think you're doing?"

"I just want to talk this out."

"There's nothing more to say. I don't want a relationship. I was never looking for one. I made that crystal clear. You got all up in your feelings."

Keith's gaze hardened just then. "That's the problem with you. Always thinking about yourself. Using people because you can. I was the only one who tried when we were married."

Nancy gawked at him like he'd suddenly sprouted three heads. *Not this nonsense again.* "You've gotta be kidding. That was almost twenty years ago, and we were so young and naive."

"And you haven't changed one bit." Keith pulled his lips to the side, studying her. "I thought maybe we'd end up back together after your other two marriages, but no. Then there were all the different guys, and who was right there after all of them?" He pointed at himself. "I'm the last one standing, Nancy baby."

"It's not like you've been a saint the last twenty years."

"But I haven't married any of them. We keep coming back to each other. It's like some twisted magnetic pull. We need each other."

"It's called codependence." Nancy sighed, knowing she needed to finally end things with Keith.

"Codependence." He mocked her. "You're going to get old and die alone if you don't let someone love you."

His words nipped and stung, but she knew the drill. Keith was fine as long as he got his way, but he could be awful and spiteful when he didn't. Their season had passed, and this was her sign to move on—maybe for good this time. "I've heard enough." And she had. "Keith, I guess I reached out for the human contact and stayed because of the wedding nostalgia." She waved her hand at him dismissively. "Maybe I haven't changed, but look at you. You've reinvented yourself more times than Madonna." She considered brushing it all off as a joke, knowing how harsh she could be. "Know wh—"

"So bitter all the time." Keith scowled at her. "You can be such a bi—"

"Enough." It was past time for him to feel her bite. "Getting to know the various versions of you throughout all these years has been exhausting." She started down the hallway to the front door. "Exhausting."

"You'll hit me up when you're horny, because you know I'm the only one who knows what you like. I'm pretty sure my neighbors heard."

Nancy turned slightly without missing a beat. "Honey, you need to know when a woman is faking. There's a huge difference between 'ohmigod, yes' and 'over, right there, a little more, not there, harder.' Felt like I was giving directions to a tourist." And with that, Nancy Jewel strutted out the front door, forcing herself not to turn around and take it all back.

CHAPTER 2

It was a relief to have her car at Keith's house so she could make a proper exit. Date or no date, she always made sure to drive. Being stranded or having to rely on an Uber or Lyft was never an option. With her luck with men, she needed the ability to leave at a moment's notice.

You're going to get old and die alone if you don't let someone love you. It was her biggest fear and insecurity. To hear it spill from Keith's mouth both enraged and tore at her. If he was her favorite ex, what did that say about the rest of them—about her, besides solidifying her position on commitment? Giving herself to someone simply wasn't for her. His words echoed in her head as she climbed into her Range Rover, her hands trembling as she fumbled with her keys.

It took her a few minutes to get settled behind the wheel as she imagined how destructive Keith's words could've been if she'd actually loved him. She'd never give that ability to another person, ever. Shaking it all off, she remembered to call Lina, hoping to catch her at a boring part of the campus tour. Her bestie always knew what to say to make her feel better.

Nancy immediately dialed the number.

Lina picked up on the first ring. "You're so late. We couldn't wait any longer. Mimi didn't want to miss the residence hall part."

"I know. Forgive me?" Nancy could use all the girl time with the one person she trusted more than anyone in this world. The one person who had her back no matter what. The one person who understood and called her on her bullshit . . . the one out of the two of them who still kept in touch with Ashish. "Dinner tonight?" Nancy asked, suddenly thinking about Ashish. He'd started out as Nancy's divorce attorney, then Lina's divorce attorney turned family friend, and had become Nancy's previous frienifit. She ignored the whisper of sadness when she thought of him and continued her conversation with Lina.

"In Atlanta, right?"

"Um, sure."

"Nance, did you forget about Danny's honor society award thing tonight? Please tell me you remember."

"Of course I remember." Of course she had *not* remembered. She wanted to kick herself for forgetting something so major. She'd forgotten to add it to her calendar—the archaic handwritten daily planner she'd reordered every year for the last ten years. Its familiar lines were an old friend. Ashish had urged her to evolve like the rest of the modern world by using the calendar app on her phone, but technology and Nancy didn't mix. Nancy knew enough to shop online, check email, and work a few dating apps. It was all she cared to put her energy into. It wasn't like she'd ever fall for those "foreign lottery win" or "surprise IRS refund due to an error on their part" email scams.

With the hours she spent on her laptop researching, updating her lectures, inputting grades, and grading papers, there was something satisfying about jotting down dates and times, something physical and tangible. To look forward to. To remember afterward. Every date. Every time. Birthdays, anniversaries, weddings, appointments, meetings. She reveled in how simple her life seemed cataloged within the neat boxes and defined lines.

Honor society. Nancy beamed as if Lina's son were her very own kid. It was a bittersweet feeling—excited that the boy whose diaper she used to change was now being recognized at his high school but also sad to realize he was growing up and there was no going back. She'd noticed that bittersweetness more and more recently as she witnessed her various friends' and coworkers' kids graduating from high school and college. She was helpless to do anything about it while also very much hopeful for their futures.

"Nance, you're still coming tonight, right?" Lina asked.

"Definitely. Won't miss it for the world."

"Danny's going to be thrilled. The address is in the calendar-invite email." Lina paused. "Never mind. I'll text it to you." There was a mix of annoyance and jesting in her voice. "Shall I also send the horse and buggy?"

They both laughed. It was music to Nancy's ears, hearing Lina's soprano trill-and-snort of a laugh. Nancy relished in treating her friend to one more moment of happiness. One more day of good after Lina's scare over a year and a half ago, when Lina's now ex-husband had attacked her, choking her so badly he'd nearly killed her. Actually, he *had* killed her. She'd had to be resuscitated and had been hospitalized for several weeks while Nancy and Ashish helped with the kids.

Nancy had sworn to do whatever she needed to give Lina nothing but sunshine and rainbows. "I'll see you tonight. Dinner's my treat. Wherever Danny wants."

"And you can tell me all about why you missed our coffee date this morning."

"Girl, you wouldn't believe the drama."

"Try me." Lina told someone she'd be right there. "Hey, I better go before I lose Mimi and the group. But Nance, there's—"

"Go, go, go. We'll talk later." Nancy ended the call, wondering where they were on the campus tour and wishing she could end classes early to meet up with them. Her fingers itched to write Danny's big night into her planner when she thought about the rest of her day, but it was on her desk at home, and she was in her car headed straight to class to keep from having to cancel it. How had she forgotten to add such a major event? She chewed on her question, thinking back through the past few months. Her gut gnarled when it hit her—Lina had told her about it shortly after her nonrelationship with Ashish had imploded.

It had been early September, and despite living in Athens, Georgia, and teaching college classes at the University of Georgia, Nancy had spent the weekend in Atlanta with Lina and the kids. They'd all been at brunch to celebrate the beginning of the school year when she'd spotted Ashish. She hadn't wanted to let him know she'd still been hurting and missing him since he'd called it off weeks prior, so she put on her brightest smile and most confident walk as she strutted out of the restaurant. He hadn't even bothered to text her afterward. A dull ache pulsed in the center of her rib cage where her heart should've been, but it had shriveled up a long time ago.

By the time Nancy claimed her marked parking space at the university, her melancholy had grown and mutated into grumpiness. Ashish had hurt her. Keith had hurt her. And now who knew what idiot would be next in her joke of a love life.

Love life.

Nancy scoffed at the idea of love. Having a PhD in psychology with an emphasis in neuroscience, three gloriously failed marriages, and a ridiculous amount of matches and pairings on her assortment of dating apps, Nancy knew more than anyone that love wasn't real. The concept of there being a match for everyone in the world was as impossible as an honest politician. The butterflies and heart palpitations most people felt for their loved ones were nothing short of a chemical cocktail of hormones and pheromones. Some cocktails were cosmopolitans, some were Molotov.

That brief idea annoyed Nancy even more than the fact that she had to go directly to class in her sexy mermaid dress instead of returning to her house to shower and change into proper attire. Her dress felt tighter and seemed shinier than it had when she'd slipped it on earlier. It felt like her personal neon sign that read WALK OF SHAME.

Thankfully, she'd found her wool peacoat buried under random junk in her back seat. Fastening several buttons on the coat made her look a little more acceptable. It was knee length and a soft orangish-yellow shade that'd reminded her of a sunset in Aruba. She'd purchased it on clearance at 90 percent off but hadn't had the heart to wear it more than once after one of her Tinder hookups told her he'd saved her contact information as "Puke Jacket Chick" because the color reminded him of vomit.

Once inside the psychology department building, Nancy stuffed her hands into her pockets and slinked down the hallway. Her first class was on the main floor, so she'd have to pass Beckett's office to get there, and her boss's gloating over the lost bet was the last thing she needed this morning. "Ha!"

Nancy hung her head in shame. Reluctantly, she fished in her purse for the twenty-dollar bill she owed her department chair.

Beckett leaned in their office doorway, beaming. "This is gold. Pure gold."

"Just take the money and go back to work. Nothing to see here."

"With the smack you said last week?" They stroked their shadow of a beard. "What did you say again? Time was as foreign a concept as my fashion sense." They gestured to their new outfit, making a show of their dark, tailored jeans, checkered shirt, and camel corduroy jacket. It all matched and fit them like a glove.

"Someone went shopping." Nancy pursed her lips, impressed. "Looking good, I'll give you that. Here." She forked over the cash. "But don't pretend like I was the only one trash-talking. You had a little bite too. It's what we do. It's how we get along."

Beckett shrugged. "Guess so."

"But I do have to say, dayum, Beck. If I knew you could wear something other than your grandparents' clothes, I would've messed with you sooner." Nancy smirked at her dig. "Holy wow!"

"Yeah?" Beckett asked timidly, fingering the buttons on their jacket.

Nancy patted their shoulder. "How much did you lose? Twenty pounds?"

"Sixty-five."

Nancy already knew Beckett's true weight loss; she just wanted to hear them say it aloud. She wanted them to acknowledge how far they'd come, especially with everything they'd been through. Early in Nancy's tenure, Beckett had suffered a mild stroke that landed them in the hospital and subsequently an outpatient facility for several weeks. They'd had to relearn everything.

Shortly after Beckett's stroke, Nancy had gotten wind of the university's plan to replace Beckett with a new department head. Upset at the possibility of losing a great boss and pissed that the university would do something so backhanded, she'd spearheaded a "Keep Beck's Head" campaign to keep Beckett as the psychology department head through their recovery and beyond. It had gone viral within the student body, gaining so much attention it'd landed Beckett on the front page of the *Athens Journal* as well as a few spots on the local news. Beckett had later confessed to Nancy that it'd been what they'd focused on throughout their recovery.

"Hey, I'm proud of you. So proud of you. Let me know if you want some company next time you're shopping," Nancy said and meant it.

Beckett's lower lip trembled as the moment lingered between them, in all the unsaid words a knowing that far surpassed Beckett's weight loss. Beckett sniffled. "Only if you're buying." They elbowed Nancy. "Enough with the feelings. I don't even like you that much. You're late for your Psych 422. Told them to give you fifteen minutes; then they could leave."

"You didn't." Nancy started down the hall.

"They're probably gone by now." Beckett snickered.

"Your shoes don't match," Nancy called over her shoulder, grinning at their back-and-forth. She considered turning around to stick her tongue out and say something about Beckett's hair, but she knew that would open her up for Beck to lob criticism at her stupid dress.

Nancy stormed farther down the hall and into her lecture hall, her stilettos clacking against the epoxy floors just as students were stirring to leave. "Class is not canceled." She adjusted her dress, hoping it would look longer. Less club, more library. "Thank you for waiting. Please take your seats." She caught several eye rolls and sighs. "Save the energy for your papers and pull up the chapter notes for this section." With that, she launched into her lecture without missing another beat.

Sometime later, Nancy's phone rang midway through explaining the classification of mental illness.

"Ugh, another call," a high-pitched, nasal voice echoed through the lecture hall. Nancy scrambled at the sound of her obnoxious ringtone, digging furiously through her purse as students chortled. It was another unknown phone number. *Jeez, spammers are busy this morning,* she thought, then quickly shifted back into professor mode for the remainder of her class time. It was rinse and repeat for two more class periods.

By the end of her final period, she reminded her students that their papers were due before Thanksgiving break in another two weeks. Several grumbles rose, music to her ears. She hadn't gone into teaching to make friends or people-please. She was there to make sure her students learned, and writing papers was one way to verify they'd done just that.

The majority of her class filed out immediately after dismissal. A handful stayed behind, crowding around her in a sloppy line of sorts. Nancy assessed the line, roughly estimating how to best triage the students according to their current grades. Pinching the bridge of her nose, she prepared herself to be peppered with questions. The first few kids asked about the paper. A few needed clarification on some of her lecture points. The next several offered various excuses about why they'd been failing her class thus far. The effort to pretend to care grated on her as much as dealing with Keith had. It wasn't like she didn't enjoy teaching or being around her students—she loved teaching more than anything and felt like her students kept her young. But in that moment, all she wanted to do was take a hot shower, change, and somehow restart her day.

Nancy slightly perched on her desk, crossing her legs at the ankles while dealing with the last of her students. She exhaled slowly as the final student turned to leave, satisfied with Nancy's response about today's lecture. Nancy mentally ran through the day's tasks, ticking them off one by one until she'd whittled her list to five things:

1. Go home.
2. Take shower.
3. Nap.
4. Make it to Danny's event.
5. Go home to sleep in my own bed.

Giddiness trilled through her at the thought of leaving campus, but when she glanced up at the lecture hall doorway, Jeremy Pressley filled it. Nancy wanted to kick herself for not immediately bolting once class had finished. Pulling herself back together, she motioned for him to come in and braced herself for excuses and/or pleas. It took five whole seconds before the excuses began to tumble out of Jeremy's mouth. He'd missed multiple classes, four assignments, one project, and two quizzes and was now begging for more time on the final paper.

"But Professor Jewel, my roommate had to—"

"You've had the syllabus since September."

"Come on. All I need is an extra week or two," he whined and pouted.

"I won't accept late work."

"It technically won't be late if we establish a new due date just for me."

She'd taught his type before—hell, she'd been engaged to his type before when she'd been a college student so many years ago. During her junior year at UGA, Nancy had been wildly in love with a political science major named Hudson. He'd treated her like a princess, spoiled her with all his attention, indulged her. He'd proposed to her at his family home when they'd visited Rhode Island over summer break with plans to marry shortly after they'd graduated. Everything had seemed so perfect until Nancy had asked him to push the wedding off until she finished her master's degree.

Hudson wouldn't hear of it because his mother had already started the wedding planning at their country club, so Nancy had broken it off right before the start of their senior year, hoping to show him how serious she'd been. Hudson's family had been so offended at her slight, and since his father had been both a trustee and a powerful alumnus, all Nancy's scholarships had been revoked.

With another peek at Jeremy, Nancy reminded herself he was certainly not Hudson, and people like him no longer had any power over her future. Stifling a yawn, she promised herself an obnoxious glass of wine much later tonight. She was totally due one. "It's my final answer on the matter."

"I need this class to graduate," Jeremy said, then held up his phone and shot a confident smile into the camera for a selfie. With a quick peek at his screen, Nancy's ears reddened when she read the caption across his Snapchat photo: "Cabo bound, biotches!"

"So that's a yes, right?" he asked, still focusing on his phone.

"No. You should've planned better. I'm not responsible for you graduating. That's on you." *Maybe I'll have two glasses of red and a cupcake.*

"I'll do anything." Jeremy lowered his eyes to her cleavage. "Anything."

Her skin rose with gooseflesh, prickly armor against his implication. She pulled her coat closed, folding her arms across her chest. "I think it's time for you to go."

"I've seen you checking me out," he said just loud enough for her to hear. He smelled like argyle, Daddy's money, and entitlement. "I've heard the rumors."

Surprise and discomfort were now turning into anger. She couldn't believe the little jerk was sexually harassing her so boldly. For the second time that morning, rage surged through Nancy's veins, hot and furious. "Leave or I will fail you right here, right now." She narrowed her eyes, daring him to say another word and prepared to reach for the pepper spray inside her purse. Professor or not, she'd take every precaution necessary to protect herself.

Jeremy hesitated, testing Nancy, then scowled and stormed out of the lecture hall, mumbling. There'd be repercussions. Nancy mentally braced herself, remembering what had happened with Hudson and how she'd lost her scholarships so many years ago. Kids like Jeremy didn't take losing easily. She jotted down a reminder to double-check his grades and make copies of everything he'd submitted, just in case it came down to something stupid.

"Um, excuse me, Professor Jewel," a small voice peeped from across the room. It belonged to Elysse Mason, a student in her early twenties with mousy dark-brown hair and a sadness Nancy could never put a finger on.

"I didn't see you there." Nancy calmed herself, exhaling. *One last student.*

Elysse picked at her cuticles. "I was wondering how my grade would be affected if I didn't finish the paper."

She'd said it so softly Nancy had to piece it together. "The paper everyone has known about since September seems to be a common topic today. What's your excuse?"

Tears welled in Elysse's round, dark-brown eyes, and for a brief glimmer, they felt familiar to Nancy.

"I'm . . . I'm having a hard time with childcare right now."

It was then Nancy noticed the heavy dark circles Elysse had tried to hide beneath mottled patches of concealer. "I didn't know you had kids."

She nodded slightly and looked like she'd fall down if Nancy blew on her. "He's almost one."

"Well, I'm sorry, but the paper counts for a third of your grade, and there's nothing I can do about the deadline. It's a hard one."

"Okay," she sniffled, deflating even more. "I understand."

As Elysse turned to leave, something warmed in Nancy's chest, and she blurted out, "But I may offer extra credit to all classes on the final." Her one good deed for the day was done, and now she was free to have a long nap before driving to Atlanta to meet up with Lina.

CHAPTER 3

For the fourth time that day, Nancy had to decline an unknown number. She had enough car insurance. She didn't need an extension on her car warranty, and she damn well didn't owe the IRS anything. Yet it seemed as though her phone wouldn't stop ringing with nonsensical spammers.

The annoyance she'd felt earlier that day had only grown, and she had half a mind to release that annoyance the next time she received another spam call. *They'd deserve it, at least,* Nancy thought, imagining how creative she could get with her use of curse words. Glancing at her phone, she hoped they'd call again just then, but the only noise was the car's heater and the engine's low hum as she sped down the highway, chasing the last rays of sunlight.

Back to Atlanta.

It should be a song, she thought. Smirking, she turned on her radio, surprised to find an Adele song playing. It made her think of what her own lyrics would be if she had to sing about Atlanta and heartbreak.

"Going back to Atlanta, again. Again. Again," she started. "If I see him, him, him. I'll need more than gin, gin, gin."

She bellowed out the words all sultry and sad in her very best Adele voice. Waving her hands all around as she really got into it. "If I see him, him, him." Little by little, sadness crept in at the thought of running into *him*. Into Ashish. It wasn't like they'd broken up or anything. They hadn't officially dated. That had been the pressure point throughout their time together. Despite not seeing other people, spending the weekends together—visiting Ashish in Atlanta or him taking the two-hour drive to Athens—and FaceTiming every night until they were ready to fall asleep, Nancy had refused to define what they'd had.

She hadn't been his girlfriend, and he hadn't been her boyfriend. She hadn't wanted a boyfriend. After a year of dancing around the subject and an epic trip to Aruba together, Ashish wanted the official commitment. He'd wanted them to start thinking about a future together. He'd wanted her to consider moving to Atlanta or for him to move to Athens. He'd wanted *more*. She'd made all the excuses. She'd done the marriage thing—she'd done it three damn times, and they'd all been disastrous. She hadn't wanted her thing with Ashish to implode like every other relationship she'd had . . . and yet it still had.

To the sad music filling her car, Nancy wondered what she would do if she saw him again. How would she act? What would she say? Had he moved on? Was he with the chick she'd seen him at brunch with back in September? Had she missed out?

"Screw you, Adele," Nancy said, then played her nineties rap playlist, turning the volume up until she felt the bass thump in her spine. The music swallowed her whole. The world became hers and Nas's, and she talked about sex with Salt-N-Pepa, and after twenty minutes, she was fully transformed for the rest of her drive.

Humming and buzzing on happy-song fumes hours later, Nancy bounded into Danny's high school. She made her way through the maze of painted concrete hallways. The scent of pine fought with decades of pubescent funk. It smelled like every high school she'd ever visited and would make the perfect official high school candle scent: Funky Forest.

"Hey, Nancy," Noah, Lina's boyfriend, called out as he ran to catch up with her. They weren't quite late, but the hallways were empty, and

Nancy could hear the buzz of people from the cafeteria a few feet ahead of them.

While Noah had been dating Lina for the last year or so, Nancy still fangirled a little over the fact that he wasn't just a regular guy. He was Noah Attoh, the famous actor from the Vengeance superhero movie franchise. Lina had met him on the set of a national talk show she'd visited with her kids, Mimi and Danny, after the kids had created a website that'd gone viral. Lina and Noah had become fast friends as she'd planned a safe escape from her abusive husband.

Unfortunately, Lina's ex-husband's abuse had escalated from coercive control, financial abuse, and verbal abuse into physical violence. Lina's attack had been captured by a paparazzo who'd gotten wind of Lina's friendship with Noah. The photos had been splashed on countless gossip websites and news shows while she'd been recovering in a hospital bed. After Lina had been in a controlling and abusive marriage to a narcissist for almost twenty years, Noah was like fresh mountain air to her.

Noah and Lina were cosmos in Nancy's chemical cocktail theory. Sweet, simple, and uncomplicated, but still gave you a good buzz. Nancy genuinely rooted for them to work out, despite not really believing in relationships. She stopped just short of the cafeteria. "Hey, how's it going? How's my girl been?"

A blush ran across Noah's face, and his eyes twinkled a little. "She's wonderful. It's going really well."

Nancy wanted to vomit at the way he and Lina loved each other. It was both sickening and awe inducing. "Glad to hear. Didn't know you were going to be here tonight."

"I just landed and sped through traffic to make it." He sank his hands into his trouser pockets like a proud parent. "Promised Danny."

Nancy's heart threatened to burst. It had taken Danny a while to warm up to Noah, but when he did, they became best buds, bonding over the silliest anime and bloodiest video games.

"That traffic was no joke. I just got here myself," Nancy said.

"I'm convinced lost souls are forced to drive round and round the 285 during both morning and evening rush hours as purgatory."

"Or hell."

He shrugged, nodded. "Hell. Definitely hell."

They both chuckled.

"Shall we surprise our boy, then?" Nancy motioned toward the cafeteria.

"One minute. I wanted to ask for your help with something." Noah shifted his weight from one leg to the other, then ran a hand across his tightly coiled hair. "I need, um . . ." He turned and mouthed something to himself. "I really want to . . ."

"Ok-ay."

"You see, well, you know how I—" He cleared his throat. "I need, no, it would mean the world to me, not that either. Argh."

"Noah. Talk like a big boy. What do you want?"

"I want to ask Lina to marry me." His eyes nearly popped out of his head as the words tumbled from his lips. He beamed like he'd won an award, a blush running across his rich, dark skin. And he had—Lina was the best award or prize any man could ask for.

While this morning had started out rough, tonight was making Nancy's feelings do all sorts of gymnastics. Her chest felt the fullest it'd been in a while. "And you want?"

"I want you to help me make it special for her."

"What did you have in mind?"

"Asking her at Christmas?"

"I thought you were better than that." Nancy smirked, remembering how she and Lina used to make fun of people who used major holidays as markers. Engaged on Christmas or New Year's Eve. Married on Valentine's Day or on dates that aligned, like 12/12/12 or 12/21/21. No matter how spectacular the holiday, anniversaries would still be forgotten because love was a fictional something.

"Or I could ask tonight during dinner?" Noah added, looking like he needed a lifeline.

"Not a fat chance. Tonight is Danny's night. Don't do that to him."

He blew out a long, frustrated breath. "I'm lost. She deserves it to be major. Massive. Grand. Help me."

"That's your problem right there. Lina doesn't want a grand gesture. Just ask her. She loves you."

"Really?" He chewed on it for a beat.

"Yeah, Noah. Just ask."

"Wow. I feel so dumb now." Tilting his head to the side, he sighed pensively. "Glad I ran it past you first."

"Ran what past Nancy?" Lina was all teeth when she appeared beside them in the hallway. Her warm-brown shoulders peeked out from beneath her colorful shawl when she adjusted it. "You didn't tell me you were coming tonight. Danny's going to freak." She poked his side playfully.

Noah kissed her nose and held her so tenderly Nancy wanted to look away.

"We were just catching up, and I wanted to surprise you guys," he said.

Nancy coughed obnoxiously. "I made it too. Where's my hug?" Nancy opened her arms wide and bear-hugged her friend. Everything felt right in that moment. Everything was going to be just fine.

"They're starting in a few. I've got us some seats, but, Nance, I need to talk to you super fast," Lina said. "It's sort of important."

"We'd like to start the evening off by thanking the parents and guardians. Please stand and give yourselves a round of applause for supporting these incredible kids," a woman's voice rang over the speakers.

"Danny first. Tell me later." Nancy hooked her arm around Lina's and made her way through the applause while Lina protested.

The cafeteria was nicer than the one from Nancy's old high school. Various food stations lined one side of the substantial space, while the opposite wall boasted a pizza oven and a full salad bar. It reminded her of the food hall on campus. Large round tables with flowing white linens dotted the checkerboard linoleum, while the honorees' photos projected onto the wall just above the podium.

Nancy wondered if the food was any good as she took her seat beside Mimi. Lina, Danny, and a few of his friends shuffled seats to make room for Noah, leaving an extra seat open next to Nancy. Lina shot her an apology.

"It's all good," Nancy mouthed. She didn't mind sitting beside her second-favorite girl. "How did the campus tour go this morning?" she whispered to Mimi as the room fell back into silence.

Mimi leaned over, inching her phone until it was between the two. Whispering as the woman returned to the microphone to go over the evening's agenda. "UGA was awesome. Definitely my first choice." She scrolled through all the photos she'd taken earlier that day while she and Lina had been on campus.

Nancy kicked herself for missing breakfast with them this morning. Their company would've been so much better than Keith's.

"We totally missed you, but that coffee shop was incredible. Their lemon pound cake . . . ohmigod, you have to bring some next time you come this way."

Lina shot Mimi a look that said, "Be quiet."

"Send a quick text to remind me next time," Nancy said softly, covering her mouth. The two giggled.

Mimi continued showing Nancy her photos, pausing at a pic of her in front of a water fountain to tell Nancy why she'd had such a dorky smile in the photo. Dorky smile or not, Mimi's eyes gleamed with the promise of a brilliant future, and she looked like she belonged on that campus. After another glance at Mimi's sweet face in the photo, awe and pride coursed through Nancy's veins.

Nancy couldn't be any prouder of her. Mimi had earned several scholarships and made all sorts of lists despite struggling through all her classes after Lina's attack had gone viral. While it'd been hard on both kids, Mimi had been the one to shut down the most. Where Danny sought outward help, Mimi had folded in on herself, collapsing under the unwanted attention and subsequent revelation about her father's abuse. She'd withdrawn and isolated herself from most of her friends and family. Most days she'd spent sleeping. It'd taken intensive therapy to get her to open up. Once she had, she'd slowly turned back into the Mimi everyone knew.

Nancy sent Mimi a silly GIF in a text message, making her giggle under her breath. Taking it all in, Nancy couldn't be happier. The kids were not only okay; they were thriving since having such a nightmare of an experience. It'd been difficult for them to process their father attacking their mom and even more so in such a public way when the video of the attack was leaked.

And now Lina was going to get married! Or at least she hoped her friend would say yes when Noah asked. That made Nancy consider getting back into dating. Maybe, just maybe, she could find someone who:

1. wasn't a complete jerk.
2. was secure in himself.
3. would be okay with simply seeing each other without anything more.

But someone like that doesn't exist.

Stealing glances of the sweet gestures between Noah and Lina made Nancy think about how wonderfully romantic her marriages had started. Sweet nothings had eventually whittled into silent dinners in front of the evening news, followed by the *Jeopardy!* / *Wheel of Fortune* hour. Passion never lasted. Who was she kidding? What was left once it was gone? Commitment? Just sticking around without any desire to actually be together?

Screw that. Nancy wanted none of that. Slipping her phone into her lap, she scrolled through her photos until she found the ones from her summer beach trip to Aruba with Ashish. The sun had kissed her skin so gently and evenly she looked like a goddess in her white string bikini, standing beside him near the picturesque shore. A faint smile played on her lips as she remembered how incredible their trip had been before he'd asked her to consider moving to Atlanta. Before he'd ruined the perfect thing they'd had. They'd had an understanding, and it was all she'd needed.

No labels.

No definitions.

No expectations.

But he'd gone and screwed it all up. To the sound of a kid botching "America the Beautiful," she seethed at his absolute nerve. Glancing back down at her phone, she ignored Lina's new text message and continued scrolling through her photo app. She quickly cropped Ashish out of a photo, slapped on a beauty filter, and used it to update her dating app profiles. She wouldn't be alone tonight.

Mimi elbowed her when Danny's name was called, and Nancy set her phone down and clapped heartily for him. Danny strolled to the front for his award. Nancy felt her eyes water. With Mimi graduating this year and Danny graduating next year, Lina wouldn't be alone, especially with Noah wanting to marry her. It was all working out, and Nancy couldn't be more thrilled.

Her phone buzzed with another text message from Lina.

Nancy squinted at her friend, who mouthed another apology, then checked her phone.

Lina: Ashish is coming tonight.

Lina: I'm sorry. Tried to tell you earlier.

She checked back with Lina, confused until she followed Lina's gaze over to the man walking up to their table. Nancy froze.

It was Ashish.

CHAPTER 4

Chill. Play cool. Relax. Breathe.

With her eyes nearly popping out of her head, Nancy had to calm down. She winced at Lina, who mouthed another apology before greeting Ashish and offering him the empty seat beside Nancy. They hadn't spoken since epically crashing and burning less than a week after returning from Aruba in August. Her suntan had lasted longer than their vacation high.

The smell of leather, cedar, and some sort of citrus greeted her like an old friend. It was his signature scent: cool, fresh, and oh so sexy. The smell alone reminded her of the many times she'd pulled him into dark corners and empty bathrooms so he could have his way with her. She felt a pull at her inner core when she glanced into his dark eyes. She was in wonder at how his presence alone still turned her into a jellyfish.

"Hey, Nance," Ashish said softly between one kid reciting a poem and another kid picking up the microphone for a speech. He was all dimples and thick, black hair wrapped in a tailored navy suit. Her fingers ached to get tangled in his strands.

"Hello, Ashish." She did her best to sound aloof. If she had learned anything from Keith, it was to leave the past in the past, for good. No repeats. No seconds. No do-overs.

"Can I see your program?" he whispered.

She slid it to him, pretending to give all her attention to the skinny redhead at the mic who droned on about her community garden project. There was something about fencing and tomatoes. All Nancy could think about was what Ashish was doing there. Why had Lina invited him? Had her best friend of a gazillion years chosen him over her?

She squinted at Lina, hoping the heat from her stare would feel like a laser to her temple. Lina's attention was on the stage.

"And none of this would be possible without Mr. Ashish Singh," the girl said, extending her hand to invite him to participate in her presentation.

Ashish joined her onstage. "I want to personally extend my thanks to everyone who supported this mission. Although real estate and contract law aren't my sweet spot, I was honored to lend a hand and witness the change in my community," he said. "These kids are incredible, and I'm so proud of them. My firm is proud of them as well and has committed to funding the rest of the project." He motioned to the little girl to change the slide to a QR code and a GoFundMe link. "You can donate as well, if you like. I have a feeling these kids will want to re-create this in other communities."

The cafeteria erupted in applause.

Flipping saint. Nancy hated how good he was. Why couldn't he be another controlling, self-centered F-boy so she could easily hate him and forget him?

From what she could ascertain, the school had created several community gardens around the area, and the kids tended to the gardens, donating the produce to local food banks. A problem had arisen when two plots of land were denied. Danny had convinced Ashish to help them legally lay claim on the lots. Ashish had filed the necessary legal documents and petitioned the courts on behalf of the kids.

"And so far, we've been able to provide free, organic produce to over one hundred and eighty families," the girl added.

Although Nancy wanted nothing more than to sulk and slide further down into trying to hate Ashish along with the rest of her day, she couldn't help but remember the times she'd been hungry as a kid. Growing up with a single mom and a father serving a prison sentence for armed robbery, Nancy and Jeff, her older brother, had seen their share of plenty and lack. When the plenty flowed, they had enough groceries and all the utilities were on. When plenty turned to lack, they resorted to fairy bread sandwiches—white bread with sprinkles—packs of ramen, and potato dishes eaten to candlelight and lanterns.

Nancy sniffled, discomfort and longing needling her. Thinking about her childhood wasn't something she allowed herself to do often. She'd blocked out most of it to focus on her present. Her now, not her then. She hadn't spoken to her parents in years and couldn't even remember the last time she'd talked to her brother. Shaking her head to empty it of the memories, Nancy opened her phone and made a ridiculously large donation to the community garden project.

When Ashish returned to his seat, Nancy's phone buzzed with new Tinder notifications. She would definitely not be alone tonight.

"Hey, Nance," Ashish whispered, leaning in so closely she felt the warmth of his breath on her neck.

She fought back against a shiver, making sure he would not see he had any effect on her still. Between the emotions over her childhood and the rejection from Ashish, Nancy needed to get out of there just then. Get far away from Ashish, leave him before he left her this time. Making a pocket of space between them, she answered, "What?"

"Can we talk afterward? Dinner, maybe?"

"I'm taking Danny and *the family* out afterward." She wanted to make sure he knew he wasn't part of the "family" anymore and that he was definitely not invited.

"Of course. Makes sense."

Nancy checked her phone, pretending to be busy.

"Can I call you later, then?"

Her breath went shallow, and every part of her wanted to say, *Of course you can call me later. Hell, you can come over too.* She said none of that. That door could never reopen. Ashish wasn't like Keith. He'd never accept her scraps and hookups. Ashish wanted her fully. He wanted her to commit to more than what she was capable of. He wanted her to love him, and more importantly, he wanted her to accept his love. The hairs on her arms prickled, and she suddenly felt too hot. Her heart raced, picking up speed with each breath. No, she could never let him back in, because she couldn't give him the rest of herself.

Nancy shook her head slightly and felt something inside her break when she accepted the fact that she had to let Ashish go for good. "Tonight's not going to work for me."

"I see." Ashish leaned back in his seat.

The two sat silent and still as statues for the remainder of the program. His whisper-quiet nose whistle sliced through the cacophony of applause, laughter, music, and various machines humming. Nancy became acutely aware of his every movement—the way he fidgeted with his silk tie, how he brushed the hair away from his eyes when it fell across his face. They both released a long breath when the stubby woman returned to the podium.

"I want to thank every student, participant, parent, guardian, and sibling. This community would not be impacted the same without your support." She placed a hand over her chest. "Now, if we can all take a moment of silent reflection in honor of the community we serve."

Nancy anticipated relief as the ceremony came to a close. She followed along with everyone, closing her eyes and lowering her head. Instead of reflecting on the community, she considered her best escape route. She'd speed-walk to her car and text Lina from the restaurant with a halfhearted excuse about wanting to reserve a table. There was no way she'd give Ashish an opening to talk to her again. She prepared herself, clutching her purse in one hand and her phone in the other.

"Ugh, another call," Nancy's phone sounded, vibrating against the table. She fumbled with her phone, now hating her ringtone. It'd been funny and cute when she'd first chosen it, but with it embarrassing her in class earlier and now here, it was now obnoxious and loud. Totally embarrassing. But she'd use it as a perfect excuse to enact her escape plan. "I'm sorry," she said to no one in particular, then scuttled out of the cafeteria. Beelining to her car, she was almost giddy at the thought of releasing her frustration and annoyance on a spam caller. In a huff, she answered the call. "Listen here, you son of a—"

"Well, that's one way to answer the phone."

Nancy's blood ran cold at the voice on the other end. All the color drained from her face.

"Aren't you going to say, 'Hi, Mom'?"

"Y-yes, ma'am." Nancy felt her entire body shrink. Her skin suddenly felt too big for her bones. "Hi, Mom. I'm sorry for answering the phone the way I did. Didn't know it was you."

"It's been a while, Nancy. I'll give you that. Thought I taught you better." Lucy tsked. "Well, *didn't* I teach you better?"

Another failure.

Another disappointment.

"Yes, ma'am." Nancy hated how small she felt around her mom. She hadn't talked to the woman in over two years and was a grown woman herself, but a simple word from her mom had the ability to shrivel any sense of self she had.

They'd had one of their usual blowups a few years ago when Nancy had drunk-dialed her mom late one night. Nancy had just finalized her last divorce and wasn't in her right mind. She found herself wanting nothing more than to hear a kind and reassuring word from her mother. She'd wanted a simple, *It's going to be okay, Nancy. You'll meet your special someone one day, and they'll love you so wholly and completely you'll finally understand why I stayed with your father through everything. I love you, Nancy. Why don't you come home for a little bit?*

Instead, Lucy had berated Nancy no less than a minute into Nancy's snotty, tear-filled moment of vulnerability:

Four decades, Nancy, Lucy had clipped. *That's how long I've stuck with your dad, and you know it hasn't been easy. I haven't had it easy at all. I had to basically raise you and your brother on my own instead of living my life.* Lucy had sighed. *And now you're going on what? Your third divorce? I mean, really, Nancy. What is your father going to say when I tell him? What is this going to do to him? Did you even think about us? I hope I can at least get my wedding gift back. The crystal vase thing set me back a few hundred dollars, but your father insisted, hoping you'd make this one work. Maybe I can sell it online or something.*

Lucy had continued for some time, each word digging into Nancy, hollowing her out even more. By the end of her tirade, Nancy's buzz had turned into sadness and exhaustion. She'd eventually fallen asleep with the phone on her pillow just to hear a voice cut through the silent echo of her house.

The next morning's light had not only brought a massive hangover; it'd brought Lucy's words back to Nancy in full force. Her foggy head hadn't been able to escape the vitriol and left a bitter taste in her mouth.

I failed with you. I just failed so much with you. I don't even know what to do with you anymore.

By the end of a full day warring against Lucy's words, Nancy had decided to barricade what was left of herself behind impenetrable barriers. Healthy boundaries, like she'd read about in all of her psychology books and what she'd taught during her section on self-care. When Nancy had confronted her mother about establishing boundaries, Lucy had scoffed at the idea and told Nancy that she'd rather have no relationship than one with limitations and expectations. *Besides,* her mother had added snidely, *it's not like I'll be cutting off any grandkids.*

After such a long break, had her mother called to apologize and reestablish a relationship with her? *Did she miss me?* Nancy wondered in the dark parking lot. Before reaching her car, she heard the sound of people talking and noticed several families exiting Danny's high school behind her. She picked up her pace. Soon the trickle of people turned into a flood. By the time she made it to her SUV at the very back corner of the parking lot, she glanced back to the entrance and locked eyes with Ashish. Her stomach turned when he started in her direction.

Nancy hated everything about today.

"How have you been?" Lucy asked.

"I'm good." Nancy cleared her throat and spoke up. "I've been good."

"Any new marriages or children I should know about?"

"No, Mom. I'm not ever getting married again, and I'm perfectly content childless." And she certainly was.

"You don't have to take that tone with me, young lady."

"I'm sorry, Mom, but you're just so—"

"So what?"

"Why are you calling from an unrecognized phone number? Did something happen?"

"I'm, um, okay. Your father . . ."

Nancy's throat felt like it was closing. "What about Dad? How is he?"

"When was the last time you visited him?"

Nancy thought about the last time she'd visited her father at Ware State Prison, where he'd been imprisoned the last eleven years. "Almost two years ago," she said softly. She'd tried to keep up her biweekly visits after establishing boundaries with her mom, but every visit had turned into her dad advocating for Lucy. He'd beg Nancy to understand Lucy or to accept her because she wasn't going to change. He'd even had Lucy show up during one of Nancy's visits. Instead of it being a peaceful family event, Lucy had arrived ready to fight and argue. The whole thing had become exhausting, so Nancy had put her dad in the same neat little box with Lucy.

Four walls.

Four corners.

Them on the outside.

Nancy on the inside, where she was safe.

Eventually, one month had turned into three, into a year, and now into almost two years since she'd spoken to either one of them. In that moment, she wished she could call her father, but it wasn't like she could just dial up the prison and ask for him.

Shame at not visiting her father for that amount of time riddled her like bullets. How had it been that long? How had she been okay with allowing so much time to pass by? She'd blinked, and now it was two years she'd never get back.

"*Hmph.* Two years?" Lucy's voice ticked up, but Nancy knew it was more statement than question.

"I've been—"

"Busy. I know."

Rolling her eyes, Nancy played along to get some peace tonight. "How about I call you later?"

"It's . . ." Lucy paused a beat, and Nancy figured Lucy had taken a drag of her cigarette. Lucy's phone calls had always been accompanied by a cigarette or two. Nancy tried hard to remember the pungent tobacco smell. It had always burned her nostrils and made her cough, but she'd liked watching the thin line of smoke curl into the air. It'd been so fascinating that Nancy used to make wishes on the curls before they'd dissipated.

"Nancy, it's your dad." The tears in her mother's voice nearly shattered every healthy boundary Nancy'd spent years cultivating. "It's cancer. I have a lawyer working to get him home, but I may need your help."

CHAPTER 5

After hours of being with Lina, Noah, and the kids during the awards ceremony and later at the boisterous dinner, the vacuum of silence in Nancy's car during her two-hour drive back to Athens was deafening. She'd made it through dinner on autopilot, nodding and laughing along with everyone as the conversation shifted around the table. She'd been able to piece together enough to keep up, but she'd felt like she was suspended in honey—slow and sticky—while everyone was buzzing frantically.

Lina had asked her several times what was wrong, but there was no way Nancy would dampen Danny's night with her problems or her tears. Or at least she expected to cry when she actually had enough time and emotional energy to process what Lucy'd told her. Being left to her own thoughts wasn't high on Nancy's list. She hated it almost as much as her annual mammogram. Tonight, however, she'd much rather get her DDD boobs squished to smithereens than consider how truly alone she'd be if Lucy had been telling the truth and her dad would be gone soon.

Nancy's eyes watered as she imagined her father, now frail and sick, lying in his prison cell all alone. She searched her memories, pulling every visit, every phone call, every moment she'd had with him. A knot tangled in her gut when she remembered the very first time she'd met him.

When she was fifteen years old, Nancy had returned home from school to bitter hospital antiseptic fumes with undertones of cheap, fake floral scents. Lucy'd had her cleaning fits every now and then, but there'd been a furious purpose this time. Lucy had brought home countless cleaning products from her job at the hospital and put Nancy and her brother to work cleaning every inch of the house. It'd taken them four days—four missed school days—to clean the house to Lucy's satisfaction.

Cleanliness is next to godliness. Don't you want to be godly? Lucy had chided them, scrubbing surfaces until her fingers were raw. She'd had them each blistered and bruised at the end of it all. Nancy's knees had gone from red to deep purple within days, and her muscles had ached. She'd never wanted to smell cleaning products again in her life.

Instead of letting the kids return to school that next week, Lucy had made them bathe thoroughly, then dress in their finest church clothes. They'd piled into their station wagon and, a few hours later, pulled to a stop in front of a prison. A thin man strolled out through multiple sets of gates and buzzers and right up to their car. Lucy had cried and hugged him, then introduced him as *Hank, your daddy.* Despite the man being an absolute stranger, there'd been no denying the matching features: sea glass–blue eyes, full pouty lips, sky-high cheekbones, and wispy blond hair. Nancy and her bother looked like someone had copied and pasted Hank twice:

CTRL C, CTRL V = Jeff

CTRL C, CTRL V = Nancy, two years later

Meeting her father had been weird enough. Going back home and having to share a small three-bedroom ranch with the man had been embarrassing because she'd had to explain his presence to her friends. At first, she'd told them Hank was her mother's new boyfriend. Hank had been fine to go along with the ruse until Lucy had overheard them at one of Nancy's sleepovers.

He's her daddy, Lucy had spewed, storming into Nancy's room. Lucy's speech had been slurred from drinking almost all night. *Her daddy, you hear me?* She stabbed the air. *Been in prison this whole time.*

Nancy had wanted the floor to open wide and swallow her whole.

Lucy had continued, despite the tears streaming down Nancy's bright-red face and her pitiful cries for her mother to please stop. The thin woman had lit a cigarette and taken a long drag. *Don't you go and try to act like your parents ain't never done anything bad. Trust me, some of your parents are no angels. Hell—* She took another drag and exhaled. The smoke curled, reminding Nancy of a delicate white ribbon. When Lucy glared back at the girls, she added, *Actually, I know at least one of your daddies ain't actually your daddy.*

The way Lucy had cackled sent Nancy running from her house. It hadn't been the first time her mother had embarrassed her so thoroughly, and Nancy knew it wouldn't be the last time. The rage and pain she'd felt surged through her calves and thighs. She'd pumped her arms to match pace. In her colorful Lisa Frank pajamas, Nancy had run until the sky lightened with the promise of morning. She'd finally collapsed in the Winn-Dixie parking lot some distance away from her house.

It'd been Hank who'd found her that next morning. Without a word, he'd joined her, sliding down the rough brick wall to sit beside her. Nancy's eyes had been puffy and red. Nancy's face had felt swollen, and every single muscle in her body had seemed to sob along with her ragged hitches.

"Nancy," Hank had finally said after several long moments. "I know I'm a stranger. I won't pretend I'm not. Your mama was angry at me for a long while when I got busted. Didn't talk to me for years. After so much time passed, we decided you kids best not know until I was out for good."

None of what he'd said made any sense to Nancy. It'd felt like word soup, and the only words holding on to the ladle were "Your mama was angry." They were the only words that made sense, since her mama had always been angry for some reason or another.

"Look, I can't apologize for your mama, but here I am, and I'm asking you to forgive me for not being in your life. I'm sorry, Nancy. Let's start over." He'd held out a hand for her to shake. "Hi, I'm Hank. I have two incredible kids that I'd like to get to know. One is a son, and the other a daughter with the most beautiful smile I've ever seen. From today on, it will be my personal job to make sure I see that smile at least once a day." He had nudged her with his shoulder. "What do you say?"

"What about Mom?" Nancy had whispered, her voice hoarse and her throat sandpaper.

"Lucy will be Lucy. I'm not her. I'm Hank, and it looks like you kids can use an extra hand with her, and, well"—he wiggled his fingers in the air—"I've got two of those."

When Nancy finally agreed and shook his hand, she'd hoped everything would return to normal. Instead, her friends had all been long gone by the time she'd opened her front door. By that Monday, she'd quickly become the brunt of jokes in her high school, and her social standing had tanked. It'd been her very last slumber party. Her last friends. Her last sense of normalcy.

Being an outcast already, her older brother, Jeff, had seemed to fare better and had moved out a few months later, just before his graduation. Nancy, on the other hand, had struggled over the next two years and quietly finished high school. She'd left her tiny South Georgia home hours after graduating with a secondhand suitcase and a bus ticket. Since Lucy had been in a fit over Nancy going to school early for a scholarship program, she hadn't even shown up for Nancy's graduation that morning. It'd been only Hank, since Jeff had his own life. Hank had taken her out to lunch afterward and had surprised her with the bus ticket—her ticket out of there.

Throughout the years, she and Hank had grown close, bonding over Lucy's capricious moods, which changed faster than the colors on Nancy's mood ring in hot or cold water. Red to blue to purple to black and back again. Happy, angry, happy, sad, grumpy, angry. Nancy and Hank had developed their own language and hand signals as warnings or all clears. Hank had been her navigator through their tempestuous home. Her lighthouse, a bright and steady beacon, through every storm.

With Jeff doing who-knows-what, Nancy had been glad to have another person around to take some of Lucy's heat off her. The guilt of leaving poor Hank to navigate Lucy's storms when Nancy had gone to college nipped at her. To make life a little easier for them, Nancy slowly eased into the habit of sending them a little money every paycheck. Twenty dollars here. Fifty dollars there. By the time Nancy had landed her first real job after grad school, she'd set up a regular direct deposit for them.

Little had she known, Hank had been having a hard time with his job and had eventually slipped back into old habits. By her thirty-second birthday, Hank had returned to prison for armed robbery. She'd kept in touch with him through weekly calls and biweekly visits. He'd been her constant—the one man she could count on because he'd always looked forward to hearing from her. It didn't hurt that he couldn't run away from her.

She laughed quietly to herself in her car, remembering when he'd called himself "her very own captive audience" during one of her visits. She did the math, putting a number to the visits she'd missed. How had she been okay without talking to him all this time? How would she feel losing him permanently? If she was lonely now, how much lonelier and emptier would she feel without her father?

CHAPTER 6

Alone.

She'd celebrated Lina's kid, not her own. She'd had dinner with Lina's family, not hers. With all the good going on with her bestie, there was no way in hell Nancy would burden her. At the end of the day, Nancy had no family of her own. Because of her tenuous relationship with her mother, who also dictated her relationship with her brother, Jeff, she'd have no one of her own left when her father died.

No one. It was like she was on a long slide that ended in an abyss of self-loathing. Her very own pity party. Maybe Keith had been right. Maybe, just maybe, there was a reason they'd kept in touch this whole time. Maybe he was her consolation prize for messing up every other relationship. He was the gum in her shoe—the thing she'd never really escape. He seemed to be her constant—that never-changing thing in her life she could almost always count on. And he wanted to be with her. Why was she fighting it? It seemed inevitable after all these years.

Tears blurred the white lines together along the road. That was how her life felt in that moment—no clear path, no clear side. All she knew right then and there was how much she did not want to be alone tonight. She pressed Keith's number, chewing the inside of her cheek and tapping her manicured fingers across her steering wheel.

"Knew you'd call," he said.

"I . . . um." The words refused to come from her mouth. Asking him if she could come over made her tongue stick to the roof of her mouth like she'd eaten the thickest peanut butter. She considered ending the call and swiping some rando on Tinder, but she didn't want a one-night stand. She wanted to fall asleep in someone's arms, if only for one night.

"I'll leave the door unlocked," Keith said. It was all the invitation Nancy needed. All she wanted: not to be alone tonight.

A half hour later, Nancy reconsidered her decision as she stood inside Keith's foyer. It was midnight on a weekday, and she had a full class schedule starting early in the morning. What was she doing, and why with Keith, of all people? She followed the soft glow of light to the kitchen and helped herself to the wine he'd left on the counter. It was the sauvignon blanc he'd brought back from his recent trip to the Willamette Valley in Oregon when they'd first reconnected this time around.

She chugged the first glass of wine, relishing in the crisp lightness. The second and third glasses went a little slower as she mindlessly doom scrolled through social media. Everyone seemed so happy, their lives more complete than hers somehow. In her head, she knew it was all fake, but in this moment, she wanted to hold on to the lie and continue to toast herself at her pity party. She raised her glass to no one in particular after she scrolled across the fourth Facebook friend who posted photos of their kids.

Her resolve grew with each glass until she felt like she'd definitely made the right decision. There was a slight buzz in her head, and she felt light and weightless walking through Keith's house to his bedroom. She paused at his door and watched him sleeping. *He's not bad looking,* she thought, trying to convince herself maybe a relationship with Keith would work this time around. There *was* a level of attraction she felt for him. She'd always been attracted to him. Physical attraction and sex had never been their problem. No matter how into him she'd been, she'd never felt like they'd connected—truly connected to where she needed to be with him. To where she felt comfortable enough to share her entire world with him—her dreams, her fears, her secrets.

She'd tried to share her fears once on their honeymoon, telling him how terrified she'd been of heights because her mom had once forced her onto a roller coaster. She'd kicked and screamed, but no one really listened to an eight-year-old, she'd tried to explain to him. Especially not an eight-year-old girl "throwing a tantrum." That had been how her mom had excused her own behavior. Once Lucy had gotten Nancy into the front seat of the roller coaster, she'd pinched her thigh so hard it made Nancy cry out. It'd distracted her enough so Lucy could fasten them both in. The mark had lasted a week; the trauma, a lifetime.

As Nancy had been explaining all this to Keith, she had felt a faint pain in the spot on her thigh; a whisper of hurt her body had remembered. Keith, on the other hand, had listened intently, nodding along and grimacing at the violence. Later, during their week in Hawaii, he'd throw his own temper tantrum when Nancy refused to go cliff diving with him.

To think she'd ever trust Keith with her entire heart again made her shudder. That sort of trust, security, and love simply did not exist for her. But he *could* be the next best thing. Out of all her weddings, her dad had given her away only when she'd married Keith. He'd liked Keith and had been devastated when they'd divorced.

Dad . . .

The sadness returned, only this time it brought impending loss along with it. Loneliness ran through her in a shiver. She darted into the bathroom, splashed her face, and took off her clothes. In only her panties, Nancy took a long look at herself in the bright bathroom mirror. With her hands on her arms, she craved someone else's touch. There was something primal in having another person's warm hands touch her skin. That was the thing: another person's hands always felt warmer against her flesh than her own. In that moment, she wanted nothing more than to be held. She crawled into Keith's bed, relieved to have another living, breathing person warm beside her.

He opened his arms for her. "What took you so long?"

She settled against his soft skin and relished in how tightly he held her. How secure and cared for she felt in that moment.

"You find the wine?" He breathed into her hair.

Nancy nodded, sure if she spoke, she'd ruin the fantasy she'd worked out in her head. Would this be how she'd feel once her father passed? Would the loneliness consume her until she crawled into a different man's bed every night just to feel less touch starved? She shivered again, tears filling her eyes as the realization of it all crashed into her. This was as good as it got. She was broken and incapable of loving properly. This was the next best thing. It had to be.

"Nancy?" Keith's voiced ticked with concern. "Come here." He held her firm, stroking her hair, then her cheek with his thumb. "I missed you too."

She wouldn't correct him. Instead, she brought her lips to his, needing to feel needed and wanted. Needing to feel soft and vulnerable. Needing to *feel*. He quickly picked up on her change, kissing her back until they were both panting. But she needed more. So much more. She needed to feel loved, if just in her head. If only she imagined the sex they were going to have was them truly making love, Keith truly loving her the way she wanted him to and her loving him back.

She kissed him harder, biting his bottom lip and eliciting a rugged moan. It was all the encouragement he needed. On top now, she wriggled her hips until they were connected. As connected as they'd ever be. They moved together, each for their own purpose: Keith, for his release; Nancy, to fill her void. To fill that emptiness she'd never shared with anyone, hollowness that called to her on sleepless nights.

In the moments after, Nancy lay there listening to Keith's breathing turn rhythmic. Somehow, she felt even lonelier than she'd felt in her car. She felt small and unimportant. She pulled the thick duvet over her like a shield to ward off the thoughts that were now filling her head. She moved closer to Keith, hoping to leach his warmth and peace. He rolled over, turning his back to her. Tears came fast, sliding down her cheeks and into her hair. Her fantasy was over.

It was time for her to leave.

CHAPTER 7

Her classes the rest of the week were uneventful. She seemed to slog from one lecture to the next. Thirty kids' faces, to the next thirty-two kids' faces, to the next twenty-eight kids' faces, to the next fifteen kids' faces in her final lab. Or it would've been fifteen if Elysse Mason would've shown up for class, Nancy noted in her planner. Maybe Elysse had been telling the truth about having a problem with childcare. Maybe Nancy could reach out to some people at the university to find out if Elysse had any options. Maybe Nancy could pay for a sitter every now and then to help Elysse out. Maybe, just maybe, Nancy was using Elysse's situation to distract her from her own problems.

Nancy waited to hear back from Lucy after calling and leaving several voice mails and texts every day since Monday. Every time her phone buzzed or rang, she flinched, expecting to hear bad news. It was like she was on autopilot. Lecture, lecture, lecture. Notes, notes, notes. Smile and nod at the kids asking questions and give them nonsensical answers because she wasn't truly paying attention. She wasn't *there*.

Ashamed at needing Keith's company every night that week, she'd woken up in her own bed with a massive stress headache after leaving Keith's house for the final, final, final-ish, final time. The throbbing pain seemed to mute everything from sounds to colors to light. She would've been better off canceling classes and staying in bed all day. At least now, her day was finished, and she could return to her bed with a pint of ice cream and something fried from the hole-in-the-wall burger place on campus. Sugar and grease were what she needed.

With her car smelling like what she imagined heaven smelled like—seasoned, smoked meat and oily french fries—she drove up to the gated entrance of her neighborhood and held out a brown bag for the guard. Its grease stain could've been a Rorschach inkblot for a butterfly. A butterfly or a ram with long horns, Nancy wasn't sure. She blinked a few times, trying to figure it out now.

The guard happily accepted his dinner, winking as he took the bag. "You're the best, Nancy."

"Am I, Tony? Am I?" Nancy smirked. It'd become their very own private joke after they'd hooked up late one night. Nancy had been in her Pilates phase and had been extremely flexible. She'd been damn proud of the positions she'd been able to pull off. After they had finished, they'd lain breathless on her bedroom floor, the thick carpet comforting the places Nancy knew would be bruised when she woke the next day. Tony had turned to her, fear and amazement in his sleepy eyes, and whispered, *You. Are. The. Best. Ever.*

Tony opened the bag and inhaled deeply. "You know pulled pork is my favorite. What do you want?" He grinned at her mischievously.

"Nothing today, but I may need a hug soon." She couldn't even bring herself to fake a smile.

Tony nodded, understanding. "I got you, Nancy. Don't worry. Just hit me up if you need me."

"I'll do that." She tapped her steering wheel. "I'd better go. You have a good night."

By the time she pulled into her garage, the loneliness had returned. Maybe she'd get a pet. A massive dog like one of those Tibetan mastiffs she'd gawked at when Ashish had shown her images of dogs he'd been interested in adopting. The monster of a dog had been the size of a small horse, with the fur of a grizzly bear. She'd shot him down immediately.

He'd started looking for a dog to adopt a month before Aruba, when he'd gotten hold of the idea of them living together. Of Nancy moving to Atlanta and them being *together*. Both contentedly childless, the obnoxiously large dog would've been *theirs*.

Moving to Atlanta hadn't really been the problem. While she loved teaching at UGA, she knew she could get the same position and salary at any of the major colleges in the city. It had been more moving in together that had given Nancy pause. Weekends and vacations had been one thing. Living together full time—intermixing lives—was another. It wasn't that Nancy didn't want to be held at night, but she couldn't imagine taking that risk again after three failed marriages.

Being a little over two hours apart, she'd liked how they'd purposely carved out time to spend with each other. How they'd scheduled calls and FaceTimes. How they'd planned where to spend their weekends—his house or hers. How they'd surprised each other with random week-night dinners. Distance had kept Ashish at an arm's length, right where she'd needed to protect her heart. It'd kept their relationship fresh and exciting. Moving in together would've stagnated their flow, suffocated them, and led to their romance's quick and painful death. It'd been a bad idea, one Nancy had bitterly opposed.

Nancy rolled her eyes, wiping the idea of a dog out of her head. She'd get a cat instead. Or maybe start with a fish to make sure she could keep a living thing alive. Her stomach growled when she climbed out of her car. She kicked off her shoes, beelined to the kitchen, ready to devour her dinner. Her phone rang. Nancy was a little disappointed when she saw it was Lina instead of her mother.

"Nance, are you sitting down?" Lina sounded like she was out of breath. Nancy could almost guess what had happened.

"Hold on." Nancy quickly washed her hands and grabbed a ton of paper towels, then sat at the table.

"Come on, Nance. I'm about to burst."

"Okay, okay, okay." Nancy took everything out of the brown bag, flattened it, and used it as a place mat. She squeezed all four ketchup packets onto the paper and swirled in one mayonnaise packet. That was her highly scientific and thoroughly tested ratio. Four to one for the perfect fry dip. If she was feeling particularly fancy, she'd add a pinch of Old Bay seasoning. "What's going on?"

"I'm in my car."

"Why are you in your car?"

"Instinct? I don't know. I'll hash it out with my therapist another time. I *need you* first."

"Lina, you're worrying me. What happened?"

"Was up all night, and the kids were doing their own thing after school today, so I went to Noah's for a bit."

Nancy was on pins and needles waiting to hear that her friend was now engaged. "And?"

"And I ended up crashing on his couch."

Jeez, it was like pulling teeth. She was ready to celebrate the good news. Nancy shoved some fries into her mouth. "Where was Noah?"

"At his studio."

"So what happened and why are you freaking out?"

"I had on this dress. It was itchy when I put it on earlier, but it looked cute, right? I couldn't get comfy enough to sleep, so I went to the closet where I have some of my clothes," Lina said in rapid fire. "I have clothes over at his place. I mean, of course I have clothes over there, we're *together* together, know what I mean? I mean, it just makes sense."

"Honey, I get it. Take a deep breath."

"I can't breathe right now. I can't focus. Nancy, I went to get something to change into and saw it."

"What?"

"A ring."

Nancy laughed.

"I wasn't snooping. I'd never snoop. I'm not a snooper. Personal space is personal space, and I'm just not like that. I was never like that. Never been like that. I'm-not-the-person-to-snoop-but-it-was-right-there-and-I-couldn't-help-myself. Who wouldn't look? Wouldn't you look? I mean, of course *you'd* look, right?"

"Lina, park the car, because you're in full freak-out mode and you need to be safe." Nancy shoved several large bites of her sandwich into her mouth, knowing she'd have to talk her bestie down and it might take a while. She heard Lina deep breathing after a few minutes.

"Is your car parked and locked?" Nancy asked.

"Mm-hmm."

"Are you focusing on breathing?"

"Mm-hmm."

"So you found a ring?"

"Why aren't you surprised? Hold on, did you know?" Lina asked.

"He told me the other night at Danny's thing."

"And you didn't warn me?"

"Why are you freaking out?"

"I don't know. I'm not sure. I can't help it. It's so major. I mean, marriage?"

Nancy quirked her mouth to the side. Wasn't *she* the one who was commitment averse while Lina wanted the fairy tale? "You . . . you don't want to be married again?" She heard nothing but the muffled sounds of soft crying. "Oh, honey. It's okay. You know this, right? You can tell him you're not ready."

"Am I broken?"

"Hell yeah. But who isn't?"

"Why don't I want to marry this perfect man? Why does the thought of something so final make me want to run away?"

"Girl, you are not running away. Listen, he hasn't asked. Maybe, just maybe, it's something he's thinking about and hasn't fully decided on himself. I mean, he *is* one of those 'be prepared' kinda people."

Nancy imagined Keith would classify Noah as a pancake person as well, while Lina was all waffle. *Ugh, Keith.*

"Um, okay. But what did he say to you the other night?"

"Honestly? He was considering asking you after Danny's thing." Nancy heard Lina's breath pick up pace. Moments later, her friend was back in freak-out mode, hyperventilating. If she didn't do something fast, Lina could pass out. "Lina, I need you to listen to me very carefully." She went into her professor mode, deepening her voice and enunciating every word. "Put your hands on top of your head and count along with me." Nancy slowly led her friend through the numbers one to twenty-five, counting in a rhythm as she trailed her finger along the thick seam on the side of her trousers. Its straight line helped her focus.

Lina's breath eased back into a natural pace. Slow and steady to match Nancy's voice.

"Now I want you to breathe along with me. We're going to inhale through our noses for six seconds, hold for eight, and exhale for six."

After several cycles, Lina spoke. "Thank you, Nance."

"Wish I lived closer. You know I'd come get you. Do you want me to come over tonight?"

"No, I'm good. And it's too late."

"What else am I going to be doing?" Nancy looked around her house, asking herself that very question. Everything was clean and put in its proper place. The only thing she'd planned to do was let the TV watch her as she waited to hear from her mother.

"I'm okay, really. Haven't had one of those in a while."

"Yeah?"

"Yeah. But I'm good. I can say no."

"You can definitely tell Noah no. You can tell the man to go to the moon and he'd do it. You know he'd immediately buy a one-way ticket on Elon Musk's next flight." The friends laughed.

"Space is a little too far. I mean, I kinda like the guy," Lina said, in her voice laughter that put Nancy at ease.

"You know what I mean. He's not your ex. And you are not the same person you were years ago. You got this."

"I got this. You're right."

"You gonna be okay?" Nancy asked.

"I am. I know what I'm going to have to do. It will be all right."

"But will *you* be all right?"

"Are you psychoanalyzing me?"

"I've been doing that since the very second I answered the phone. You know I'm a judgy bitch."

"What would I do without you, Nance?"

"I ask myself that question every day."

"How's everything on your end? Want to do brunch this weekend?" Lina asked.

There was no way Nancy could tell Lina about her father. She couldn't be a burden like that when her friend already had so much on her own plate. "Everything is fine. Good, actually." She hated lying.

"You sure?"

"Yeah, hey, why don't you head home. God only knows where you're parked."

"You're right. This parking lot is a little sketchy. I'll text you when I get back home."

"It's a deal. Be safe."

"Thanks, Nance."

Nancy heard her lie repeating in her head. She was not fine. She was anything but "good." She was a hot, flaming mess and needed to know what was going on with her father before she went insane.

She texted Lucy again: It's your daughter. News?

She stared at her phone screen, willing a reply, but there was none. She considered making the four-hour-long drive to the prison, but it would be way past visiting hours by the time she arrived.

Her imagination quickly took over. Did no reply mean bad news? Was he already gone? Did she piss Lucy off somehow, and now the woman wasn't replying out of spite? Soon, the same nervous energy she'd just talked Lina out of coursed through her own limbs. Her muscles tensed to move. Her fingers fidgeted, seeking stimuli. Something to do. Maybe Lina'd had the right idea. A nice, long drive was what Nancy needed. Maybe she'd even drive to Atlanta to check up on her friend since tomorrow was her planning day.

After grabbing her sandwich, Nancy headed to her car. She drove past campus, which was all lit up. The lights this time of night made the old buildings seem to glow and the newer ones stand boldly against the night sky. She went down various side streets and old country roads, Missy Elliott playing in the background. Naturally, she'd chosen old-school Missy over her newer music. There was something about the old nineties beats that sang to her like old friends.

Turning onto a dimly lit back road, Nancy cranked up her music. The bass rumbled in her chest and resonated in her gut as she rapped along to *Supa Dupa Fly*. Hands to the sky and car dancing, she ground her hips in the driver's seat like she was at a dance club. She felt free and light. Life felt normal for just a few moments . . . until she almost hit a person walking alongside the unlit road and swerved.

She slammed the brakes, and her car screeched to a stop. Her heart hammered in her chest. With her hands shaking and her pulse beating in her ears, she cracked her window. Despite her dry throat, she called out to the person in front of her car. They didn't answer, and it was then Nancy noticed the stroller on the other side of the person.

In disbelief, Nancy flicked on her high beams to better see, then called out again. Did the person need a ride? Were they all right? What the actual hell were they doing this far out on such a dark road? Nancy glanced around, checking to make sure she wasn't about to be scammed or robbed, but there was no one else out there except for them. Nancy squinted, then gasped as she placed the face before her.

It was Elysse Mason, the student who'd missed her lab earlier that day.

CHAPTER 8

Nancy watched, dumbstruck, as Elysse Mason adjusted her backpack and moved out of the car's path. The woman struggled with the stroller, rolling it onto the coarse gravel shoulder. What was she doing out so far from the city? More importantly, what in the world was she doing walking alongside such a dark road? Nancy sighed at the realization of how close she'd been to hitting both Elysse and the stroller.

Was there a baby inside? Did she almost hit a child?

Nancy scrambled from her car over to the woman, waving her hands above her head. "Hey! Hey, Ms. Mason!"

Elysse shrank backward, hovering over the stroller.

"It's okay." Nancy held up her hands to show she was safe. "It's Professor Jewel. From psych. You're in, like, two of my classes this semester."

Elysse blinked several times, still cowering. "Professor Jewel?"

"What are you doing out here so late? This is so dangerous."

"I-I, um. I don't . . ." Elysse started crying.

"Here, let me give you a ride." Nancy's eyes went wide when she noticed the faint outline of a small child in the stroller. "Come on." She held out her hand, ushering Elysse toward her SUV.

"Um, thank you. I don't—"

"Let's get out of the road first. Does this come off?" Nancy wrestled with the car seat, trying to figure out what button unlocked it from the stroller. Elysse pressed a reddish lever and weakly lifted the car seat into Nancy's back seat. It was like watching someone in slow motion: lift, place, click, snap, lock, tug to double-check, weep . . .

"We'd better get going." Nancy climbed into the driver's seat and waited some time for Elysse to get settled. "Where to?"

She shook her head. "I don't know. I was—" She sniffled, wiping her nose along the sleeve of her shirt. "I was going to look for a shelter or cheap hotel or something."

Nancy handed her a tissue. "Shelter?"

"My boyfriend—" Her voice filled with sobs. "I picked him up from work and we got into this big fight and he . . . he put us out of the car."

"He put you and your baby out of a car in the middle of nowhere?" Nancy felt the steam rise in her head, along with some choice words. She quickly remembered she was the woman's psych professor and held her tongue.

"I'm so sorry. He gets like that sometimes."

"No way. Do not apologize for him."

The baby started whimpering when the car moved. Elysse scrambled to soothe him.

"It's okay," Nancy reassured her. "Kids cry. It's what they do. Part of their job description, actually." She glanced over to see Elysse biting her cuticles. "Do you have any family in the area?"

Elysse shook her head. "My dad lives in Tennessee."

No family nearby. It was well past eleven o'clock. Thinking about all the hotels in the area, Nancy wondered if any had availability. If so, she'd probably have to pay for it, which also brought up the question of time. How long would Elysse need a hotel room? Did she have a job? Would she try to go back to her boyfriend? Could she call her father?

It almost felt like too much thinking for that time of the night, and yet not enough.

"There's—" Elysse cleared her throat. "There's an emergency shelter a few blocks from campus."

"The one our department sponsors?"

She slowly nodded. "I volunteered there last year. Think they stay open until midnight."

The baby whined softly, like he was giving his own opinion of going to a shelter this time of night. Nancy couldn't agree with him more. Knowing Beck would probably give her a long lecture on propriety and whatnot, Nancy made a decision. Rationalizing it further to bolster her confidence, she pictured her guest room, which sat empty 350-something days out of the year. She certainly had the space. She made sure to speak in an upbeat tone to reassure Elysse that it was okay, saying, "How about you guys stay at my place tonight? You can clean up, rest, and come up with a solid plan tomorrow."

"Are you sure?"

"Yes." It might not've been the best decision, but it was the only one in that immediate situation. "Definitely. It's late, and you look like you could use some sleep. We'll put our heads together in the morning to get a plan."

"Thank you," Elysse said in the smallest voice.

When they returned to Nancy's, she got them all settled in her guest room. Timid and road weary, Elysse thanked Nancy before closing the bedroom door behind her. Pitiful sobs were dried up by a tiny voice calling for his mama. Nancy prepared herself for a long night.

~

Bloodcurdling screams rose from the guest room and greeted Nancy the next morning. She grabbed her robe and ran to investigate, only to find Elysse perched on the edge of the bed, trying her hardest to give the small boy a bottle. He bucked and screamed, arms flailing.

"Come on, Elijah," she begged.

"Hey, can I help with anything?"

Elysse glanced up, dark, heavy bags under her eyes. Although she was young, she seemed much older in that moment. "I'm so sorry for waking you up."

Nancy recognized that look. She'd seen it hundreds of times visiting Lina when the kids were babies. "How old is he?"

"Eleven months." Elysse closed her eyes when the boy pushed the bottle out of the way with the fury of a wet cat. "I know I'm supposed to be weaning him. I'm doing the best I can."

"This is a no-judgment zone." Nancy held out her arms. "Is it okay if I try?"

"He's been fussing for the last hour." She picked Elijah up and gently slid him into Nancy's arms, sighing.

Nancy cooed, remembering the many times she'd helped Lina with the kids. She held the boy close to her chest and firmly patted his back. He wriggled for a few moments, then settled into Nancy's arms, taking the bottle when she offered it. Both women exhaled. Elysse looked like she was on the brink of crying again.

"Why don't you go and take care of yourself. Pass me his diaper bag, and I'll watch him for a little while."

"I am so sorry for intruding."

"No apologies necessary. I don't have classes today. Only a few things and I can do them all online. But I'll do them later. Go ahead and take some time to yourself. Get your head together, and we'll talk in a bit, okay?"

"Thank you, Professor Jewel."

"You're welcome. I put some things in the bathroom if you want to shower and whatnot. Do you have clothes?"

"Yeah." Defeat laced her thin voice. "I had a bag packed in the trunk, and when he saw it, he freaked out."

It was all coming together now. Nancy nodded, understanding her situation. "You were leaving him?"

Elysse shifted, folding her arms tight across her chest like she was holding herself together. "Mm-hmm. I was going to stay in the car for a few weeks until I got us settled. Wasn't supposed to pick him up last night, but he got off early. As soon as he noticed the bag . . ."

"You were going to stay in your car?"

"Only until family housing came through. They said it would be a week or so."

"But—"

"It's either that or drop out of school my last year to live with my dad in Tennessee."

"I'm not second-guessing your decisions. I'm only here to help, okay?" Nancy bounced a few times with the baby to settle him back down. "Is it okay if I take him to the living room so you can get some time to yourself?"

Elysse nodded, dropping her gaze to the floor.

"We'll be right out there." Nancy waited a beat, then carefully walked down the hallway to her living room. She opened the blinds, frowning at the thick, overcast sky. Greeting her houseplants, she rubbed a few of the leaves, making sure to give her monstera extra encouragement to grow. Its pronounced dark-green leaves stood proudly, centered in the picture-frame window. Reaching her shoulders now and as wide, it was one of her prized plants. She'd given a few clippings to Lina once, but they'd never propagated. It was all hers.

After spritzing the leaves, she plopped onto the sofa, holding Elijah tighter and imagining the life Elysse must've been trying to get away from. Nancy had left Husband #2 like that—packed up all her stuff and left their condo when he was at work.

The pipes whined when the guest bathroom shower turned on—a good sign. A washing-off-of-the-old-to-make-room-for-the-new sort of thing. Nancy wondered how she could better help Elysse's situation. Was there anyone on campus she could talk to?

Bottle now empty, Elijah straightened himself and stared at Nancy, his bright-brown eyes curious, taking her all in. With one chubby hand holding his bottle, the other one quickly found purchase on the intricate lace on Nancy's robe. He babbled something.

"Yeah, I've always wondered how they made that too," she said, then put him against her shoulder and patted his back. Within minutes, he let out several heavy burps. Her phone rang, still on the nightstand in her bedroom. "Five bucks if you can tell me who that is."

She managed to make it to her phone by the sixth ring and immediately recognized the phone number.

It was her mom.

Her stomach bottomed out, but she put on her best voice and answered. "Hello?"

"The attorney is confusing me," Lucy said. "Said something about, oh, I don't know. He used a lot of big words. Taking my money, that's what he's doing."

Nancy switched Elijah to her other hip and shouldered the phone, hoping Lucy would calm down enough to explain. "Try to think about what he said."

"I wanted you to help me. I asked you to help me, Nancy." Lucy sniffled. "Have I ever asked you for anything in your entire life? But I ask for your help once, and you couldn't even do that."

"Mom, what are you talking about? I've been waiting for you to call, remember? You said you would call me back with an update."

"Why didn't you come down here? You expect me to handle all of this on my own at my age?"

"I didn't know you wanted me to come down." Nancy eased onto the couch and put Elijah on the floor to play with some blocks from his bag. How was she supposed to read Lucy's mind? What did this mean for her father?

"He's going to die in that prison, and it'll be all your fault."

That weight was not something Nancy was willing to carry. She closed her eyes and took a deep breath, trying to keep her composure. "What did the lawyer say?"

"He took my two thousand dollars and filed some paperwork. I waited weeks to hear back. He finally called to tell me the warden declined Hank's release. Two thousand dollars. You know how long it took me to save that?"

What could she do? Who did she know? *Ashish*. He was the only decent attorney she trusted, but there was absolutely no way she'd ever tell him about her dad.

"He only has a few more months; the doctors said it themselves. And he looked so frail and sick when I visited him last week. You need to go see him, Nancy."

Would her father be upset at her for not visiting for so long? How would the conversation even go? *So, Dad. It's great to see you after all this time, but now we don't have any time left.* Time . . . it was the one thing she wished she had more of with him. Thinking back, time felt like an enemy. The time her father hadn't been in her life during his first stint. The time she'd been at college. The time she focused on herself and carried on with her life and career. No time to visit him. No time for a quick coffee when he'd come to town. No time. More stolen time when he'd been arrested again in her thirties. Fifteen years initially, then eleven more years taken away from her. So many, many months. And now their time was going to come to a close.

An end.

"Did you hear what I said?" Lucy asked. "You need to go see him."

Nancy bit the insides of her cheeks until she winced. Anger rose in her chest. Anger at her mom for being the reason she'd stopped going to visit her dad and for trying to control her relationship with her father. Anger at her dad for always having taken her mother's side and never standing up for Nancy. But if Nancy were to be honest, most of the anger was directed at herself for not learning how to ignore her mom and still keep her relationship with her father. She needed to learn to just play the game so she could at least see her father one last time.

"Nancy?" Lucy asked.

Nancy cleared her throat. "I heard you."

"And?"

"I'll make some time to go visit him."

"What about the lawyer?"

"I'll see what I can do on my end. Can you have him send me everything? I'll text you my fax number, email, and address, just in case they need to mail anything."

"I'll do that."

They sat in silence for several beats. They'd always had this strange awkwardness between them—Nancy not quite knowing what to expect from her mom, and Lucy not quite knowing how to be a mother to her. At least that was what she'd told Nancy so many times: *You ain't come with a manual. How am I supposed to know what hurt your feelings? Your brother wasn't like this.*

Thinking about her brother made her wonder where he was and how'd he been faring. "Where's Jeff?" Nancy asked.

"Jeff and Amy have been busy staying clean and working."

Nancy cringed at the pride in Lucy's voice. She'd never heard her mother use that tone when talking about anything she'd accomplished. Not when she'd graduated from high school top of her class, with enough scholarships to cover all four years. Not when she'd graduated from undergrad and grad school magna cum laude. Not even when she'd landed a teaching position at a college.

"Five kids so far, you know," Lucy said.

Five kids.

Melancholy filled Nancy. She had five nieces and nephews and didn't know any of them. It wasn't like she and Jeff had grown up to be close or anything. They'd been raised more like competitors than siblings, constantly trying to one-up the other for a morsel of Lucy's attention. A drop of her affection.

Jeff had been everything right when Nancy had been everything wrong. He could've done no wrong in Lucy's eyes. Not when he had been arrested and imprisoned for selling drugs when he was twenty years old. And not even when he'd spent his thirties in and out of jail, prison, and rehab. Jeff was the golden boy and would always be Lucy's favorite.

Eventually, Jeff had been nothing more than a stranger Nancy had heard bits of news updates about from Lucy or Hank, but never from him. She didn't even have his cell phone number. With five kids, she'd imagined someday he'd want them to know their aunt. By the amount of fun she had with Mimi and Danny, she was a pretty damn good aunt, if she did say so herself.

Nancy's fingers twitched with pettiness. "So why isn't Jeff helping you?"

"Don't get to see them much since they moved to Virginia a few years ago."

"*Hmph,*" Nancy snarked.

"Trust me," Lucy added. "I wouldn't be calling you if Jeff were around. Do you really think I'd actually ask you for anything if it weren't serious?"

That hurt. She didn't want to admit it to herself and thought she'd built an impenetrable force field around herself when it came to Lucy, but the woman's words stung. Another reminder of how worthless and inconsequential she'd been to her mother.

Elijah banged the blocks together on Nancy's coffee table. She flinched with each strike, noticing a tiny indentation in the reclaimed wood each time. The banging brought her back into the present. Into her living room and the larger problem at hand: her dad. She reclaimed her time, reminding Lucy of her boundaries. "Hey, Mom. I'm going to go. Call me when you have more details, okay?"

Lucy mumbled something.

"Okay, bye then." Nancy ended the call, closed her eyes, and inhaled deeply, feeling the pressure in her lungs. Slowly, she released, mentally pushing Lucy out of her head. Crawling over to the boy, Nancy still felt some kind of way at how passive-aggressive Lucy had always been to her. She dug through Elijah's bag for something soft and stuffed as he banged harder on her table. "Bunny. Who wants a bunny?" She offered him a furry stuffed animal, holding the rabbit out by its ears. Dropping the blocks, he reached for the bunny. In one swift move, Nancy gathered the blocks and returned them to his diaper bag. She sat back, watching the boy play with his bunny now, lifting and closing the pocket flap, pulling on the bunny's shoelaces, squeezing its fluffy tail until it squeaked. *Why couldn't life be that simple?* she wondered.

"You like that bunny, don't you?" she asked, smiling.

Just then, Elysse made her way to the living room. Her damp hair clung to her ears and hung in tight, coiled curls. Her gaze was sullen, and the way she gripped her phone, her fingertips white and her hand trembling, filled Nancy with concern.

"Everything okay?"

"He's going to take Elijah."

"What do you mean 'he's going to take Elijah'?"

"Brandon called. Said he was going to get a lawyer." Elysse sniffled, her eyes filling with tears. "Told me I am an unfit mom. He's gonna take Elijah away from me since I want to leave so badly." She darted over to her son, picked him up, and clutched him to her chest.

Fiery anger coursed through Nancy. She knew his type, which meant she also knew he'd make good on his word. Pulling her lips between her teeth to keep from spewing every vile word that was building up in her throat, she seethed. Oh, the compound curse words she imagined saying about Elysse's boyfriend were going to be her most creative yet.

She felt antsy watching the woman rub her son's head and whisper to herself. *Was she praying?* Nancy tamped down even more on the bad words, all too aware that she was not just some lady who'd helped Elysse out; she was Elysse's psychology professor and had to maintain a level of professionalism, no matter how hard she had to fake it.

"What can I do?" Nancy asked after a few moments, needing to talk. Needing to help. Needing some sort of action plan to feel useful.

"You've already done so much. Thank you." Elysse lowered the boy to his wobbly feet and held one of his chubby hands. His other hand gripped her calf. She sniffled, clearing her throat. "I'll call some shelters today and make sure we're gone by this evening."

"I'll have no such thing," Nancy blurted out. "I mean, if you've already put in the application for family housing, I can call around, if that's okay with you." Nancy clapped her hands, remembering the semicute guy from housing she'd fooled around with. "I think I may know someone in that department. Want to help yourself to some breakfast and coffee while I make a few calls? Might take a bit."

"Are you sure?" Elysse asked.

"Positive. Fridays are my planning days."

"Do you think the university has someone who can help me on the legal side?"

"I doubt it," Nancy said; then Ashish's face flashed in her head for the second time that morning. She mulled it over for a beat. He *had* helped Lina out of a bad situation and was excellent at his job. She figured he owed her a solid anyway for the way he'd treated her. *Why not?* "I think I might have someone who could help."

Hope flitted across Elysse's face.

"Go ahead and make yourself comfortable. Rest." She wondered if he would even do it pro bono. While calling Ashish would take only a few minutes, building up the courage to dial his number and make the ask would take quite some time. Time and maybe some liquid courage.

CHAPTER 9

By late afternoon, Nancy was a sweaty mess. Walking the four blocks from her place to the café in unseasonably warm, muggy weather hadn't been the best idea, especially since the sky had been threatening to burst wide open all day. But with the uncharacteristic nervous energy pulsing through her, she needed all the movement she could get.

Instead of Ashish being normal and handling everything for Elysse's situation over the phone, he'd insisted on meeting Elysse and Nancy in person, since he'd already been at the university for a conference. As much as she didn't want to see him, she couldn't decline his offer. He *was* the best attorney she knew, and it wasn't about her. It was about Elysse and Elijah. At least that was the lie she'd told herself to justify how quickly she'd given in when he'd asked to meet.

Now, only feet away from the café, she wondered if hiring a different attorney would be a better decision. Would she be violating some sort of student-teacher rule if she paid money for a good cause? Furtively peeking at her reflection in the shadowed window, she sucked in her gut and thanked her booty-lifting panties for rounding out her backside a bit more. If only she felt as great as she looked.

"Hey, Professor Jewel!" Kenny, the barista, shouted from across the counter when she opened the door. His red hair seemed redder with the burnt sunset reflecting off the high-gloss wooden countertop. His now shoulder-length hair was pulled into a high man bun, but to her, he resembled a Ken doll no matter how he'd changed his hairstyle. Although he'd graduated earlier that year, he'd stayed on at the café to help his father run it.

"Hey, Kenny. I'll take my usual when you get a moment." She spotted Ashish at a corner table. He waved her over. "Has that guy ordered anything yet?"

"Not yet."

"Add a dirty chai and a lemon bar to my order, then." Nancy smirked slightly, knowing just how to get under Ashish's skin. "And, Kenny, can you call it a 'chai tea' when you bring it to the table?"

"Sure thing. Give me a few minutes to get it all out to you."

"Thanks." Being devious made her all giddy. Very specifically recalling all the times Ashish had gotten annoyed by people calling chai "chai tea" when the very word *chai* meant tea. She bounded to the table, bouncing on the balls of her feet. It was sort of a dick move, but the way the vein in the center of his forehead throbbed when he was annoyed always brought a smile to her face. Plus, he'd automatically get the joke, and maybe, just maybe, he'd be willing to work with Elysse for free if he knew they were on good terms.

Ashish stood to greet her, opening his arms, then quickly closing them. He straightened his dark-gray slacks and eventually settled on an awkward handshake. "Hi, Nancy."

Stay in control, she reminded herself as her hand filled his. The smooth warmth was such an oddly familiar sensation. It'd been a long time since they'd been on her body. She cleared her throat . . . and her mind. "I went ahead and ordered for the table." *Total boss move.*

"Oh, thanks for that. I was going to get a—"

"Lemon bar?" She raised an eyebrow.

"You got me." He motioned for her to sit and followed suit. "Thanks for meeting me. Tell the truth, I needed an excuse to get out of tonight's networking session. You look great, by the way."

She shot him a sideways glance, not quite expecting the compliment. "Um, thank you. Elysse will be here shortly. She had some paperwork to drop off before the housing department closed."

"Okay, so fill me in. How can I help?"

Nancy gave him the quick-and-dirty details of what she knew about Elysse's situation, omitting the part where she almost hit the woman and her kid with her car. She also left out the key detail that Elysse was one of her students. They'd deal with the conflict of interest another day. As Nancy gave him the last bit of information about Brandon threatening to take Elijah away, Kenny approached their table, delicately balancing their order on a tray.

"Here you go, Professor Jewel." He placed her double espresso onto the table and presented her with a small creamer and a packet of honey. Just the way she liked it.

"And here's your *chai tea*." He winked at Nancy, then lowered a dainty cup-and-saucer set of dark, creamy liquid.

Ashish's eyebrow ticked up. Just as Nancy had predicted, the vein buried between his thick eyebrows grew.

"Thanks, Kenny." She smirked, inhaling the rich, fragrant spices infusing the area. It brought back so many memories of them together. He'd made chai every morning instead of coffee. Chai and a warm hug against his bare chest on mornings they'd wake up together. Eventually, she'd associated long hugs with the spices. She'd guessed if hugs had an actual smell, they'd smell like chai.

"Let me know if you need anything," Kenny said.

"I'm sure this is perfect." She almost wanted to change her order, but after a swirl of honey and a small pour of creamer, her double espresso was exactly what she needed.

"Chai *tea*?" Ashish asked with a knowing look in his eyes and the hint of a smile across his full lips.

"Couldn't help myself."

"You never can."

"Can you blame me, though?" Nancy laughed.

"I guess not." Ashish sliced into the soft, creamy lemon bar and brought the spoon to his mouth.

"I know, right?" Nancy smirked. She'd had the lemon bar too many times to count since Kenny had introduced it last spring.

"Want some?" Ashish asked. "It's so good."

Nancy shook her head. She had to keep it professional. "So, Elysse? How's your caseload?"

"Straight to business." He wiped his mouth, disappointment lingering in his eyes while he put on a serious face. "Forgot about that."

"She'll be here in a few minutes, and I was hoping you'd consider at least helping her file the necessary paperwork."

"What is it with this student? Why are you so involved?"

Nancy'd asked herself that same question. Why hadn't she taken the woman and her son to a shelter? "I don't know." She waved him off. "I mean, I have a heart, Ash."

"I know. It's a lot larger than you let on."

She grimaced. Was he trying to pick an argument with her? Was he trying to annoy her so she'd say something stupid, giving him an instant out? She sipped the rest of her coffee, pretending to ignore his last statement. "I don't know all the specifics, but I can spot a powder keg when I see one, and this is definitely a powder keg. I mean, you remember what happened with . . ." *With Lina.*

She knew he was thinking about how close they'd been to losing Lina at her ex-husband's hands once he'd been served divorce papers. Ashish had tried to talk Lina out of being present when her abusive husband was served—no, he'd begged her not to go through with it. Lina'd had her mind set. To her, it had been the only way to truly escape someone so devious with such deep community ties. She wouldn't have had a chance in any courtroom in their county, since her ex-husband had personally known the judges.

One of the coffee machines behind the counter beeped several times, reminding Nancy of when she had sat bedside in the hospital, praying to anyone who'd listen for Lina to wake up. The beeping had been as endless as Nancy's tears.

Ashish cleared his throat, bringing Nancy back into the present. "I'll never let anything like that happen again," he said, his eyes steely and his jaw solid.

Nancy knew he wouldn't. She checked her phone, hoping Elysse would be there soon. She'd missed two phone calls—one from her mom, the other from Elysse. Her phone dinged with a text from Elysse.

Elysse: I'm so sorry Professor Jewel. Elijah had a blowout at housing and smeared it all over his stroller!

Oh no! Nancy remembered the times she'd helped Lina when one of the kids' diapers had failed. Amazed and horrified, she'd always wondered how someone so small could produce half their body weight in poop. And baby wipes had been woefully inadequate. Elijah probably needed a bath. His stroller needed a water hose.

Nancy: Are you still on campus?

Elysse: I'm getting a ride back to your house, if that's okay.

Nancy: That's perfectly fine. I'll meet you there.

She signaled Kenny for a box.

"Everything okay?" Ashish asked.

"That was Elysse." She put her phone facedown and ran her fingers over the textured case. Its rough rhinestones gave her something to do to keep from thinking about the larger implications of having Ashish back at her house. A sick feeling gurgled in her stomach when she recalled the very last conversation they'd had as friends with benefits, a eulogy of sorts for what could've been and what was.

"Nance?"

"Yeah. Her son's diaper exploded. We'll have to meet her at my place. I mean, if you still have to talk to her."

"I'd prefer to meet her, if that works for you."

Nancy nodded. "I have some work to catch up on anyway. I'll give you guys some space to talk." She rose from the table without waiting for Ashish. He could meet her there. As much time as he'd spent at her place, he certainly knew how to get back there.

Before she reached the door, lightning carved a bright path across the ominous sky, followed by a heavy downpour. It was like Zeus had popped a massive water balloon with a whip of lightning, stopping Nancy in her tracks. She instantly regretted walking instead of driving to the café.

CHAPTER 10

Of course Ashish had an umbrella, Nancy thought for the tenth freaking time in as many minutes. Arms firmly crossed, she glowered in the passenger seat of Ashish's Volvo. At least she was damp and not as soaked through as she would've been if she had walked the four blocks back to her place. That was what she focused on instead of participating in small talk to make the situation less awkward.

Or less painful . . .

Her thoughts drifted to the last time Ashish had been in her house. The last time they'd been *together.* Tears pricked her eyes, but she'd never allow herself to cry over him again. Shaking off the thoughts and shaking off the pain, she straightened and held her head high as they approached her neighborhood's guard station. Motioning for Ashish to roll down the window so she could overtly flirt with Tony, Nancy leaned over slightly and tightly crossed her arms to give herself more cleavage.

"Hey, Tony!" she said a little too happily.

"How's it going?" he asked, looking at the clipboard in his hands.

"Walked to campus and forgot my clicker, can you?"

He held up a finger to her, focusing harder on whatever was on the clipboard. "Hold on a sec."

"Everything okay?"

"You seem to have a visitor."

"Yeah, I already added her to my list."

"My shift just started, but there's a note here." He glanced over to the visitor parking area. "Looks like the visitor claims she's your mother, and it says here she's been belligerent and was warned that the authorities would be called if she kept it up."

The sky suddenly felt darker, the rain heavier.

"Would you like me to let her in?" Tony asked.

Nancy felt Ashish's gaze hot on her face, knowing she'd lied to him about her family. While he'd introduced her to his family multiple times and had included her in their family dinners, he'd eventually asked about hers. She hadn't wanted to explain where her father was and how awful her mom had been. It'd been easier to simply lie and tell him they'd both passed away. She'd felt bad about it at first, but how could her parents ever compare to his lovingly perfect and normal family?

"So do you want me to let her in?" Tony asked again, his arm hovering over the gate control.

"Are you sure she said she was my mom?" Nancy pulled at ropes.

"Well, who the hell do you think I am?"

Nancy's gut bottomed out at her mother's voice now slicing through the din of rain pummeling against the guard gate structure's copper roof. She turned to see her mom, smaller than she'd remembered, the hollows of her cheeks shadowed beneath her black umbrella.

"It's fine, Tony." Nancy sighed.

"I'm not going back to my car. Saw you through the window and wanted to make sure these people"—she pointed a finger toward Tony—"told you I was here."

"Now, ma'am—"

"I'll ride with you." Lucy had Ashish's back door open before they could protest. The pungent smell of tobacco and smoke filled the car when she climbed in. "Let's go." She patted the back of Ashish's headrest.

Speechless, Nancy nodded, still unable to return Ashish's gaze when Tony opened the gate. Ashish slowly pulled out from under the awning and back into the heavy downpour. Rain beat down on the car's roof like a million tiny marbles hitting metal. They drowned out whatever Lucy was saying. Nancy was grateful to have the extra time to prepare mentally for dealing with her mom . . . and Ashish.

Unfortunately, the drive to her place took only a few minutes. Five minutes tops in the rain. Nancy's brain ran through a thousand different scenarios of how she'd maintain her boundaries with her mom, and a thousand more of how she'd explain everything to Ashish. Not that she had to explain anything; they weren't close like that anymore. But just in case he asked, she had to have a convenient excuse handy. She stole a peek at him when he parked and another when they slogged into the house, dripping wet and soggy.

"Hmm," Lucy muttered, slipping off her shoes and placing them beside Nancy's and Ashish's near the front door. She wriggled out of her jacket—one arm, then the other—until it dropped to the floor. She took longer to pick it up than Nancy preferred, leaving a small puddle on her hardwood floors.

Lucy glared at Ashish as he closed his own umbrella. He placed it in the stand delicately beside her own. "Thanks, but we should be fine," she said, waving her hand.

"Um . . . okay, then." Ashish walked farther into the house like he'd done a hundred times before. He looped his messenger bag over the same chair he'd always chosen.

Lucy approached him, hands on her hips. "What do you think you're doing?"

Ashish's brows furrowed.

"What. Do. You. Think. You're. Doing?" Lucy sounded out each word, overpronouncing like she was talking to someone who didn't quite understand English.

"Mom, chill."

"I thought you paid Uber drivers on the app thing."

Ashish snorted, shaking his head slightly.

Nancy rolled her eyes, trying her hardest to keep it together. "Mom, this is Ashish. He's, um . . ." She searched for how she'd explain his presence without giving too much away. If she said they'd dated in the past, Lucy would ask more questions. If she said he was there to help Elysse, Lucy would pick and prod until fully inserting herself into Elysse's situation.

"I'm a friend of Nancy's, and I'm just here to talk to one of her students." He offered his hand. "Ashish Singh. Not an Uber driver, although the idea of driving random people around and hearing their various stories intrigues me." He shrugged. "Maybe in another life." He flashed one of his most genuine smiles. It was almost warm enough to melt the iciest of hearts. It'd melted Nancy's many times in the past.

"Well, you should've said something earlier." Lucy half shook his hand, then turned and busied herself with inspecting Nancy's place.

Nancy watched the scene play out, biting the insides of her cheeks. She had to tread lightly with her mom, knowing how unpredictable her moods could be. The last thing Nancy needed was for her mother to embarrass her even more. It was one thing to explain to Ashish why she'd lied about her mom and another thing entirely having to deal with being so exposed if he ever found out her father was in prison. He'd definitely look at her differently, and that was the last thing she ever wanted. How would she even play that off? In that moment, all she wanted was for her mother to leave and for Ashish to pretend he'd never met her.

"So you live here all alone, Nancy?" Lucy asked, more statement than question.

"Yeah . . . can I get you anything?"

"Oh, you *do* remember how to be hospitable." Lucy pursed her lips and continued on farther into the living room while Ashish rummaged through his bag. "I'll take some sweet tea, if you have any."

Nancy's lips tightened. She couldn't remember the last time she made or bought sweet tea.

Lucy seemed to pick up on it. "*Hmph.* I'm sure you have wine." She slowed near a bookshelf and inspected the books and framed photos. Grimacing, she plucked a shiny silver frame from atop a stack of mindfulness books and flipped it over. "You're not in any of these." She opened the back and peeled off the photo. "You didn't even change the pictures out? You got strangers on display?"

For the second time that night, Nancy couldn't bring herself to look at Ashish. It'd been something he'd noticed when they'd first started hanging out—her not switching out the photos from store-bought frames—and had eventually become a running joke between them. He'd even teased that he'd change out the photos to ones of them.

He cleared his throat, pulling out some papers from his bag. "Anything from Elysse?"

Nancy checked her phone. "Not yet."

"I can't believe it." Lucy dropped the frame facedown onto the bookstack in a clatter. "You'd rather show strangers than your own family? Strangers, Nancy?"

"Mom, it's not like that. I—"

"Somehow I knew coming here was all wrong. I knew you didn't really care about me and your father." She wrung her hands together. "You were always so different. Never really like a daughter."

Nancy cringed, trying her hardest to deflect the painful arrows that were now piercing her weakened armor. She braced herself with the kitchen counter. There it was: her own mother never saw Nancy as her child, never saw Nancy as an extension of herself.

"I mean, I at least expected to see a picture or two of your dad, since you liked him more than me, but it's like we don't even exist to you."

"Mom, it's not like that."

"Do you treat your parents like strangers, young man?" Lucy asked Ashish, her eyes watery.

"No, but Nance doesn't really do sentimental," he said.

"Oh, tell me about it. No wonder she didn't have any friends in high school. I once begged the doctors to give her an MRI to find out if she had a heart in that chest of hers."

More arrows. More pain.

Ashish stood, drew up his height until he looked like he belonged in her space. "She has a massive heart, and it's the purest one I've ever come across."

Nancy blinked. Had Ashish stood up to her mom on her behalf?

He continued, stealing a glance at her. "She doesn't do sentimental because she cares about the here and now. Not the past. She"—his face suddenly lit up, and his gaze seemed like it lingered on a distant memory—"she lives for every single second. She thrives in every moment. Yesterday doesn't even exist when she's in her zone."

"Sounds like you're a whole hell of a lot more than friends." Lucy frowned. "Are y'all together?"

"Mom, no."

Lucy harrumphed.

Nancy had to stop the madness and take control of the situation. "Why are you here?"

"Your father."

"Did something happen?"

"He's dying!"

Ashish's brows softened.

"I know. I know, but did *something happen*? Like, since we last spoke?" Nancy said, trying to keep it all together.

"You sent me your address for the lawyer, and I figured I'd come in person." She motioned to her bag near the door. "Brought the paperwork he filed and the thing from the warden."

Nancy flinched at the word. Ashish had certainly heard it, and now she couldn't meet his eyes. How would she explain *warden* being used in reference to her father's situation?

Lucy picked up on Ashish's questioning look and quickly pounced on her opening. "Her daddy's in prison."

Old, familiar tension surged in Nancy's legs. Her thighs begged to run far away from this conversation. Away from Ashish now that he knew. "Mom, don't—"

"Not a big deal or a secret. People mess up all the time. Just so happened Hank's dumb ass got pinched twice." Lucy leaned on the nearby armchair's back and crossed her arms matter-of-factly. "Armed robbery. But don't you worry, not like it's genetic or nothing."

Don't say it. Don't say it. Don't say it.

"Then again, maybe it is. Her older brother landed in jail for a little while. Now he's trying to stay clean, so we'll see. Maybe that's why Nancy chose not to have any kids. She'd probably be a terrible mom anyway." Lucy snorted a laugh, like something she'd said was funny and not cruel. "It makes so much sense now. Nancy, you remember that time you had to carry a bag of flour around and pretend it was a baby for school?" She clapped her hands, fully laughing and pleased with herself. "I was trying to help you with something, and you yanked it away from me so hard it burst. Then you screamed and cried and said you'd be a better mom than me one day." She smirked, serious again. "When's that one day, huh?"

Nancy was sure she saw disgust run across Ashish's face. There it was—the thing she'd kept hidden for so long. The part of her she didn't want to share with anyone, especially Ashish. She couldn't open herself for the taunts and jeering like she had in high school. She couldn't allow that part of herself to be laid bare before someone like Ashish.

She'd crafted her life perfectly enough without the added drama and toxicity that always followed her mom. And now Ashish knew it all. He knew her ugly and her gross. Her chest ached with stifled sobs. She suddenly felt fifteen again and wanted to bolt from her house and sleep in a Winn-Dixie parking lot until her dad came and rescued her.

Until he protected her from her mom.

CHAPTER 11

There was a clattering at the door.

"I'll get that." Ashish hurried over to help Elysse with the baby while Nancy and Lucy had a silent standoff: Nancy willing her mom to stop; Lucy running her tongue across her teeth, gearing up for round two.

"I'm so sorry it took so long, Professor Jewel." Elysse was soaked through.

"It's okay. This is Ashish."

"I'll help." He rolled up the sleeves of his shirt and grimaced at the stroller just outside the front door. "Starting with this stroller. Nance, is the hose still out back?"

"Yeah."

"I'm on it." He disappeared through the front door, into the dark with the stroller.

"How about you and Elijah go get cleaned up and comfortable. Have you eaten yet?"

Elysse didn't meet her eyes.

"Actually, you're just in time. I ordered pizza earlier. Should be here soon." She lied and quickly pulled out her phone. "Let me check." She pretended to check but instead placed an order for two large pies and some drinks. "Yup. Thirty minutes. Think they were slammed or something."

Lucy made a grand gesture of extending her arm out to Elysse. "And I'm her mother."

"Nice to meet you." Elysse waved instead of taking Lucy's hand. "I'm all wet and gross. I'm sorry." She shifted Elijah to her other hip.

"It's quite all right." Lucy started toward Elijah. "And who is this handsome little man?" Without warning, she reached for the boy to hold him.

Elysse's eyes widened. "Um—"

"Hey, Mom, they really need to get out of those wet clothes." Nancy intervened, not wanting her mom to push herself on them. "Go ahead and get cleaned up. Pizza should be here by the time you're done."

Elysse exhaled. "Thank you."

One.

Two.

Three . . .

Nancy counted to ten, watching Elysse shuffle down the hallway to the guest room. Inhaling, she steadied herself, preparing for whatever else her mother had in store.

Dad. She reminded herself to play nice. All this was about her dad, not Lucy.

"You really enjoy embarrassing me, don't you?" Lucy said on the way to the front door. Nancy held her breath, hoping she'd be upset enough to leave altogether. She had no such luck. Instead, Lucy stopped in the foyer and fished through her bag.

"You obviously don't want me here," Lucy said, then produced a thick manila envelope. She brought it into the kitchen, slammed it onto the counter. "Here's everything from the lawyer."

"Thanks." The stack of paper was heavy in Nancy's hands. It seemed to carry an indescribable weight.

RE: Compassionate Release Petition for a Terminal Medical Condition

Dear Warden Buchanan:

My name is Hank Jewel and I am an inmate housed at Ware State Prison. This letter serves as my request for compassionate release in accordance with Program Statement 5050.49, Compassionate Release/Reduction in Sentence: Procedures for Implementation of 18 U.S.C. § 3582(c)(1)(A).

This petition is specifically made as to the Terminal Medical Condition category discussed in Section 3(a) of the program statement.

Something caught in her throat. Seeing her father's name on the document made it real. She'd been worried that her mom had been melodramatic about him being a little sick—maybe a cold or something—to worm her way back into Nancy's life without any boundaries. But there it was in front of her: terminal diagnosis.

Dad.

Her heart cried out for him again. Anger, rage, sorrow, and guilt all combined deep within her. Why hadn't she visited him sooner? Why had she been so stubborn when her mom chose no contact over healthy boundaries? Nancy placed the papers on the counter and closed her eyes, allowing the cold granite countertop to anchor her in place.

Lucy exhaled heavily, her nose whistling in the space between them. "See. Bet you thought I was lying this whole time," she said, her voice just above a whisper and sprinkled with tenderness. Ever so slowly, Lucy slid her hand over Nancy's.

Nancy's eyes fluttered open at the sensation of Lucy's hand on hers, clammy and foreign. In that moment, Nancy focused on one of her mother's prominent veins. Plump and blue beneath her pale, translucent skin, the vein crawled up and over deep wrinkles. It underlined the heavy splattering of age spots from one side of her hand to the next.

She followed it all the way up her thin arm until it disappeared into her checkered blouse. Nancy hoped it carried love from Lucy's heart to hers.

Nancy cleared her throat. "He's really not doing well, is he?"

"He doesn't have long left."

Nancy felt a tug in her chest as tears begged for release. Could she cry in front of her mother? Would Lucy comfort her? She sniffled.

Lucy held her hand firmer. "Doctor said he might have two or three months left."

The tears were pounding at Nancy's will. "That's all?"

Lucy gently held both of Nancy's hands, and in that moment, Nancy considered collapsing into her mother's arms for a much-needed hug. Was this the event that would finally bring them closer? A shared loss could do that to people. They could trauma bond. It wouldn't be the healthiest option, but it would be better than what they had now. Maybe they could even grow from this. In a tear-filled blur, Nancy peeked at her mother. With her own watery eyes, Lucy gave the warmest, kindest smile Nancy had ever seen. Hope lit in Nancy's chest like a match to kindling, small but with the promise of a larger fire. A warmer burn. A more welcoming hearth to sit beside.

"He didn't want me to tell you." Lucy shrugged matter-of-factly. "Didn't want you to make a fuss over him. You know how stubborn he is."

Nancy nodded, glad Lucy had told her. She would've hated to find out too late.

Lucy snorted, a slight smile dimpling her cheeks. "That's one thing that man will never change. Once he makes up his mind, it's like it's set in concrete. I couldn't get him to change his mind when you were a baby, you know."

Nancy furrowed her brows, confused.

"That was when he went in the first time. I think you were three or four months old. I was still nursing you, and let me tell you, you were a greedy baby. About wore me out wanting to eat every hour or two." Lucy's smile widened as she looked off into some distant past. "Hank

81

thought it was hilarious. Called you a baby bear. You had this big round belly and chunky legs. He would pretend to nibble the rolls on your arms to make you laugh."

She patted Nancy's hand. "You'd squeal and flail about, giggling like it was the funniest thing in the world. He was the only one who could make you laugh like that. Your brother tried a few times, but you'd just cry."

Nancy found herself laughing along with Lucy. Hand in hand, she took the journey with her mom down the memory highway. It felt good to be at peace, for once. To have both of their white flags raised in solidarity.

"There was this one time your dad went to nibble on you, and you bucked so hard from laughing, you slid right out of my arms and onto the floor. Hit your head so hard on the tile it took some time for you to even cry. Hank immediately sprang into action. He got your brother dressed and helped me to the car. Took us straight to the emergency room as the goose egg on your head grew bigger and bigger. I had to pinch you every few minutes to keep you awake."

Nancy had never heard this story before. Without thinking, she ran her fingers over a raised, bumpy area near her hairline. She'd come to think of it as a birthmark all these years.

"No, that's not from the fall," Lucy said. "Turns out, you were just fine. That scar came from the six stitches you needed afterward. We got into an accident on the way back home from the hospital. We didn't have car seats and stuff back then."

Nancy noticed how her mother's voice trailed off. She waited for more of the story. More of how her dad made her laugh. More of how normal and happy they'd been. Hanging on Lucy's last words, she closed her eyes to take in the moment, grateful to know she wouldn't be alone after her dad passed. She'd have her mother.

"They arrested him later that day after clearing up the accident mess. Said he had an outstanding warrant."

She realized then that her mother had probably always blamed the baby version of Nancy for taking Hank away.

"Know what, Nancy?" Lucy said softly, a change in her voice.

Nancy knew if she looked at her mom just then, she'd break down. "What?"

"If your daddy dies in that cold, hard prison all alone and help-less"—she removed her hands from Nancy's and clasped them in front of her—"it will be all your fault. I will never forgive you."

Nancy waited a beat to see if her mom was going to make light of or take back what she'd just said. Or even apologize. A beat dragged on to a moment. Her heart picked up pace, and she quickly recoiled from her mother. "My fault?" She'd heard enough. She'd heard all she wanted to hear. "How would it be my fault?"

"You didn't come when I told you I needed help," Lucy said matter-of-factly.

"You didn't ask for me to come home." Nancy felt her pressure rise. Her ears popped. "I can't read your fucking mind!"

"Your language."

"My language, Lu-cy? How about your toxic behavior?"

"There you go trying to blame me for everything that is wrong in your life. I'm not toxic. You are. Just look at how you keep people away. Look at all of your divorces."

"Don't deflect."

"I'm not deflecting anything. I'm simply saying you're the toxic person here. You're the one who hasn't seen her dad in years, and now you only care because he's dying."

Rage claimed every single cell in her body, and she felt as though the top of her head would blow up like in the old cartoons she'd watched. "You need to leave."

"And now you're kicking me out in a thunderstorm? I bet your friend would never do that to his mother." She wrung her hands. "See, I knew you didn't care about your family."

Nancy dialed Tony's cell. He picked up on the first ring. "Hey, Nance."

"Don't ask any questions. I need you to come pick my mom up and take her to her car, please."

Tony waited a few seconds, then said, "Give me five minutes."

"Thanks, Tony."

"Anytime."

"Fine by me." Lucy threw her hands up like it didn't matter. She tapped the legal packet in front of Nancy. "That's your copy. Can't say I never gave you anything."

Nancy seethed so hard she shook watching her mother don her shoes and jacket.

"Now I remember what I was thinking when I noticed your picture frames." A light playfulness in her voice. "I thought: here's a woman who seems so put together and perfect on the outside, but she's so empty inside she can't even see herself living in her own home."

That was the death blow that claimed the very last fragment of what Nancy thought of as her heart. Her own mother didn't love her. Lucy had never loved her and would never love her. Every interaction proved it to be a fact. Nancy switched off her emotions and took a more pragmatic approach to the situation. While she wanted nothing more than to take the nuclear option on her mother, she was still Professor Jewel and had both a student and Ashish in her home.

Nancy's eyes felt hard, her body rigid. "Thank you for this information, Lucy. I will see what I can do on my end." She used her professor voice. "I believe Tony is outside. Thank you for visiting."

Lucy scoffed, clearly disappointed she hadn't elicited the reaction she'd wanted. She shook her head on the way to the door. "That's why you'd rather have strangers than yourself. You can't face yourself."

Nancy thought she'd completely crumble when Lucy closed the door behind her. How could her own mother treat her like that? Or worse: Would Nancy start treating people like that? Would she end up alone and bitter like her mom? That was what Keith had said . . . maybe he was right, somehow. She hated the idea of him being right about anything, but she hated the idea of her mom being right more.

So empty inside.

Nancy looked around her house. She noticed all the artwork and trinkets she'd picked up on various trips abroad—trips she'd mostly taken by herself. She took note of her houseplants, brilliant hues of green. Her monstera—her prized plant—stood above the other assorted greenery. She'd considered adding another monstera but could never bring herself to add another plant that might eventually overshadow the one that had been with her longest. She reached for a wineglass—one out of the other five she rarely used.

"I'll take a glass. Red, right?"

She turned to find Ashish on the other side of the counter, his shirt soaked through.

"Saw your mom leave." He looked from one side to the next, his wet hair grazing his eyes. "Please tell me you didn't throw that box of my stuff out."

Nancy thought about his box of stuff. The box of random items that were not hers after he said he could no longer keep seeing her without a commitment. The leftover box he'd never claimed. "It's in the linen closet." Her voice was too shaky and thin.

"Nance?" He moved closer to her. "Are you okay?" He swiped a thumb across her cheek. "Why are you crying? What happened?"

She felt them then, thick tears trailing down her cheeks, wet snail tracks mottling her makeup. She also felt the heat from his hand on her face, familiar and very much wanted. She turned to him, raw and broken. *Empty.*

His other hand found purchase on her cheek. With his thumbs, he delicately wiped her tears away.

"I'm here. Talk to me." His dark eyes bore into hers. She'd always looked away when he stared at her like that. It'd felt like he'd been trying to peek into her very soul. But she couldn't look away this time. She wanted him to see. She wanted him to notice. She wanted him to verify that she wasn't empty when it was all she felt.

"Nance," he whispered. "Come here." He pulled her into his chest. Despite having been in the cold rain, his chest was warm. When his arms wrapped around her, something released within her. More tears found their way through her barricade until she couldn't tell where his shirt was wet from rain or because of her. His hug was firm and solid, something she'd always loved.

She shivered, feeling his lips brush across her forehead. Her body reacted as with muscle memory and ached for a taste of him. Judging by the bulge pressing against her stomach, his body seemed to remember her as well. She tilted her head slightly.

"Nancy," he breathed. "I'm sorry."

She didn't need words just then. They held no weight to her. She'd heard apologies all her life, and they'd been nothing more than noise to fill silent spaces. She didn't want Ashish to fill the silence. She wanted him to fill her. She needed to be held and kissed.

Her hand slipped around his neck until her fingers tangled in his thick hair. He shivered, leaning his head back into her hands. Gently, her nails drew tiny circles across his scalp. His grip on her tightened. Taking her cue, she pulled him to her until their lips touched. She pressed herself against him, kissing him deeply.

When they parted, he was looking into her soul again. Eyes deep like an unending well, his heavy brows knit. She turned her head slightly. Softly, he brought it back until they were gazing into each other's eyes once more. She trembled, tears bubbling back up.

The doorbell chimed.

Disappointment filled Ashish's face. She broke their embrace, knowing all too well a one-night stand was not what he wanted. It wasn't what he'd accept, and yet it was all she could offer. Her legs tensed to sprint out the door again. She had to find an excuse to not be near him just then. He adjusted himself while Nancy headed toward the door.

After setting up a pizza station on her counter, Nancy busied herself. Nervous energy swept through her body. Between her dad, Lucy, and now whatever had happened just then with Ashish, her house felt ten times smaller. Cramped. Stuffy. She tried hiding out in her bedroom, but her chest was heavy. The water felt too hot and too cold when she splashed her face in the bathroom.

She needed fresh air.

She darted into the living room, grabbed her car keys from the rack near the kitchen, and called over her shoulder, "I'll be back later. Elysse should be out shortly."

She sprinted to her car, tapping the steering wheel as the garage door rolled open. Rain beat down hard on the roof of her car as it sliced through the various roads. There was a discomfort she couldn't find words for. Hurt from her mom? Grief from the impending loss of her dad? Confused feelings over Ashish? They all made her want to crawl out of her skin.

Nance. The way Ashish had looked all the way inside her terrified her most. That level of intimacy was something she could never return, and eventually he would be disappointed, like he'd been months earlier.

There it was: she was a disappointment. To her mom. To her dad. To Ashish. Probably to Lina, even, as often as she flaked out on her friend. What was wrong with her?

Keith.

There was at least one person who expected very little from her. His arms tonight would be just the Band-Aid she needed. All it took was one call to let him know she was en route to his place.

Keith met her at the door, towel in hand. While she should've felt relief or excitement about being with him, she felt nothing. Was she as broken as her mother had said? Had the emptiness claimed her entirely?

Keith helped pat her back with another towel. "That's some weather, isn't—"

Was she a shell of a person forever trapped in an endless black hole? She swirled around and kissed him, hoping to find some emotion she could pull on. Furiously searching for *something*, she yanked his shirt over his head and kissed his shoulders and chest. Did she even want him sexually anymore?

Of course she wanted to smash; it was what she did. Screw and leave. It was her signature move. She didn't need anything more. She'd never needed anything more.

She tugged at his belt, then unbuttoned his jeans. At least he wanted her. She kissed a trail down his body until he was in her mouth.

"Oh shit, Nancy." He braced himself against the steel-looking monstrosity of a table near the door. His fingers played in her hair as they moved together until he was oh so close. "Come here." He groaned, pulling her to her feet and taking control of her body.

His tongue teased every part of her until he walked her back and bent her over the couch. The leather squeaked with each stroke when he took her. Nancy dug her fingers into the pillows, hoping to *feel*. Needing to feel. "My hair. Pull," she begged, praying that would do the trick. Keith complied, palming her head and tugging her head back to meet her lips.

"Harder," she panted. She'd settle for pain if she couldn't feel anything else.

"Nancy, I'm—" he grunted.

She clenched around him, trying to leach an ounce of pleasure. Nothing. Panic rose in her chest, and soon her breath caught in her throat. Grasping for any other feeling besides emptiness and now fear, Nancy waited for Keith to finish. She slid to the floor, clasping her knees to her chest. What the hell was wrong with her?

"Come on." Keith held out his hand for her to follow him to the bathroom.

She felt oddly disconnected from her body, a stranger in a poorly fitting coat as she went through the motions until they were lying side by side in Keith's bed. In the dark, Nancy waited for Keith to wrap his arms around her and pull her close. She needed him to hold her.

Instead, light snoring sounded from his side of the bed. She rolled over and gripped her pillow, the trickle of tears sliding into her hair.

Her mom was right about her.

CHAPTER 12

The next morning found Nancy in her own bed, tightly cocooned in three layers of covers. She vaguely remembered driving back home and crawling into her bed. She was grateful to be home. Rolling to her side, she rubbed her eyes. Lucy's words flooded back into her head like a bad dream: *You're the toxic person here. You're the one who hasn't seen her dad in years, and now you only care because he's dying.*

Pulling the covers over her head, she inhaled deeply to the count of six, then held for four and exhaled slowly. Needing to dislodge everything her mother had said, Nancy repeated her affirmations, first in her head, then out loud. "You're brave, brilliant, and badass. Boss up, babe."

Over and over she whispered it to herself, growing louder each time. Tossing back the blankets, she had to busy herself to keep her mother's criticism at bay. She sprang out of bed, dressed, and went to make coffee.

"Good morning, Professor Jewel," Elysse said, biting into a leftover slice of pizza. She sat cross-legged at the table, her laptop open with what Nancy assumed was a paper.

"Morning. Where's Elijah?"

"He was up earlier. Just put him down for a nap. Last few days have really worn him out."

"I can imagine." Nancy waited for her Keurig to bless her with the good stuff. "Was Ashish able to help?"

"Yeah. He's gonna help me file some documents and thinks it's going to work out in my favor." She beamed, finally looking her age. "Said he'd stop by this morning to get me to sign some stuff, if that's okay with you."

"Yeah, that's totally fine." She faked a smile. She absolutely did not want to see him again. "My apologies for leaving last night. I had something I'd forgotten about."

"I understand." Elysse pointed at the folded lined paper on the other side of her laptop. "Ashish left that for you."

"Oh, okay. Thanks." Nancy tried not to move too quickly to reach for it. She'd left so abruptly after they'd kissed. What had he thought? She slid the note into her back pocket, needing to read it without an audience, and slowly drifted back into her bedroom. Leaning against the bedroom door, she pulled out the note and unfolded it.

Hope you don't mind, but I noticed the papers you left on the counter and read through them. I'm so sorry to hear about your dad. You know I'm here if you need to talk. I have a coworker who's done release requests before. Would you mind if I reached out to see what needs to be done to get him home? Give me a call when you can.

Ash

Nancy's feet sealed themselves to the floor. It was her worst nightmare come true. She'd done everything to ensure he'd never find out about that part of her life. Her past. Then it hit her: he'd read through her father's file, discovered every horribly embarrassing detail, and still wanted to help. How was she supposed to feel? Was she capable of feeling anything anymore? She sighed, more confused than ever.

"Um, Professor Jewel?"

Nancy snapped out of her spiral and rejoined Elysse at the table. "Yeah, Elysse?"

"Well, Student Services said it could take up to a week to find a place for us, and you've been really cool about letting us stay here, but Elijah can be fussy sometimes, and we don't want to inconvenience you." She looked away. "My dad is sending me some money for a hotel."

"I'm glad you got in touch with him."

"Yeah, he, um . . . it was really hard, but he understood."

"You know dads are kinda cool like that." Nancy remembered the many times Hank had helped her out of a pinch. "They try to act all tough, but they can be softer than Jell-O sometimes. My dad was like that when I wanted to go to college away from home. My mom was totally against me being so far away, but Dad understood. I'd come home after school all angry when I felt like they weren't supporting me with my college decision. But after I grumbled and stomped around, he'd always find some way to let me know he heard me." Nancy's chest swelled. She leaned on the table, crossing her legs at the ankles. "I didn't even know how I'd get into college, to tell the truth."

She got all animated talking about her dad. It made her feel lighter, somehow, thinking about his goodness and kindness—the best parts of him. "He gave me the money for the application instead of making me pay for it with my little part-time job at the movie theater. Said it was the least he could do for letting him watch all the movies for free. He was actually in the theater the day I got my acceptance letter to UGA." She could still smell the greasy popcorn and old, stale odor of recycled, air-conditioned air. "I had it sent to my job to make sure nothing happened to my mail." Nancy couldn't believe she was telling Elysse so much, but she also couldn't stop her word vomit.

"My manager came out of her office—she was this cute old woman with the most beautiful silver hair I'd ever seen. You won't believe how many times I wanted to just reach out and touch it. I imagined it felt like Christmas tinsel. Do you even know what that is?"

Elysse nodded along, her eyes wide with wonder.

"My manager came sprinting from her office with my letter from UGA, and Dad had just gotten his bucket of popcorn for some movie. I think it was one of the *Austin Powers* or *Star Wars* movies—the prequels, not the good ones—but that doesn't matter. There was a drug store next door, and Dad begged me to wait for him to get a disposable camera. I was ready to jump out of my skin by the time he returned. It was so corny and cheesy, but all my coworkers gathered around while I ripped open my acceptance letter. Dad took all these ridiculous pictures—think he had three cameras full. He was so proud of me he asked my manager to let me off early and then took me out to dinner instead of watching the movie he'd come in for. I got pizza grease all over that letter, but it was so worth it. He beamed all night, so proud of me."

"That's really awesome. My dad is like that. I just don't want to"— she picked at her dry cuticles—"I don't want to disappoint him, know what I mean?"

Nancy knew all too well what she meant. Images of her own father flickered in her head, and a sudden urgency gripped her. She needed to go see him today. She sipped her coffee and said, "You're far from a disappointment."

Elysse's eyes glimmered. "I was scared, but I'm glad I did it. He wants me to stay in school."

"I don't blame him. You're a great student."

"Thank you. And, um, thank you for helping me. I can't—"

"It's okay. Just turn in your paper on time and we're good. I was thinking about heading out of town later today, anyway, so this works out."

Elysse closed her laptop and slid it into her backpack. "I'm gonna pack and clean up while Elijah's asleep. Would you mind giving me and Elijah a ride later?"

Nancy checked her phone. "How does an hour sound?"

~

A little over an hour later, Elysse was loading her son's car seat into the back of Nancy's SUV. She had a bounce to her walk and a lightness in her face that Nancy had never seen before. Something in Nancy wanted to do more for them, but there was a line of professionalism she didn't want to cross. After all, she'd see the girl in her class on Monday.

Nancy had tidied up the house and packed an overnight bag and was now joining Elysse in packing the car. She guesstimated the trip to Waycross, Georgia, would take a little over four hours and imagined all the music she'd play to keep her mind busy. She figured she'd spend the night if visiting hours were over by the time she got there. That would allow her enough time to visit all Sunday.

She put the key in the ignition. Her Range Rover turned over with a hearty growl; then her phone rang.

"Hello?"

"Hey, Nancy."

She hadn't paid attention to the guard gate number but recognized the voice. "Hey, Tony."

"I have an Ashish Singh here for you."

Nancy smirked at his formality. Tony knew Ashish from his weekly visits and had even joked about being jealous. Nancy guessed Tony had figured out they weren't seeing each other anymore, and the call was more of a check-in of sorts. Tony was always looking out for her.

Nancy checked her mirror, making sure she looked decent, then said, "Oh yeah. I forgot he was coming."

"You good?"

"I am. Thanks for asking. It's okay. You can let him in." Nancy cringed. Seeing him was the last thing she needed to do before visiting her father. Her mind was already all messed up.

Moments later, Nancy greeted him at the door with a pasted-on smile. She forced herself to ignore how her body was reacting to being near him again. "Hey. Let me get Elysse." She spun and started away from him.

He reached for her, closing the door with his foot. "Nance, hold on."

"Last night was a mistake. I get all weird and forget how to make rational decisions around my mom, that's all."

He squared his shoulders to her, lowered his head. "I'm sorry to hear about your father. I can't imagine what you're going through. I'm—"

"Thanks, but I'm good."

He tilted his head to the side, giving her a look that made her want to confess her deepest, darkest feelings. "I'm here if you need anything. I heard back from—"

"Ah, here's Elysse." Nancy motioned to the young woman entering the kitchen to clean out Elijah's bottles.

"Oh," Ashish muttered.

Nancy gave them space to go over the paperwork. Ashish used his professional voice, calm and sincere, but also very much assertive. She listened from her room, busying herself. She changed her sheets, cleaned her bathroom, and folded laundry that was balancing on a chair in the far corner of her room. There was a satisfying hum in her busyness that was louder than whatever she'd felt about Ashish being in her house again. It drowned out her anxiety and gave her something to focus on.

Her mind eventually drifted to thoughts of her father. Of her mother. Of Jeff and what he'd been up to all her adult life. The four of them had never been a close family. They'd had their moments, here and there, but nothing ever lasting.

Maybe it was the soft wafting of lavender scents from the laundry that brought to mind the time Lucy had it in her head to start a laundry service for extra money. Her mom would come home from her job cleaning the hospital all day, and she, Nancy, and Jeff would sit for hours folding baskets upon baskets of clothes. Other people's clothes.

Lucy had seemed nicer back then. That or maybe Nancy was being sentimental. The way Nancy remembered it, the TV had always been on to one of Lucy's nighttime shows, but instead of watching it, they'd take turns creating the silliest stories. A week before they'd picked Hank up, it'd been Lucy's turn. She'd regaled them with an epic saga of a dashing knight rescuing a queen from her cruel and decades-older husband, the king.

The knight was in the king's employ and carried out only the most dangerous tasks. One day, the knight found the princess, bruised and beaten, and vowed his allegiance to her. He brought her trinkets from his travels and news from her family. Soon they fell in love, and the brave knight was forced to fight the king. But the princess was wiser than both of them and took their fight as her way of escape, stealing away during their battle.

Luckily, the knight survived and found her. They had several happy years together that produced two children. But the king eventually caught up with them, demanding restitution. Being true and brave, the knight gave of himself and was locked away for eternity.

Nancy thought back to how sullen Lucy had been telling that story. She'd tried to cheer her mom up afterward by fixing her a massive banana split. The bowl had been piled high with scoops of ice cream, chocolate syrup, sprinkles, and whatever else Nancy had found in the pantry. Among the mountains of folded clothes, the three of them had enjoyed the treat. It'd been one of the last times they'd been somewhat happy.

Nancy's stomach roiled as she considered how she would deal with Lucy if the woman was at the prison today. One way or another, she'd figure it out. She checked the time and realized she'd have to get on the road soon to make it to the prison before visiting hours ended.

Elysse and Ashish were making small talk about her goals after school when Nancy met them in the living room. Elijah shot her a wide grin from the side of his mother's hip, two tiny teeth dotting his gums.

"Everything set?" Nancy asked.

Ashish nodded. "I think I have enough to file some initial requests. Elysse here was telling me about her plans."

"Definitely going to make each of them happen. She's a bright student," Nancy said.

Elysse beamed. "I don't think I'll ever be able to thank you enough, Professor Jewel."

"Like I said earlier, it's nothing." She checked her phone for something to do with her hands. "We better get going."

Ashish folded his arms across his chest. "Where are you guys headed?"

"My dad got me a hotel until I can get a place in the residence hall, and Professor Jewel was going out of town, right?"

Nancy's lips tightened. "Yeah."

"Heading to Lina's?" he asked.

"No." She looked off. "To Waycross."

"Oh. Okay. Um, well . . ."

"I'm going to change Elijah before we leave. Thanks again, Ashish." Elysse slipped away.

"Going to see your dad?" Ashish's voice was sturdy enough to hold her upright, if she'd ever let him.

"Yeah."

"I, um." Ashish scratched his head. "I reached out to my colleague, and she sent me everything I'd have to do to request his release."

Nancy didn't know what to think or feel in that moment. Should she be relieved that he had asked for help with the request? Glad he wasn't judging her? Fearful he might use this against her in the future?

"If it's okay with you?" Ashish asked.

She heard herself swallow a boulder. "Thank you, Ash."

"Just had this thought, actually."

The way he raised his eyebrows questioningly made Nancy want to grant him permission to have his way with her.

"Would it be okay if I tagged along to better assess the situation?" Ashish cleared his throat. "I mean, I was going to try to get in a visit anyway, but it wasn't going to be for a few weeks. Once I go back to work on Monday, I'll be pretty slammed."

"A few weeks?" Her dad didn't have a few weeks. Every moment they waited was one less moment her father would be comfortable. "It's, like, four hours away, and I was most likely going to spend the night," she said.

"I'll get my own room if you let me tag along. And I'll pay for gas." He held up his hands. "Strictly professional. Not trying to pressure you or anything here. This just seems so convenient and cuts the timeline down substantially."

She felt off. Out of sorts, like she'd ventured into uncharted land without a compass or a map. How was she supposed to react or feel? Within two days, Ashish had not only discovered she'd lied about her parents, but he'd met her awful mom and was about to meet her dying father and maybe, just maybe, help get him out of prison.

CHAPTER 13

The ride should've been smooth and quiet.

It should've given Nancy time and space to process, to piece together the fragments of emotions—bits and pieces of excitement, fear, hope, grief, sorrow.

She should've been singing at the top of her lungs to give herself something to do other than play car bingo in her head. Red car. Red car. Red car. Red car. Red car. BINGO!

Instead, Nancy gripped her steering wheel until her knuckles where white and her hands numb as she followed her GPS's light-blue pathway from her house to Ware State Prison. The clean lines and clearly marked buildings and roadways made her trip seem so simple. So sterile.

Turn right.

Keep straight.

Turn left at the light.

Drive another thirty miles.

Your destination is on the left.

She wished for that level of disconnect. Numbness. It was so much better than the mess of feelings surging through her. And Ashish's presence in her car made it that much worse.

She'd agonized over her decision at first, immediately wanting to take back her offer when he initially suggested to tag along. Two birds, one stone, right? But now, with the final turn onto the foreboding road leading to the prison, she wanted nothing more than to drop Ashish off before reaching the entrance.

She was unsure of how she'd react to seeing her dad in failing health, unsure of how she'd feel being vulnerable in front of Ashish. Having Ashish there was a mistake. No, so much greater than a mistake. A tragedy waiting to happen. She slowed to a stop, her hands shaking as she shifted the car into park.

"Would you prefer I wait out here until you've seen him?" Ashish asked softly. It was one of the few things he had said the whole drive. Four hours, twelve minutes of silence between them save the occasional *Can I turn that station?* or *Is this okay?* or *I'm grabbing a Coke—do you want a Sprite?* when they'd stopped for gas.

She couldn't blame him. It wasn't as though she'd opened herself to any small talk or niceties. Driving the route without breaking down emotionally had been hard enough.

Ashish ran a hand through his hair, inadvertently fluffing it a little. "You know, I didn't really think this through." He snorted, as if just realizing it himself. "All I was thinking this whole time was: get there, assess his situation, make some on-the-ground contacts, and submit the request. Maybe even ask to personally meet with the warden, if possible. Or at least set up an appointment while I was there."

He rubbed his forehead, sighing. "I'm sorry, Nance. I didn't even think about what you would have to deal with when you got here. Honestly, I didn't even think about how difficult this would be for you until just now." He reached for her trembling hand. It was pale and clammy. He rubbed it between his own hands. Together, they watched the stark, white tips redden and plump back to life. "Asking to tag along was probably not my best idea. I'm so sorry, Nancy."

She laughed.

No, Nancy burst out into hysterics until she was snorting and wheezing. He'd figured this out *now*? Jeez, she knew guys could be clueless, but he was four and a half hours too late to change his mind. If she had to suffer, so did he. *"Oooh,"* she laughed, wiping her eyes with the back of her hands. "Yeah. I'd say." She snorted. "Totally not your best idea, dude."

That made him join in her laughter. It felt good laughing like an absolute idiot for a moment, ignoring the fact that they were outside her father's prison, where he was probably lying in some depressed makeshift hospital bed or cell, clinging to life.

Yeah . . .

She was losing her mind but still couldn't stop laughing at the ridiculousness of it all. Tears poured down her face, and for the first time in a long while, she didn't care. She slapped her belly, laughing with her entire gut until her core hurt and her arms were oddly sore. The laughter seemed to wring out every emotion she'd carefully curated, bottled, and corked. She laughed through her pain. Her loneliness. Her sadness. Her grief. Her loss. She laughed and cried and laughed and cried.

"Whooooo," she exhaled, sniffling, and caught Ashish gazing at her with a tenderness that made her instantly want to recoil. However, she did no such thing. He'd see her today. For the first and probably last time, she'd let him actually *see* her.

He wiped her tears with his thumbs. She leaned into his hand, relishing how safe she felt in that instant. How comforted and protected she felt in that space. Then the real tears welled up and poured from her, heavy and hot. He reached for her, holding her, as she cried into his shoulder.

After some time, the windows fogged against the mid-November chill. All that was left were Nancy's soft, ragged breaths. "Thank you, Ash," she said.

"Guess it's why I'm here," he whispered into her hair.

Sometime later, with her eyes puffy and reddened, Nancy entered the visitors' area with Ashish trailing behind her. They went through the motions of showing their IDs, going through various metal detectors and scanners, and being screened for contraband. Thankfully, her name was still on the visitors' list, while Ashish was able to gain entry because of his job.

They were ushered through several locked doors, down a few sterile, brightly lit hallways, and buzzed through secured entrances to the visiting area. Two things had always rattled Nancy when she'd visited: the sound of thick, solid doors slamming and locking behind her, essentially locking her in, and the smell. It hit her instantly, making her gag. Chlorine, piss, and body odor assaulted her nose, burning her chest. She shook her head, feeling her eyes start to water. Ashish cleared his throat a few times.

"Let's see." The security guard checked the clipboard. "Hank Jewel? He's down there." He pointed to a round metal table with built-in seats.

Nancy staggered back a bit into Ashish when she saw her father. He looked like he'd stepped into a time machine and aged ten years in the two she hadn't seen him. Her legs took over, leading her to his table. He stood, opened his arms for her, but caught himself. No physical contact.

He hugged her with his eyes instead, his lips spreading wide across his gaunt face. His eyes brightened with each passing second, as though her sheer presence brought life to him.

"Hey, Dad." Nancy felt her resolve completely shatter. She wanted nothing more than for him to hug her and tell her he was going to be okay.

"Where's my smile?" Hank asked.

Nancy felt her bottom lip tremble.

"Now, don't you start that. I'm just fine. You hear me?" Hank struck his chest. "I'm fit as a horse." He coughed. "Just getting old, baby. Just getting old."

Hank motioned for them to sit. "And you are?"

Ashish held out his hand to shake, then brought it back to his side. "Ashish Singh. Nancy told me you might need some help getting back home to, um, to be more comfortable."

"Bah." Hank waved Ashish's statement off. "That's Lucy talkin' nonsense. Ain't nobody lettin' me outa here."

"Dad, don't say that."

"Mr. Jewel, if it's okay with you, I'll still like to see if an early release is possible given your current health challenges," Ashish said.

"You do whatever will make this one happy," Hank said. "Nancy Bear, you still haven't given me one of those smiles I love so much." Hank pulled a silly face, showing the few teeth left in his mouth.

She felt both sorry for him and also very happy to see him. Sniffling, she shot him her best smile, feeling Ashish's hand warm on her back, steadying her.

His face lit up. "There it is. All is right in my world now."

"How is your world, Dad? Have you still been receiving the commissary money?"

"I have, and thank you for that."

"And your health?"

"Your mama got to you, eh?" He scratched his cheek.

"How bad is it?"

"Doc says it's lung cancer, but I don't believe him much. I ain't never smoked nothing before." He coughed.

Nancy stilled, watching his entire body fight against the forceful barks until he wheezed. His hands shook afterward as he weakly adjusted himself in the seat. She really *was* going to lose him soon.

"How's everything with you and your mama?" he asked.

"Same as usual," Nancy mumbled, a pit in her stomach as she remembered the last conversation she'd had with Lucy.

"Now I know she's a bit difficult, but she loves you," Hank said.

Nancy scoffed. "That's not love."

"Having you and your brother put her in a weird place. I don't think she ever got over it."

"Yeah? I didn't ask to be born. And I refuse to excuse her behavior. She's an adult, Dad."

He looked pained. Hurt, even. "All I've ever wanted is for you two to get along."

"Dad, you can't possibly—"

"Nancy Bear, please?" He coughed again.

"I'll try," Nancy mumbled, hating that he always advocated for her mother. All she wanted was for her dad to acknowledge the way her mother had treated her, but Lucy could do no wrong in his now-cloudy eyes.

"Promise?" He held up his crooked pinkie finger like he'd done so many times before.

Nancy wished she could hook her pinkie through his. She changed the subject instead. "Did you ever finish those books I recommended?"

"Read them all in a matter of weeks," he rasped, then cleared his throat. "The last one reminded me of the time all of us packed into Lucy's old station wagon and went on a road trip to the Grand Canyon. Took us damn near two weeks just to get there because of all of the stops and trouble."

Nancy smirked. She thought back to their epic road trip and could point out the similarities to *The Odyssey*, primarily how their two-week trip had turned into a four-week, nonstop nightmare. They'd had tires blow out, the car broken into, their stuff stolen more than once. On the way back home, they'd ended up stuck in some tiny town in Texas for six days while the car was being repaired.

"Come on, you know we had some fun back then." Hank looked off wistfully. "We camped out in that town in Texas and made the most of it."

"I got chiggers so badly, I still have marks on my legs," Nancy said and wanted to take it back when her father's smile slid from his face. "But then Jeff and you had a chance to go hunting with some locals."

"Man, Jeff was a crack shot. I was so proud of that boy when he got that buck. And Lucy, Lucy and you had some good times in that little swimming hole."

The swimming hole was a small lake where all the locals visited. Nancy happened upon it one afternoon when she'd gone for a long walk to be away from her mom. She'd made fast friends with some of the girls and soon was splashing around, salvaging what was left of her summer vacation. When Nancy had returned back to their campsite all wet, Lucy had demanded answers. The next day, Lucy and Nancy had gone to the lake together. Lucy had made sure to pack sandwiches and drinks for Nancy and her new friends. The next few days had seemed to be perfect, with Lucy and Nancy swimming at the lake while Jeff and Hank hunted with the locals. Nancy had even slowly lowered her walls to let her mom in little by little, until Nancy had confessed that one of the boys had asked her out. Lucy's demeanor had changed almost instantly.

The next day, Nancy had left for the swimming hole only to find her mother on the muddy banks in one of her bikinis. Lucy had made a show of passing out the sandwiches she'd made for the kids, talking loudly and exaggerating her movements just enough to have Nancy's red bikini slowly inch up her butt. Furious beyond words, Nancy had found the boy who'd liked her and went off with him back to his house. She'd lost her virginity that day and returned back to their campsite to find her parents packing up the station wagon to leave first thing in the morning.

Nancy had spent the rest of her trip praying for her period, despite using a condom.

"Hey, Nancy Bear, where did you go?" Hank asked in the brightly lit prison visiting area, his furry eyebrows tightly knit.

The memory of the lake flitted from Nancy's head. "Nowhere. I'm here. Tell me about your treatment plan."

"There is none. I'm stage four, they say, but I tell you I'm fine."

"Are you serious?" Nancy's voice ticked up louder than she wanted, and a flurry of questions rose in her throat. Would treatment help?

Would they be able to get his cancer in remission? Could he live longer? Why wasn't he fighting it?

There was Ashish's hand on her back again. Centering her. Focusing her on what was right there. She wasn't there to fix her dad. She was there to see him. To spend time with him. She settled back into herself and inhaled deeply.

"I'm just fine. So glad you came to visit me, though. Catch me up on what's been going on with you," Hank said.

The three talked until visiting hours ended. Nancy promised to visit in the morning, and Hank promised that he'd get better. She waited, watching her father slowly rise and shuffle out of the visiting area. She'd done it hundreds of times in the past, but this time had a strange feeling to it. He seemed to walk in slow motion. One step here. Another step there. Pause to brace himself with the back of a chair or edge of a table so he could cough without tipping over. Nancy caught herself wondering how her father—the man who'd been so strong and formidable—was now a shell of what he once was.

She didn't realize she was crying again until a guard handed her some tissues when they exited the prison.

CHAPTER 14

Left leg.

Right leg.

Left leg.

Right leg.

Each step she took was one step farther away from her dad. One moment less with him when he already had few moments left. Two years. She'd wasted two years trying to prove a point to her mom about nonsense boundaries. Boundaries that were nothing more than thread in a raging sea. Meaningless. Useless. She'd kept her laurels only to be robbed of her greatest treasure. Time had shown her his hand only to pickpocket her heart.

She had half a mind to call Lucy and apologize for everything she'd ever thought, said, or done. Maybe, somehow, her dad's illness had been her fault. Her doing. His body had managed to take in all the animosity she'd felt toward her mom. It'd festered into his illness. His love for both of "his girls," like he'd call them, his downfall.

Nancy was winded by the time she took the final steps to her car, her arms lead when she raised her hand and clicked the key fob to unlock the doors. If she'd been wrung out earlier in the car, visiting her dad had shredded her into a million mismatched pieces.

"Hey." Ashish was by her side, reaching for her keys. "I'll drive."

Climbing into the passenger seat was agonizing, each movement painfully slow and clumsy. She leaned against the window as Ashish started the car and pulled away.

Goodbye, Dad.

"You haven't really eaten much all day. How about we grab some food and head to the hotel?" he asked. "I can even, um, hang for a little while. Maybe we can catch that random chick flick you've wanted to watch."

She wanted to laugh. Felt like laughing, even, but couldn't muster the energy to do so. It'd been one of their many inside jokes. She'd had a bad habit of not remembering the names of movie titles she'd wanted to watch and would always describe them as some random chick flick she'd seen advertised. It'd made it into their vernacular. On nights they'd been sitting around scrolling for a movie, he'd nudge her and ask what random chick flick she had heard about and wanted to watch.

But she couldn't think of any random chick flicks she'd want to watch. How could she watch anything and be entertained when her father was suffering? She cringed, remembering the hacking and gasping her father had done and how it'd drained his body.

How could she ever be happy?

"So what do you think about getting him home?" Nancy managed to ask. She needed to know if Lucy had been on a wild-goose chase or not. Did he have a fighting chance?

"I wasn't really able to make the contacts I'd hoped for, but that's top of my list for tomorrow. I'll give you two some time alone to visit while I work."

"That wasn't an answer." She sat up, tugging against the seat belt when it snapped her back in the seat.

"I mean, the request is pretty simple and straightforward. I didn't see anything from the previous attorney as to why it was denied."

"What does that mean?"

Ashish dipped his head. "Are you sure he even filed it?"

Nancy closed her eyes and moaned. It was like Lucy to get scammed. She wouldn't put it past her mom to have "hired" someone she'd fast-friended who'd *told her* he was an attorney. She'd always been the type of person to pick up strays—shiftless people looking for an easy target. "Oh God. Two thousand dollars didn't even sound right."

"She paid him two grand to file a simple request?"

Nancy frowned at the disappointment in his voice. "Ye-ah . . ." She fished for her phone. "There's only one way to find out." *Hell, why not?* she thought and dialed her mom.

"Hello, Nancy."

"Hi-ya, Mom," Nancy said in a sarcastic singsong. Her palms felt warm. No, her palms itched and felt hot, matching her entire body. "Went to see Dad." She said it like a big middle finger to her mom. Like, hey, I visited him, and now you don't have anything to hold over my head. Take that.

"Okay. Well, I'm glad you got a chance to see him." Lucy was quiet for a beat. "Would you like to stop by here for a visit? I'm making dinner. Nothing fancy, but it's enough for a few people. I usually do that, you know. Cook for a few days, if not a few people."

The smile in her mother's voice snuffed out Nancy's earlier annoyance. She considered visiting Lucy for a moment. "We might stop by a little later. Have to check into the hotel first and unpack the car."

"That'll work. I don't get much sleep anymore," Lucy said. "Hold on. Who's this 'we'?"

"Ashish came along to see if there was anything he could do legally for Dad."

"Hmm. And how would he know what to do?"

"He's an attorney, Mom."

"And . . . you didn't think to tell me when I was in your house?"

"I didn't think it would matter."

"You didn't think." A statement, not a question.

A dig, but Nancy let it pass, remembering the purpose for calling. "So, um, Mom." Nancy sat up a little higher in her seat. "I was calling to try to find out some more information about the lawyer you hired. Can you give me some more details?"

"What do you want to know? I gave you everything he gave me."

"How did you find him, and when did he file the request?"

"I met him through someone I knew. I don't know the date. It's on the paperwork," Lucy said. "I mean, what are you insinuating?"

"Ask her who he submitted it through." Ashish whispered so only Nancy could hear him.

"I just wanted some background for Ashish," Nancy said. "Maybe the name of the person that guy submitted the request through."

"I don't know any of that."

"But you had to pay him in advance? Two thousand dollars?" Nancy tried her hardest to not sound like she was picking a fight.

"Yes, Nancy. I paid him. That's how it works. You have to give people money for them to do anything around here."

"I know, Mom, but how did you pay him?"

"Cash. How else would I have paid him? I don't have cards and accounts like you. I'm making it out here best I can. Can you do any better? Should I have asked you to pay him? Would you have paid him, or would you have asked a thousand questions and micromanaged everything?" Lucy said.

"I would've taken care of it if you needed me to." Nancy was getting nowhere.

"Does that Ashish think he can do any better?" Lucy blew out a breath.

"He's not sure yet, but he said it's pretty straightforward. He doesn't understand why it was declined."

"You know how things work out here. It's the good ole boy system." Lucy paused a moment. "I don't want to talk about this anymore."

"Oh, okay, then."

"Jeff just sent me some more pictures of the kids. You won't believe how big they've gotten. Remind me to show you when you're here."

Hearing Lucy dote on Jeff's kids like she was grandmother of the year nipped at Nancy. "Of course I won't believe how big they are. I've never seen them. Haven't heard from my own brother in twentysome-thing years." She sat up straighter, unbuckling the seat belt.

The car's annoying seat belt alert sounded.

"You know, I'm a pretty good aunt to Lina's kids."

"Nancy. Honey, what's gotten into you?"

Nancy wasn't quite sure why she'd gotten so annoyed when Lucy mentioned Jeff. He was practically a stranger to her. Would she even recognize him if she walked by him on the street? Would he recognize her? "Why do you throw Jeff around like a prize? He's my own brother, and I don't even know him."

"A prize? Nancy, what is this nonsense now?"

"I'm serious. I want to know how you can always be so nice to Jeff and cruel to me. Last time I saw you, you were so belittling." Where was all this coming from? Why was she getting so far off track? And all while she was on speakerphone in front of Ashish too!

"I didn't belittle you. You could never take any criticism. So sensi-tive all the time."

"I'm not sensitive."

"You most certainly are." Lucy snickered. "Bet you went to see your dad and spent so much time crying and feeling sorry for him and yourself."

Lucy won. Nancy sat back into her seat as Ashish parked outside the nearest burger place. Her stomach growled at the smell of grease and charred meat when he exited the car.

"Am I right?"

Nancy had nothing to say.

Lucy chuckled. "Yeah, like I said, you're weak. You called me to find out if the guy I hired is a real lawyer and to take out your anger, but you need to be angry at yourself. You're the one who abandoned him when you got married to that guy with the kids. What was his name? Oliver or something? You stopped coming to see us. Stopped talking to your dad. He got bored. Missed you."

"That's not fair. I really tried with Ollie." And she *had* tried, but Husband #2 had come as a family starter pack: a widower looking for a replacement for the woman he'd loved with four kids all under the age of five. Lina'd tried to come help Nancy when she'd been able, but she'd been juggling her own small kids at the time. A few years into the marriage, and he'd guilted Nancy into not working so she could stay home to raise the kids while he traveled for work, traveled for his football/basketball/hockey/baseball weekends, and traveled for his church retreats. Nancy had felt like she'd been a breath away from drowning.

"Dad was arrested for trying to help *your* friends," Nancy said. "He thought he was driving a U-Haul to help them move. Move *their* stuff, not a bunch of stolen merchandise."

Lucy snorted. "He was hoping to see you that weekend. Don't you remember? He was supposed to install some shelving for you, but you canceled at the last minute."

Talking to her mom was useless. She'd never see the truth. "Shelving was code for helping me leave Ollie," Nancy admitted. Ollie had started to get controlling, and the week before he'd punched a wall near her and told her she'd never live up to his first wife during one of their arguments. Instead of immediately leaving, though, Nancy'd given him another chance.

"That's what you do. You leave so you don't have to deal with life. Marriages and family are real life, Nancy. Wake up!"

In a matter of minutes, Nancy had gone from brave and bold to nothing. Her mom had the uncanny ability to make her regret every decision she'd ever made. "Mom, I'm gonna go."

"And you've proven my point. You have to face life one day, Little Nance."

Nancy ended the call without another word. Her brain felt like her mom had opened her skull with a can opener and used a hand mixer on her gray matter until it was fluffy peaks. Up, down, left, right? They were all the same to her now. Nothing quite made sense, and she'd even forgotten the reason why she'd initially called her mom.

CHAPTER 15

"All they had were chicken sandwiches. I'm sorry." Ashish handed Nancy a paper bag and a cup carrier with what looked like two milkshakes.

"Thank you," Nancy said, the conversation with her mom still fresh in her mind. She needed to process the whole situation. Get it out of her head and into the open. Maybe hear another perspective on how to best deal with Lucy so she could be with her dad.

Grease, salt, and sugar, Nancy thought, looking down at the food in her lap. *Lina would be proud.* Nancy texted her friend.

Nancy: Miss you. Could use some girl time. We need to catch up.

Lina: Same here. Tomorrow? Brunch?

Nancy: Can't do tomorrow. Next weekend? Let's run away.

Lina: I'm down with running away.

Lina: Is it bad? Do we need to Thelma and Louise it?

Nancy: Not that bad.

Lina: Sleepover at your place next Friday night?

Nancy: Hell yeah!

Lina: Deal. Love you, girl!

Nancy: Same. xoxo

Thankfully, six lanes of traffic separated them from the hotel. Ashish skillfully navigated her SUV, the setting sun drawing shapes across his face. She let him get the bags while she carried the food to check in, feeling some kind of way when he checked in to his own room, like he'd said he would.

He followed her to her room, setting her bags down. "Mind if I?" He motioned to the restroom.

She shook her head, exhaling. "Go ahead. It's been a long day." Nancy slipped off her shoes and jacket, then dipped into the bathroom after Ashish and opted for a shower, needing to cleanse the day from her scalp to the soles of her feet. No matter how hard she scrubbed, the smell of the prison lingered. For some reason or another, she hardly remembered the prison ever smelling the way it had. It'd never registered before. It had been neither pleasant nor unpleasant. It'd just smelled like confinement. But today it'd carried hints of desperation and remorse.

Wrapping her hair and twisting the towel into a turban of sorts, Nancy caught herself in the bright mirror. She saw her dad's eyes in hers, smaller and encircled by laugh lines of all sorts: deep crow's-feet at the corners, wispy wrinkles underneath, and crinkles on the bridge of his nose. He'd spent so much of her past being jovial about one thing or another that laughter had etched itself deep within his flesh.

And here she was, perma RBF with frown lines. Her heart ached to hear one of his laughs. The ones that'd started deep in his belly and wound their way out in a thick baritone *he, he, he, he*, which had always reminded her of a redneck version of Santa.

That was how she'd start the conversation about her father with Ashish—talking about Hank's Santa laugh. She owed Ashish at least a little bit more about her dad. Hank was more to her than just a dying prisoner. He was a real, complicated man, a loving father, and a cheerful person, overall. She planned the conversation in her head, pulling on her flannel pajamas.

When she opened the bathroom door, Ashish was gone. She paced around the room a bit, hoping Ashish would eventually knock, but there was just silence. Silence and her thoughts. They circled around her day, spokes on a wheel with Ashish at its center. He'd been there when she'd packed the car. He'd been there for the drive down. He'd been there, holding her up during her visit with Hank. He'd even heard everything between her and Lucy and hadn't once criticized her. He hadn't gotten upset at her for lying about her parents. And he hadn't batted an eye at her colorful parents and all their baggage.

He'd seen the ugly she'd carefully hidden and masked from him for so long, and he hadn't run from her. What did it mean? How was Nancy supposed to process it all? Maybe, just maybe, she could let him in fully, eventually reveal the Nancy she'd kept safe and protected behind her fortressed heart.

Her first revelation would be telling Ashish more about Hank. Sniffling, she cleared her throat. Since the real Ashish wasn't there, Nancy had the conversation with her imaginary version of Ashish. "My dad was, no, *is* a pretty incredible person."

She told Imaginary Ashish so many wonderful things about Hank. Like how he could fix anything from cars and boats to household electrical stuff and plumbing issues. Her mom had been well pleased when he'd ticked everything off her house-repair list. He'd even improved things that hadn't broken. A smile played on Nancy's lips as happy memories of him filled her head. That was how she wanted to remember him: strong and capable, not sick and weak.

Her stomach growled.

She slumped onto the firm sofa, one leg under the other, recalling more happy memories of her dad. She noticed the bag of food. It was still full. Had Ashish lost his appetite? Did it have anything to do with her drama? Biting the insides of her cheeks, her mind started a slow spiral of what-ifs. What if she'd read it all wrong? What if he'd tagged along out of pity? What if . . .

The door lock clicked and opened just then, pausing her descent into self-doubt. Ashish entered her room, his hair wet and his white shirt perfectly fitted to his body. "I left a note," he said.

"I didn't see a note." Nancy fought against the cheek muscles that wanted to smile at him.

"Wrote it on the bag." He pointed at the *Went to shower. Be back in 10* scribbled on the wrinkled bag in light-blue ink. "Didn't know how long you'd be and thought you could use some time to yourself." He shoved a hand into his gray sweatpants. "But I wanted to check on you. So, I, um . . ."

"It's okay, Ash. I get it. Thank you." Nancy patted the seat beside her, glad for his company. "Hungry?"

He sat beside her, split open the bag into a makeshift place mat for their food. "How you holding up?"

"I'm better, I guess." Nancy handed him the chocolate milkshake and took a sip of the vanilla one while Ashish tore open four packets of ketchup. "Was just thinking of some pretty cool times I had with my dad."

"Like what?" He squeezed the ketchup onto the bag and swirled in a packet of mayo.

"What do you mean?"

"If you could only remember one memory of him for the rest of your life, what would it be?" he asked, mindlessly dipping a fry into the mixture.

Nancy was amused at how second nature it'd gotten for him to make her fry sauce. She'd almost forgotten his sweet little gestures—the simple things he'd done for her that'd become so routine for them. His asking about her dad, however, was definitely not routine. It made her feel like she was about to step out on an iced-over lake. One step away from shore and she wouldn't be able to tell where the ice was feet thick or dangerously thin.

"Didn't mean to make you uncomfortable, Nance. You don't have to explain anything."

"It's okay." She owed him at least one story to humanize her father. To let Ash know he was a good person who had made a bad decision. "Let's see, one memory for eternity?"

"Yes."

One memory of her dad stood out from the rest. She hesitated, scared of what Ashish would think of her, terrified of him using it against her one day. Her heart picked up speed, and her mind chased after it, hurtling through a hundred different scenarios of how her vulnerability could be a weapon or a tool to manipulate her in the future.

Ashish slid his hand over hers, giving her just enough courage to open her mouth and share a fragment of herself with him.

"It was the second Christmas he'd been home. Jeff, my older brother, was—"

Ashish's eyes went wide for a moment at the mention of her brother. She knew he was thinking she had managed to hide an entire family from him.

"Jeff was gone. He had graduated from high school by then and was in another city. I heard from him a few times that year." It felt weird talking about her brother. "It was just me and my parents. It was my senior year, and I lettered in academics, so all I wanted was a letterman jacket." Sitting beside Ash, Nancy could still feel how badly she'd wanted that jacket.

"Money was tight. Money was always tight for my parents, and they used to take odd jobs here and there. I worked, but my mom decided to charge me rent, so I only had enough for lunch money most weeks. When Dad learned I wanted a letterman jacket, he worked as many hours as he could." She remembered finding him asleep on the couch to keep from waking Lucy up after working double shifts at the local Taco Bell.

"Christmas morning comes, and I have one box under the tree. It was my letterman jacket. Dad was so proud to gift it to me. He made such a massive deal about it. Mom was angry, because in her eyes, I was only going to wear it for maybe six months, since I was graduating later that year. She hated the idea of wasting that kind of money. Dad wouldn't hear of it."

"Wow. Do you still have the jacket?"

She shook her head and left it like that for him to think she'd tossed it in the garbage. There was no way she would ever tell him her jacket had mysteriously ended up in the washing machine with a load of towels. The red-and-black leather and wool had been washed on hot with ample bleach until it was unrecognizable. Her mom had used it as an arguing point for all Nancy's future requests. Lucy'd had a knack for using everything as evidence to prove whatever point she'd been trying to make. Everything could and would be used against her in the court of Lucy.

Nancy rubbed her arms, wishing to take back the memory she'd shared with Ashish, wishing she hadn't pulled back the curtain and allowed him to peek inside. She waited a beat. Two, three more beats, not quite sure what to do with her hands or her body. Not sure where to focus or what type of look she should have on her face.

"Thank you for sharing that with me," Ashish finally said. He glanced down at the food. "How's your shake?"

"Bet it was pretty good a half hour ago." Her voice was a little too happy. A little too fake.

"Same for this food." He waved a soggy fry at her. It drooped pitifully. "But it's edible and I'm ravenous."

And just like that, the awkwardness was gone. She'd had worse meals. Cold, greasy fries and stale chicken sandwiches with wilted lettuce were the perfect sad dinner for her sad state. It was almost poetic.

They ate in a silence that grew more comfortable the longer they were together. When they finished, Ashish bagged everything up and tossed it in the garbage. Without prompting, he sat back down, flicked on the TV.

"Movie? Show? News? Reality?" he asked.

She pulled her legs up beneath her, finding a comfy position. "Something mindless."

"Reality show it is then."

"That works."

Within minutes, they'd landed on a dating reality show. Contestants were forced to answer a series of trivia questions while being pummeled by paintballs in order to earn certain privileges on the show. The privileges ranged from eating and sleeping to going out on dates and even calling their family members. One of the cast was on-screen, crying about not having bathroom privileges. Another did a confessional about what went down when she'd landed date privileges with one of the married men.

"This is so stupid," Nancy said.

"Want me to turn it?"

"No way in hell. I'm so here for all the train wrecks. Makes me feel better about my life."

Little by little, they migrated toward each other. Ashish wriggled, placing his arm over her shoulder. Laying her head on his shoulder felt like second nature. It was just something they did when sitting together. He was like a familiar pillow. How was she supposed to find a comfortable position without him? He didn't seem to mind, returning the gesture, his head on hers.

The drama escalated on the reality show they were watching. An episode in and they were both hooked. By the third episode, Nancy was fully in Ashish's arm as he drew little circles up and down her shoulder while she traced doodles on his thigh. So familiar and natural. It felt good to be held. Felt good to not be alone.

Felt good to *feel* something again.

"Hey, Nance, can I ask you something?" He stopped drawing circles.

"Yeah?"

"You ever think of how we'd be now if we were still seeing each other?"

Was he serious? She tilted her head to better see him. His heavy brows made his dark eyes darker. Deeper, even, especially with how he gazed at her. It made her tremble. She fought against freaking out to hear what else he had to say.

"I think I made a mistake," he whispered, looking through her again, his piercing gaze finding the tiniest kinks in her armor. She wanted to turn her head away from him. Away from his confession. What did it even mean? Did he miss her? Would he be okay with going back to how they'd been, or would he still want more?

The way his finger so delicately grazed her skin with the lightest of touches made her want his touch everywhere. Rows of goose bumps blossomed in its wake. A shiver trickled from deep within her core outward.

"I'm so sorry." He outlined the delicate curves of her face to her lips, where he traced the peaks of her Cupid's bow. Her body grew warm all over.

Her heart raced, anticipating more of him. Wanting so much more of him. She tangled her fingers in the thick hair at his nape, eliciting a low, guttural moan that sounded like a plea. She leaned up, bringing her lips within a whisper of his, breathing him in.

Sliding his hand down her back, he grinned mischievously against her lips as she arched into his touch like a cat being stroked. The feel of him was something she already knew, but this was different. She couldn't put her finger on what that difference was.

Bringing her to his chest, he held her close. Her head in the hollows of his neck, she breathed him in until their breaths were in sync. In. Out. In. Out. Allowing herself to imagine their heartbeats also matching, Nancy relaxed further in his embrace. He tightened his grasp. Being this close to him felt good, safe, like everything was going to be okay for once in her life. She bought into the lie for a few moments, letting her shape conform to his.

Some people would say kissing is intimate, but to Nancy, hugging—actually giving up all boundaries and personal space—was far more intimate. She hadn't been hugged and held so tenderly in so long.

Not even in the latter months of their relationship had Ashish held her this fully and wholly, encompassing all that she ever was and would ever be.

Deep down, she knew it wouldn't last.

Deep down, she knew Ashish would eventually want more of her.

Deep down, she knew she'd disappoint him again.

Wanting to feel the protection of her boundaries—those invisible walls surrounding the more vulnerable parts of her—she wriggled a little, coming up for air. Fighting her body, she pulled away from him even more.

"You okay? Did I do something wrong?"

She shrank back from his touch, making more space between them. "I can't, Ash."

His head slumped between his shoulders.

"Please leave, Ashish," she said with a finality that expanded to more than just this moment.

Inhaling deeply, he stood, adjusted himself. "I'm sorry, Nance."

CHAPTER 16

Sleep had refused to visit Nancy. She'd sat in the dark all night, lit by the television's glow until the sky outside slowly lightened. Morning met her exhausted in every way. Her mind felt like it'd run an obstacle course: over, under, through every possible scenario at least ten times. Physically, she felt like she'd failed the obstacle course and had to attempt it over and over again until she had nothing left.

After forcing herself out of bed, Nancy shuffled over to the window and drew the curtains. Squinting against the bright sunlight, she took in the flurry of fall colors painting the trees from the highway all the way into the horizon. The scenery breathed life into a quote by Lin Yutang she'd had in her office that spoke of the seasons and the colors of life. Of how spring is young and innocent and summer is too proud. Of how the yellowing of autumn leaves parallels life as one matures and grows mellow, richer in the wisdom of approaching age, and yet tinged with sorrow and a premonition of death. Of how out of the richness and experience of life emerges a consonancy of colors: the greens of life and strength, orange of sweet content, and purple of acceptance and passing.

While she had displayed the quote as a beautiful arrangement of words, she'd never quite understood the full meaning behind it until now. The greens and oranges and purples outside her window bled into each other as tears claimed her eyes once again. Her father had been green and strong and vibrant in her youth. As she grew up and her own green matured, Hank's orange shone, content and brilliant as they grew closer. As they became family. And now, in his own twilight, Hank's purple was a deep and knowing hue filled with purpose.

Nancy stilled, imagining the life cycle of leaves. Once they turned purple, slowly, they dried out as the last bit of life relented. When they fell, they danced along the wind as it caught their final moments back to the earth. Nancy remembered once trying to put fallen leaves back on the old oak tree in their neighborhood. She'd scooped handfuls, searching for the perfect leaf—the one that still had some shades of green in its veins—to try to attach back to the branch.

Chewing on that memory made her remember how Lucy had made fun of her for trying to rescue the leaves. Lucy had said Nancy's efforts had been as futile as mopping the beach. Lucy hadn't been wrong. None of the leaves would ever reattach. Never come back to life. It'd done something to that ten-year-old version of Nancy. It'd hardened her in a way, changed the way she'd hoped for things.

It hit Nancy as she stood in the window, the soft sunlight warming her glistening face: words were a lot like leaves. They sprouted and grew, but once a word or a leaf fell, there was no putting it back. Once a leaf fell, it died. Decayed. Harsh words were the same, causing decay and little deaths when they fell.

Nancy started at the rap against her door, her heartbeat quickening. "Nancy?" It was Ashish. "I'm heading down to check out and grab some coffee. Would you like one?"

She wiped her face and cleared her throat. "I'm good. Almost done. I'll meet you downstairs."

~

At the prison, Nancy beelined to the visiting area without a word to Ashish. Facing him was the last thing on her mind. She'd already done it a thousand times in her head throughout the night, and each scenario ended the same: he would never accept her scraps. He was a full-course-meal-and-doggie-bag sort of guy. Picked over bits and pieces would never fully satiate him.

The dance through security and the various locked doors was easier this time. The smell wasn't as bad as it had been the day before. When Nancy finally saw her dad up close, he even seemed healthier and more vibrant than before. It was strange, because she never considered herself a glass-half-full type of person.

"My Nancy Bear." Hank held out his arms, then brought them back to his side, knowingly.

"Hey, Dad."

"Where's your friend?"

"He's talking to some people here about your situation." *And avoiding me like the plague because I'll never be able to really love him.*

He smirked, motioning for her to sit across from him. "Good luck to him."

"How are you?" She shifted on the cold metal bench.

"It's like the sun is shining brighter now that you're here."

She wanted nothing more than to grab his hand. "I'll stay as long as they let me."

His eyes watered, and his kind smile returned. "So tell me about this feller."

"What do you mean, Dad?"

"This Ashish. Sure, he's here to help, but there's something more there." He waggled his finger at her.

"We were sort of seeing each other, but we're not anymore." She wanted nothing more than to not have this conversation with her father.

"Why not? He seemed like a pretty decent person." He blew out a long breath, coughing at its tail. "A lot better than that Keith guy or even the one with the kids."

"Oh my gosh, Dad. That was so long ago. You know I was married again after that, and I've dated a hell of a lot since then."

"I know. I know." He threw up his hands defensively.

"Have you ever considered I'm perfectly content being single?" She ticked off items with her fingers. "I mean, I love traveling, have an amazing job, great friends, and don't have to deal with anyone's drama." This was all true. She *was* content with her life . . . or she *had* been until the call from Lucy earlier in the week when she'd learned about her dad's illness. She had never considered being truly alone until then. She'd never thought about how her life would be without her father—the one person on the planet who loved and accepted her no matter what.

Hank waited a few beats, nodding. Pulling his bottom lip in between his teeth, he nibbled on a patch of dryness, looking at Nancy with such tenderness and care.

She turned away from his glare, then returned it. "Dad, I'm fine."

"Okay, Nancy Bear. I'll respect your feelings." When he crossed his arms, his sleeves rose, revealing his almost skeletal biceps. "I only want you to be happy, that's all."

"Like I said, Dad, I'm fine." She couldn't take her eyes off his bony arms. Sadness crept into her periphery, waiting for an opening. She shook her head, then remembered the last conversation she'd had with Lucy.

You're the one who abandoned him when you got married to that guy with the kids.

"Can I ask you something?" Nancy asked.

"Anything."

"Why did you help Mom's friends that weekend? You didn't even know them."

It was his turn to look away now. Only, when he did, he sniffled and wiped his eyes. "It's a long story."

Swiveling her head from side to side, Nancy shrugged and shot him one of her *"Yeah, and . . ."* looks, raising her brows high. "I guess I'm *your* captive audience now."

He chuckled. "Ha. Good one."

"Come on, Dad. I need to know. Talked to Mom yesterday, and she said it was my fault for canceling on you that weekend. Please?"

Hank slowly brought his hand around his mouth in thought. "Lucy said it was your fault, eh?"

Nancy nodded.

"That's the farthest thing from the truth." Lowering his hands to the table, he clasped them together tightly. "Your mama was married real young before I knew her."

This was news to her.

He pulled his lips to the side. "I worked for her husband, actually. He was the meanest summabitch I've ever met." A heavy cough tore through his chest. Catching his breath, he continued. "I, um, I helped her get out of that situation and ended up owing him dearly." He shrugged. "That's how I ended up in here both times."

More. She wanted more of the story. More time to listen to him regale her with every detail she never knew. Looking at him, weak and leaning against his arms on the table, she knew he didn't have the energy to do so. She changed the subject. "Hey, I'm really sorry for not visiting sooner. I got into it with Mom and she—"

"She what?"

Nancy's entire body snapped straight, hearing her mother's voice.

Hank clapped. "I got both my girls here. And on a Sunday too. God must be smiling on me."

Lucy patted Nancy's back for her to scoot over. "Good morning, Nancy," she said, sliding onto the bench so that she was sitting directly in front of Hank, Nancy to her side.

"Hi, Mom."

Lucy fussed over Hank, patting his hand, ignoring the "no physical contact" rule. "What? You think *he's* gonna try and break outa here or hurt someone?" With a flick of her hand, she waved off an approaching guard.

"I'm okay, Lucy. Don't bust his balls."

She held his hands in hers, tenderly stroking her thumbs across his thin skin. "I have another appointment with that lawyer tomorrow afternoon."

"The one you already paid?" Nancy asked. *The one who probably scammed you?*

"Yes," she said. "Says he knows someone."

"Nancy Bear, you didn't tell her about your friend?" Hank asked.

"I did." The heat from her mom's stare made her shiver.

"That Indian fellow?" Lucy asked.

"Ashish? Yes, Mom."

"He's here, actually," Hank said.

"Does he think he can help get you out?" Lucy asked.

"I don't know, but I told you I'm fine where I am. Only have another two years on my sentence, anyway. I'll be home to you before you realize."

Nancy hated how cheerful he sounded. She hated how delusional he was to believe he had two years left. "Dad, stop. Ashish will help to the best of his abilities. He can only do so much, and nothing is guaranteed."

"Where is he?" Lucy asked. "Are you sure he knows what he's doing?"

"He's somewhere in the prison, and yes. I trust Ashish. He's highly capable." Nancy said a silent prayer for him to meet the right people to get her dad released.

"And if he doesn't?" Lucy asked.

"Then I'm fine where I am. How many times do I have to tell you, Luce?" Hank said. "I'm perfectly—"

An ear-piercing alarm screeched, making Nancy cover her ears. Heavily armed guards flooded into the area, forcing the prisoners back to their cells.

"Sounds like a riot or something," Hank said, standing, looking like he'd been through it several times before. He saluted them. "I love you girls. Take care of each other."

"Hank," Lucy called, reaching out for him as he walked away.

"Love you, Dad," Nancy said.

"I need you to follow me this way," a guard called out to Nancy and her mom.

They quickly shuffled behind the line of other visitors back the way they'd come. Nancy felt her mom's trembling hands press against her back. She hadn't been afraid until then. The idea of being trapped in a prison along with rioting prisoners put the fear of God in her. After reaching back, she grabbed one of Lucy's hands, squeezing firmly.

Ashish met them outside, a flash of relief crisscrossing his face. He looked down at Nancy clenching her mother's hand and back up at her. She gave him one of her *"I have no idea"* looks, shrugging her shoulders high.

"You guys okay?" Ashish asked when they gathered near her car.

"Yeah," Nancy said. "We're good."

Lucy clenched her chest and started to cry. "My poor Hank is in there. In there during a riot!" She bawled. "What if something happens to him?"

"Mom, he's going to be okay. I don't think it was even his unit." She patted Lucy's back.

"I hope so. I really hope."

"It's all we can do right now," Ashish added.

Lucy's sniffling dried up. She dotted her eyes with a tissue. "*Is it all we can do?*"

"Mom, Ashish is trying."

"And what are *you* doing? You saw how sick he is."

"I'll do whatever I can. I want him home as well."

Lucy snorted. "That's all you have after two years?"

"Come on. I'm trying here. Can we not do this now?"

"I'm sorry for inconveniencing you." Lucy adjusted her sweater. "I'm sorry for being such a bother."

Guilt Trip 101 had nothing on Lucy Jewel. Nancy sighed. "You're not a bother. How about we go get some lunch?"

"I'm fine. I can't eat right now."

"Oh, okay. Then, um . . . I've got to head back. I've got work tomorrow, and Ash needs to get on the road."

"Figured as much." She pressed her lips together, then started toward her car.

CHAPTER 17

One week.

All it took was one week to unravel the perfect life Nancy thought she'd curated. A week ago, she'd been content and ignorant of her father's diagnosis. She'd had healthy boundaries with her mother, and her zero-contact policy had protected her from Lucy's attacks. Today, however, she was standing before her full class, lecturing about biological theory, wondering if she was doomed to become just like her mother. According to the lesson notes she'd taught from over the last decade, at least, Darwin believed most human behavior was impacted and shaped by their genes, DNA, and other hereditary factors.

It hadn't hit her until she started reading from her presentation slides. The thought of behavior-coded DNA being passed down from parent to child. Generational patterns. Preconditioned responses. No running. No hiding. *You get what you get, and you don't pitch a fit.*

"See, Darwin believed—" Nancy faltered, freezing midlecture. "Darwin b-believed . . ." She realized she shared some traits with her mother. She was rash and had the propensity to get a bad attitude. She also loved being the center of attention and didn't really consider other people's feelings. A pinprick of panic needled her.

"So, Darwin." Her voice cracked, but it felt like more of a crack in her facade. "Who can explain Darwin's theory?" She held herself together with mental duct tape and a prayer to not flake out in front of her class. She pointed at Elysse's raised hand, exhaling when the girl started speaking.

The last thing she ever wanted was to make people feel as small as her mother made her feel. Nancy tensed her legs when she realized they were shaking. She had to get her crap together and keep it together for another eleven minutes. But the more she thought about the parallels to her mom, the more she began to freak out internally. Sweat beaded on her forehead, and her classroom suddenly felt like a sauna.

It was then she noticed the thirty faces gawking questioningly at her. *Pull it together already.* Making a show of checking her watch, she exclaimed, "How 'bout we call it a day? Don't forget your papers are due Sunday by midnight. We'll have a few more classes this week for any questions you may have," she said in her professional voice instead of the frantic one trying to break through.

Leaning her weight on the small desk nearby and crossing her legs at the ankles, she slowly exhaled as her class filed out. Although she didn't really want to, she canceled classes for the rest of the day and opted for office hours instead. A few students stopped by throughout the day, but other than that, she had time to gather her thoughts and get her head right.

One week of classes and then it would be Thanksgiving break. She considered her options now that her parents were back in her life. The last two Thanksgivings had been more like Friendsgivings, spending time at Lina's and hanging out with the kids. She wanted to do nothing more than spend the week in Waycross, visiting her dad daily and maybe spending some time with her mom, but the thought of spending time with Lucy spiked her heart rate.

Whatever she chose would be the wrong decision. It wasn't that simple. If she went to Lina's, she'd upset her mom and disappoint her dad. If she chose her parents, she'd be subjecting herself to her mother's attacks. It would be a nightmare.

After her final student session, she started home. *Home . . .* she chewed on the word. The concept. What was home to her? After her mom had pointed out her generic picture frames, her house had felt different. Like, maybe Lucy had been right about Nancy. Nancy didn't quite feel like she belonged in the life she lived.

Emptiness tapped on her shoulder, reminding her of its constant presence. And now she didn't want to go home. She also didn't want to be alone. At the next stoplight, she scrolled through Tinder for an acceptable match. None of the guys felt right. She didn't feel quite right about being with a random stranger.

With no other choice, she dialed Keith.

"Hey, Nancy," he answered.

"Doing anything tonight?"

"No, but I know what I could be doing if you were here," he said playfully.

"Want me to pick up dinner?" She felt weird asking something so routine. They didn't really do dinner.

"Already ate, but you grab something on the way."

"Okay. See you in a bit." She chewed on the inside of her cheek, playing back their conversation, not fully convinced she should make good on her word. Before the next light, Nancy turned into the parking lot of her favorite pizza restaurant. Inside, she found a space at the bar and ordered a small pizza to go and a beer for her wait. With the promise of Thanksgiving next week, the restaurant felt emptier than usual. Nancy figured some students had gotten a head start on their holiday break. She would've taken advantage of the extra time if she could have. Or at least that was the lie she told herself as she sipped her beer and watched the football game splashed across several overhead televisions.

"What are we having?"

Nancy's spine stiffened at Jeremy Pressley's voice as he claimed the adjacent barstool. She clenched her jaw when his knee bumped hers.

"Get her another one," he told the bartender, flashing a crisp twenty-dollar bill. "On me." He slapped the bill onto the glossy countertop.

Nancy put her mug down a little too forcefully and watched the amber liquid slosh about from one side to the next, churning up a little foam. She waved the bartender off. "No. I'm not accepting it." Turning slightly to Jeremy, she added, "If you want to talk, you can come to office hours after the break."

He looked over one shoulder, then the next, and shot her a confident grin. "It's a public place. I'm just trying to have a beer with a beautiful woman."

Nancy sat up straighter. "Who is also your professor." She slid off the stool, grabbing her purse. "This is highly inappropriate behavior. I don't think it's funny or clever or anything."

"I could show you some different behavior if you'd like. What are you into?"

Nancy tapped the counter for the bartender's attention. "Jewel. It's a small pizza. Can you check to see how much longer?"

Jeremy mirrored her movements until he was now standing, his back against the bar, facing her. "So your place or mine?"

"What exactly do you hope to gain from all this, Mr. Pressley?"

"I think we got off on the wrong foot the other day." He shot her a smile she was sure he'd used thousands of times to get his way. "But I *really* need that extension."

"Already discussed this. I'm not allowing any extensions." She didn't owe him an explanation and yet felt like she should put it out there. She crossed her arms. "If I allow you to turn it in late, I'll have to allow everyone the same opportunity. With late papers, it messes up my schedule, and I end up behind on submitting grades. Some of my students need this class for winter graduation."

"I need it to graduate this spring. Come on, no one else needs to know."

"Why can't you turn it in on time?" She needed to hear his ridiculous excuse.

"I'm leaving for Spain in the morning. My family does it for Thanksgiving every year."

"And?"

"And I haven't even started it yet." He scratched his head. "I'm swamped with my other classes."

"You've had the syllabus since September. You should've planned better."

Anger flashed in his eyes. "My parents are alumni."

"Okay. You'll need to turn this paper in on time if you want to join them."

"I can't fail this class."

"If memory serves me correctly, you've missed quite a lot of assignments already. You can't afford to miss this deadline."

"I CAN'T FAIL THIS CLASS!"

The tone of his voice made her flinch.

Jeremy closed the space between them and got uncomfortably close to her, dipping his head to hers. "Are you sure there's nothing I can . . ." He ran a finger down her arm.

She jerked away from him, shaking with rage and fear at his boldness. His entitlement.

"Hot for the teacher, Jer?" two of his fraternity brothers cackled, joining him at the bar with their phones held up.

"Think about any *extra credit* I can do." Jeremy's whisper had a dangerous tone.

She needed to report him as soon as possible. But what would she report? What proof did she have? That would be the first question Beckett would ask. Fuming, Nancy wanted nothing more than to slap the grin from his cocky little face. She opted to ignore him instead, focusing all her attention on the football game. When the pizza came, she lingered a few seconds as the wide receiver caught the ball and ran through several defenders into the end zone for a touchdown. She joined in as the restaurant erupted in cheers. When she went to reach for her pizza box, Jeremy snatched it up.

"Say 'please,'" he said, smirking.

"No. Give me *my* pizza, Mr. Pressley," Nancy said, unamused and growing more upset by the second.

"Come on, I'm just having a little fun." Jeremy snickered.

"Fun is working on your paper so you can graduate." Nancy held out her hand and gave herself a mental high five when she felt the warm box being placed on her open palm.

"I can show you—" Jeremy started saying. Nancy turned and exited the restaurant without another word.

Instead of going to Keith's, Nancy stopped by her favorite greasy spoon. She picked up a milkshake for her and a burger and fries for Tony. Together, they watched the rest of the game in the guardhouse.

CHAPTER 18

The rest of the week droned on without incident. Without excitement as she counted down the days until she could see her father. Until she could spend quality time with him.

It was like she'd been in a bad version of *Groundhog Day*—her days repeating the same humdrum pattern over and over again until she either gave in or gave up. She chose to give up, canceling her Friday office hours to stay in bed and Netflix. It'd been the last day before Thanksgiving break anyway, and campus had been a ghost town.

She'd carefully managed Lucy's calls and texts since leaving the prison, keeping the promise to her father . . . *until now,* she thought, wishing she had an old-school corded phone to twirl her fingers in the springy coils for something to do besides letting her mom gaslight her. She was half a second from hanging up on the woman.

Sighing for the tenth time in as many minutes, Nancy said, "Hey, Mom, I have to go."

"So now you don't have any time for me?"

"Come on, we've been on the phone for the last twenty minutes. You told me all about my nieces and nephews, and I agreed to buy tickets for both you and Dad to travel to Virginia to visit them when he's released."

"You're keeping track of how many minutes we spend on the phone? I am truly sorry for taking up so much of your precious time."

"It's not like that and you know it." There was no winning with her.

"Do you have plans tonight or something? Going out with that lawyer?" Lucy asked.

"I told you and Dad both—we are not together."

"Why not? You know I visited Hank earlier this week, and he was wondering the same thing. Said you were happy all by yourself or something." Lucy snorted a laugh like it was the silliest thing she'd ever heard in all her life.

"I am content." Nancy rolled her eyes, wishing her mom would just get her once in her life. "I have an incredible career, wonderful friends, and I love the freedom I have to travel. I don't need a man or a marriage or children to define my happiness."

"But every woman wants to be a mom, Nancy."

"I don't. I thought I did, but truth is, I really don't want to be a mom."

Lucy grumbled something unintelligible. "Let me guess, it's my fault, right? You don't want kids because you think I'm such a bad mom."

Not too far from the truth, Nancy thought.

"But everything is always my fault anyway, so I guess I'll bear the burden of this as well."

Nancy switched the phone to her other side, ready to end the call, but she wanted to hear more about her father. "Anyway, how was Dad this week? Is there a doctor for him?"

"There's a few of them. Nurses too. Most times, he visits the hospital. I think that's how his cancer got so bad. They don't let them see medical people routinely. Not like we do." There was a long pause. For a second, Nancy thought the line had gone dead.

"He's not doing well and I miss him. I can't lose him, Nance." Lucy sniffled. "I know he's been in there for a while, but he's the reason my heart beats."

Now it was Nancy's turn to take time to process what was said. She'd never heard Lucy talk about her dad like that. She'd never known the woman to be capable of loving anyone other than herself. Hell, if

Lucy Jewel could love someone, maybe there was hope for her after all. Nancy considered it a beat longer. Were they finally having a moment? "Hey, can I ask you something?"

"Sure, honey."

Nancy almost choked up at how sweet and sincere Lucy sounded in that moment. She decided to lean into it. "How . . ." She swallowed hard. "How do you do it with him being away for so long?"

"He loves me, and I need him as much as he needs me."

Nancy's mouth dropped to the floor at her mother's confession. The idea of Lucy Jewel needing anyone made her world feel topsy-turvy. Was her mom being vulnerable and honest with her?

"And I know I'm hard on you kids sometimes. I just want you guys to be happy," Lucy added.

If Nancy wasn't already a drinker, this would've pushed her over. Finally, a confession of how difficult Lucy had been as a parent. Hope filled Nancy as she considered having a real relationship with her mother.

"Thank you for your transparency, Mom," Nancy said.

"I'm always transparent with you and your brother. I tell it like it is, but you say I'm hurting your feelings or pushing your stupid little boundaries."

Damn. Less than a few minutes. But she'd gotten a glimpse into her mom's softer side. It was gone sooner than it'd lasted. Disappointed, Nancy armed herself for another argument. "My boundaries are healthy."

"You throw the words around like they're supposed to do anything. The only boundary you have is your ability to block out anyone from loving you." Lucy paused. "Now that I think of it, Hank may be in prison, but you're the one who's locked up."

"That's enough." Nancy stood, pulling her cardigan tighter around her shoulders like a protective coat.

"See, you can't handle it when someone tells you the truth. You don't really want transparency."

"I'm gonna go now."

"As expected." Lucy huffed.

With that, Nancy ended the call, wanting to throw her phone across the room. Why had she accepted Lucy's call earlier? Why had she talked to Lucy for so long? Why had she allowed Lucy the chance to get cruel again after opening up to her?

Nancy wanted to pull her hair out. Checking the hour, she was more than ready for girl time with her bestie. Lina must have needed the time as well, because she'd texted her every day that week to remind Nancy to jot it down in her planner. Lina had even called twice that Friday morning, once that afternoon, and once when she had gotten on the road.

Nancy paced her house, walking on the balls of her feet, waiting for Lina to come through her front door. When she finally did, Nancy greeted her with a giant bear hug, exhaling. "About time."

"Girl, don't get me started." Lina dropped her bag and wriggled out of her coat. "Traffic was ridiculous. And the kids had all these last-minute things they had to do or ask or show me."

"Alcohol?"

"I thought you'd never ask."

Lina got the glasses out while Nancy picked two bottles of pinot grigio from her collection. They met at the counter, perching on stools.

Nancy held up her glass. "And now it's officially ladies' night," she said, clinking her glass to Lina's.

"Let the debauchery begin!"

After bringing the glass to her mouth, she took a sip and choked, staring at Lina's hand. "Oh my God, Lina. You didn't tell me!" Some wine dribbled down the side of her mouth. She wiped it with the heel of her palm and fumbled with her glass before steadying it on the counter. Her eyes went wide when she reached for Lina's left hand.

Lina blushed. "I was going to tell you tonight."

"Okay, so talk. What happened? I thought you didn't want to."

"Remember how I found the ring and freaked out." Lina held out her glass for a refill.

Nancy obliged, filling the glass. "Yeah, you did. What happened?"

There was something in Lina's gaze that made Nancy uncomfortable. Did she not want to get married to Noah? Was that it? Was she making her friend uncomfortable by prodding? Had their relationship changed?

"It happened a few days later." Turning the ring on her finger, Lina looked down at her glass. "The kids were at their friends' houses, so I went to Noah's. That Sunday morning, he made pancakes for brunch, and there was a note on the side of my plate with a giant question mark."

Nancy leaned in, happy to hear Noah had listened to her advice.

"When I asked him what it was supposed to mean, he took out this ring and asked if I'd marry him."

"And?"

"Of course I said yes." There was a little more behind Lina's half smile. It was like the joy of it all hadn't reached her eyes.

"What's going on with you?"

"What do you mean?"

"C'mon, Lina. You didn't want to get married. Said you weren't ready and all. What changed?" Nancy finished her glass, her stomach rumbling for food now. "Dinner?"

"Yeah. I ordered Thai at the light. Should be here soon." Lina focused on her phone screen.

"Perfect. I was craving some drunken noodles."

Downing her second glass like it was water, Lina smirked. "Drunken noodles sound kinda perfect right now. Ordered that, pad thai, and some curry."

"I love you." Nancy laughed for a brief moment, glad for the lightness between them, but she couldn't let Lina change the subject. She held the wine and, before pouring it, asked, "Seriously, though, are you okay with this?"

"Why wouldn't I be? Noah's kind and intelligent. We have so much fun together. He adores the kids. I would be crazy if I didn't marry him." Lina grabbed the wine and filled her own glass. She took a long sip. "Wouldn't I?"

"Glass down, Lina." Nancy used her professor voice.

"I'm good, really."

"Look into my eyes and tell me you want this. Tell me you're one hundred percent ready to marry Noah without any reservations."

With watering eyes, Lina turned her head from Nancy. "I love him, Nance. Why don't I want to marry him?"

"Maybe the same reason I couldn't commit to a real relationship with Ashish." The truth came out of her faster than she had time to process. Were she and Lina both commitment averse? Had her mom been right?

"But I'm okay with the idea of being in a relationship. We've been together awhile now." Lina looked back down at her ring. "He's planning this ridiculous New Year's Eve party where we're going to officially announce our engagement."

"Just tell him you really don't want this."

"I do." Lina's voice cracked. "I want to be with Noah."

"Being with him and marrying him, being his wife and him being your husband, are two different things. It's okay to just be with him."

Lina rose. "I need to use the bathroom. Can you get the food when it comes?"

"Yeah, I'll get the food," Nancy mumbled, watching her friend escape the conversation. Hurt and a little upset that Lina hadn't been honest with her or honest with herself, Nancy shuffled to the door when it chimed.

The two friends ate, drank, and watched movies under a blanket of awkward tension that neither had enough energy to confront. When Nancy went to bed that night, her mother's words haunted her. If Lucy was able to actually love and commit to someone for the long haul, did that mean Nancy was irreparably broken because she couldn't seem to?

CHAPTER 19

There's something to be said about someone who works all week and doesn't sleep in on Saturday morning. Sleeping in is like a consolation prize—rolling over to face away from the sunlight to catch a few more hours of precious sleep, suppressing the body's circadian rhythm.

If only it worked for Nancy this morning. After a restless night fighting with her covers—ripping them off all sweaty and panting, to rolling herself in them until she couldn't move—Nancy was up with the sun, doom scrolling through her social media. She needed something for her brain to do other than worry about her friendship with Lina.

They had a habit of doing this push-and-pull dance of sorts, seasons of being close like sisters and seasons where they barely spoke to each other. Nancy started to worry their close season was expiring. With everything going on with her parents, the last thing she needed was to lose her best friend. Her sister . . . again.

Nancy knew the signs, remembering how Lina had slowly pulled away from her so many years ago. Little by little, to keep the peace in her marriage, Lina had gone from calling Nancy throughout the day to once a week, then once a month, then long stretches until they hadn't seen each other or talked in over five years. Nancy had tried to maintain their relationship, but her calls and texts would go unanswered. She'd eventually relented to sending birthday and holiday cards just to let Lina know she'd always be there for her.

While Nancy had known and understood Lina's predicament with her controlling and abusive husband, the hurt and loss was still felt. Nancy had had to go through her own divorce alone and, with it, lost contact with her dad because of Lucy's controlling ways.

Nancy's divorce from Husband #3, Michael, three years ago had been another disappointment, but she'd seen it coming faster than a bullet train. Michael had taught philosophy in an adjacent building. She'd dated him for something to do. Something to keep her from getting bored. They'd had chemistry, but not love. She'd been resigned to a loveless existence for some time. What they'd had was a mutual love for travel. They'd figured why not marry, just in case something happened on one of their adventures.

A year and a half into their marriage, or what Nancy liked to think of as sixty-eight thousand Delta miles later, Michael had fallen in love with his teaching assistant. It'd been so cliché and unprofessional, but he'd sworn she was the love of his life, and who was Nancy to deny his right to love when there had been none between them?

Nancy dressed, stilling to hear if Lina was up and about. Rolling her eyes, thinking about Michael and his stupid wife and stupid kids and their perfectly happy, stupid marriage, Nancy convinced herself she would work everything out with Lina. She headed to the stupid kitchen to make coffee for them both.

Lina had already beaten her. "Morning."

"Morning. Get any sleep?" Nancy asked, testing the waters to see if there was any weirdness left between them.

"Slept okay, I guess." Lina fidgeted with the belt on her thick terry cloth robe as coffee poured from the Keurig into the mug below.

"We good?" Nancy asked, but wanted to take it back when she noticed Lina wasn't wearing her engagement ring. She hadn't wanted to pee in her friend's cornflakes; she'd been genuinely happy for Lina. All she'd wanted to do last night was make sure Lina wanted to get married instead of simply going along with it.

Lina nodded. "Yeah, we're good."

"Then why did you take that beautiful ring off?" Nancy helped herself to the Keurig once Lina had her coffee.

"I've been thinking." Lina took her time pouring creamer into the cup. Rings of white bloomed and swirled into the dark liquid until it matched Lina's skin tone. "I don't think I'm ready to take the step toward marriage. Honestly, I don't think another marriage is for me."

Relief tingled across Nancy's face. "That was all I was saying last night. Please know I wasn't trying to be a hater or anything."

"I know, Nance." Lina held the mug between her hands. "That's why we're friends. You call me on my bullshit."

"I can think of a few more reasons why we're friends, but I'll give you that."

They shared a laugh.

"Gummy Bear, Lina." Nancy invoked the pledge of the sacred gummy bears so Lina would know how serious she was in that moment. During college, they'd agreed to be besties for life. Over a bowl of vodka-soaked gummy bears, the pair had pledged:

1. To always remain friends,
2. To never allow a lover to come between them,
3. To never name kids or pets after each other,
4. To never cut their own bangs no matter how tough life got,
5. To get tattoos of a bicycle together,
6. To hire strippers for their funerals, and
7. To always tell the truth, especially if the other person mentioned gummy bears.

"I promise I will talk to Noah and let him know my reservations," Lina said.

"You *can* say no to him. He's legit a good guy and will understand."

"Yeah? You don't think it'll cause friction or make him think I'm rejecting him or anything?" Lina winced.

"Not at all. That man only wants you to be happy." Nancy set her coffee down and approached Lina. She held her friend's hands in her own. "Look at me." She waited for Lina's eye contact, needing to remind her friend that her ex-husband could never hurt her again. "He is not David. David is in jail where he belongs. He no longer has power over you."

Lina shivered and looked like she'd cry for a brief second.

Nancy continued. "You have the right to tell your boyfriend no. He's a grown man who will not throw a temper tantrum. Be honest with him. The both of you deserve that, at least."

Nodding, Lina looked away and picked up her mug. "You're right. I *can* tell him no." She set the mug down a little too hard on the granite with a loud crack. "It's been almost two years, and I'm still caught in David's mind games. When is this going to end?"

"They don't call it PTSD for nothing." Nancy reached for her friend again, this time holding her hand firmly. "You won. You're alive. Your kids are thriving. Hold on to that. Don't shrink again, Lina, not even for someone like Noah."

"I won. I'm alive. Mimi and Danny are freaking awesome little buttheads." She smirked. "I know what I have to do." Her stomach rumbled, echoing in the silence that fell as her proclamation hung in the air.

"I'm glad you know what you have to do. Right now, it sounds like we have to get some food." Nancy made it light to get Lina to smile.

Within fifteen minutes, the friends were in the car heading to one of Nancy's favorite brunch spots. The promise of crispy bacon and fluffy pancakes had both of the women's stomachs making all sorts of noises. A hearty breakfast was the perfect remedy to a night of drinking too much. More importantly, she was glad she had cleared the air with Lina. Now there'd be no off-season between them.

Nancy eased into the restaurant, prepared to order her usual short stack with bacon and eggs, only to be told they would have an unusually long wait for a table. Two charter buses of high school band kids had beaten them by only minutes.

"Want to go somewhere else?" Nancy asked a few minutes into waiting. The smell of the food made her hangry.

"Hold on." Lina squinted, staring into the dining area. "Is that—"

Nancy caught Ashish's dark hair just then. What was he doing back in Athens? And with Elysse, Elijah, and her dad, maybe? Her eyes went big as a plan formed in her head. They were sitting at a large round table with several seats, and only three of them were occupied. "No. We are not leaving." Nancy motioned for Lina to follow her. They wove around tables toward their mark until Elysse spotted Nancy and waved her over.

"Hi, Professor Jewel," Elysse said. "Say 'hi,' Elijah." She encouraged the boy to wave. The bags under her eyes were smaller, and she looked healthier, like she'd slept for the first time in a year. "This is my dad. Dad, this is my psych professor. The one I told you about."

The man stood and reached out his hand to Nancy with the kindest eyes she'd ever seen. "Teddy Mason." He was a little shorter than her with a round belly. "Thank you for everything you've done for my Ellie. You've been so kind."

"We're a family here, and Elysse is one of the brightest lights in my class," Nancy said in her professional voice.

"Do you have a table?" Teddy asked.

"Not yet," Lina said.

"Why don't you all come and join us? We haven't ordered yet. Been here gabbing for a while."

"Good to see you guys." Ashish moved the paperwork from the seat beside him. "Yes. Please join us."

Lina quickly claimed the seat beside Teddy.

The pancakes. Do it for the pancakes. Soft, buttery, sweet pancakes, Nancy reminded herself as she sat next to Ashish. She inhaled a deep breath of him, her lips remembering how his felt.

Nancy cleared her throat to control herself. "What are you doing back in Athens?" she asked Ashish.

"Guest lectured yesterday. Turns out I was a hit at that conference last week. Didn't know anyone was paying attention to my rambling." Ashish wiped his hands on his pants. "I think the university is trying to woo me into a teaching position, and I figured why not check in with Elysse to give her an update on the case."

Nancy blinked. Ashish on campus? Ashish living in Athens? Ashish being within a stone's throw from her? What was she supposed to think?

"My dad made him come to breakfast with us," Elysse said.

"It's the least I could do. You all have been so generous to my little girl," Teddy said.

"We usually do the holidays together since we lost Mom a few years ago." Elysse wiped her son's fingers with a baby wipe.

"I'm so sorry to hear about your loss," Nancy said, a strange pinch in her gut as she considered the fact that people might soon be saying that to her, if Lucy was right about Hank's prognosis. How would she react to such sympathy on the passing of her father? She shook her head, dislodging the hovering sadness and grateful to see the waitress approaching their table.

They placed their orders and fell into comfortable conversation. When the food came, it brought Nancy's good mood along with it. A good mood and a sugar high. She found herself laughing at Ashish's dad jokes and leaning into him more and more as they carried on their own conversation about what it was like working at the university. Nancy tried to convince herself it was to better hear him when what she really wanted was to be near him. Each minute they spent talking was one in which she allowed herself to imagine how they could be if he lived nearby.

But she knew better than to stoke the ember of hope into a flame. That fire would never burn again.

CHAPTER 20

Thanksgiving week was usually Nancy's catch-up time. It felt like a hyphen connecting the rush of school happenings in the fall to the frantic end-of-the-year push. Nine days, including both weekends bookending the holiday workweek.

In years past, Nancy had spent the holiday at her parents' house or with whatever boyfriend or husband she'd been with. Last year, she'd spent a glorious week at Lina's, stuffing herself until she needed to sleep and then shopping with the kids. This year found Nancy feeling like a child with divorced parents. Plan was, she'd grade papers the first part of the week, then spend Thanksgiving Day at Lina's and the weekend visiting her parents in Waycross.

Although she hadn't finished grading all the papers by Thanksgiving Eve, she was ready for some company and decided to head to Lina's early. If she was honest with herself, she was ready to eat her fill of all the desserts as they came out of the oven.

She was almost giddy as she pulled into Lina's neighborhood. Lina had bought a fixer-upper last year. Every time Nancy visited, she noticed something new here and there. New floors and paint here. New decorative trim and lighting there. It'd been new cabinet knobs and pendant lights her last visit.

Nancy smiled to herself, thinking about how far her friend had come. She felt pride at seeing Lina reclaim every part of her life, even transforming her living space room by room, square inch by square inch, into a home that reflected her personality. *Her home.*

"Hey, Meems. Were you waiting out here for me?"

Mimi met her on the porch with a hug after she parked. "Hey, Auntie Nance. No, I'm waiting for my friends."

"How's your mom?"

"She's okay, I guess."

"Epic shopping tomorrow night?"

"Definitely."

Nancy hiked her bag higher on her shoulder, noticing the cute new welcome mat at the front door. It read: WE ONLY ANSWER THE DOOR DURING GIRL SCOUT COOKIE SEASON. Nancy could go for some Thin Mints, but the aroma of baked goods and something cinnamon had her attention when she entered the house.

"Auntie Nance is here," Mimi called and went back to sit on the porch.

"Hey, Nance. Come to the kitchen." Lina's voice was strained.

Nancy inhaled, deeply wishing to bottle how delicious the house smelled. She hung her bags on the nearby hooks and kicked off her shoes. Following the scent to the kitchen just as Lina set two pies on cooling trays, Nancy high-fived herself. *Just in time.*

"Hey, Nance. Hungry?" Lina asked, reaching in the oven for another pie.

"Of course. How could someone not want to eat with all this food?" She counted at least six pies on the counter. "Need help?"

"Yeah. Put on those pot holders and grab that last one, please." Nancy followed her instructions and reached into the oven for the final pie. The crust was perfectly brown and begging to be eaten with ice cream. "I'll just put this one in my car, okay?"

"I have one for you over there." Lina motioned to the table, where a dozen or so pies sat.

"Um, are you working something out? Rage-baking or stress-baking or something?"

Lina laughed. "Not this time. I'm helping Danny with desserts for a community thing tonight. It's for honor society."

"How many did you make?" Nancy tried to count them all.

"So far, fourteen apple, sixteen cherry, twelve sweet potato. Guess it's a good thing I had that double oven installed a few months ago."

"Holy crap. Have the kids been helping?" She grabbed a glass from the cabinet, poured some water, and handed it to Lina.

"Thanks." Lina pulled off her pot holders and took a long drink. "They've been in the kitchen all day. I just gave them a break."

Nancy heard her but couldn't say anything as she focused on the engagement ring on her friend's hand. Nancy had thought, no, Lina had said . . . Nancy bit the insides of her cheeks, tempering her imagination. That weird awkwardness between them was something she never wanted to return. She'd confront her about it later.

Lina seemed to catch Nancy gazing at her ring. She put her glass down, shoved her hands deep into her frilly apron pockets. "I-I haven't had a chance to talk to Noah yet."

"Hey, I'm not judging you. It surprised me just now, that's all." She cringed at how strange a dance they were doing. "So tell me about these pies and when I can eat one."

"How about now? I promised the kids, anyway. Apple or sweet potato?"

"Both."

Lina smirked, then took out some plates while Nancy got the spoons. They fixed plates for everyone and chose to eat outside on the patio for some fresh air. Fresh air for the kitchen. Fresh air for their friendship.

"This is so good," Nancy said, shoveling another spoonful of sweet potato pie into her mouth. It had the perfect blend of cinnamon and nutmeg. She eyed the apple pie on her plate and considered mixing the pies together. Sweet apple potato pie à la mode sounded good to her.

"Thanks. Danny has to drop them all off in an hour or so." Lina twirled the ring on her finger in thought.

Danny bounded onto the patio. He seemed taller that he'd been a few weeks ago. "Hey, Auntie Nance." He side-hugged her.

"How are you?"

"Tired. I had to peel everything. I don't ever want to see another apple or sweet potato in my life."

Lina snorted a laugh. "It wasn't that bad."

Danny held up his hands. "They're still red."

"*Awww*, poor baby. Guess you'll be in too much pain for our annual epic shopping spree," Nancy said.

"I'm sure I'll be all healed up by tomorrow." Danny shot her one of his million-dollar smiles.

Lina ruffled his hair. "Why don't you go and start packing everything. Use cardboard between the layers like I showed you."

Danny grumbled something and shuffled away.

"I don't see why he's being so dramatic. *I'm* the one he volunteered to make the pies." Lina stretched, twisting her torso from side to side in the chair until her back popped and cracked. "I need a massage."

"Are you all done?" Nancy asked.

"For tonight. Noah should be here in a bit. We're supposed to have family movie night."

The way Lina averted her eyes when she mentioned Noah broke Nancy's heart. Did her friend think she didn't want them to be together? "I'm glad you guys are having family movie night. What movie?"

"Um, *Die Hard* to properly kick off the holiday season."

"That's a good one." Nancy felt like she wasn't quite invited. Was she interrupting? Was she not welcome like she'd been in the past? "I was thinking, um . . . to turn in early tonight. Have some papers to grade since I'm going to, um . . ." She thought quickly since she hadn't yet told Lina about her parents. Nancy hadn't found the right moment yet. She couldn't have told her at Danny's dinner. She couldn't have called her up to tell her afterward, because Lina had been freaking out about the possibility of being engaged. And now Nancy couldn't tell Lina because Nancy didn't want it to seem like she was trying to take over Thanksgiving or overshadow Lina's engagement. It just hadn't ever been the right time. Nancy hadn't wanted to burden her friend with her own sad news.

"After our epic shopping spree, I'm planning to sleep until Monday," Nancy recovered in a light manner and almost believed herself. So now they were both keeping secrets from each other. Regret brought a sadness that slowly crept over Nancy. Their season *was* closing, and she'd be all alone again. More alone than ever once her dad passed.

Nancy sniffled, her appetite drying up. She rose, faked a yawn. "Actually, I think I'm going to go to bed a little early. Did you need me to help with anything before I turn in?"

Lina gave her a taut smile. "No. I think we're good. I put everything in the guest room for you. Just let me know if you need anything, 'kay?"

"M'kay. Night."

"Night."

Walking to the guest room had a finality to it. Like, this would be the last time she'd visit for a while, if ever again. Once inside, she felt fat tears slide down her face.

After some time, she settled on her new revelation, bolstering the thick walls in her chest. If that was how it would be between them, then Nancy would have to learn to be okay with it. She'd loved Lina from a distance once; she could do it again. She opened her laptop, logged in, and began reading through the papers from her classes.

The quiet hum of working was exactly what she needed to get her mind off everything else. She hyperfocused on each word, each sentence. She double-checked the students' references, and for some of the stronger papers, she entered them into the plagiarism-checker program for good measure.

Minutes turned into hours; her room slowly darkened. By the light of her laptop, Nancy went through the rest of her papers and entered the grades. The next one she opened belonged to Jeremy Pressley. Surprise and fascination found her as she read through his paper. It was succinct, had a strong thesis with supporting arguments. He'd even cited more than the mandatory five references.

"*Hmph*, Jeremy Pressley. Guess you had time after all," she mumbled to herself, double-checking his references. They were legit. She wondered why he'd made such a fuss out of turning in his paper if it was going to be so stellar. With his past performance, however, something was off. Nancy decided to run it through the plagiarism checker, just in case.

Sure enough, multiple sentences and entire paragraphs came back with 90 to 100 percent matches in the database. He'd definitely plagiarized. Nancy wondered if he thought she was dumb enough to not put it together.

She contemplated her next steps carefully. Reporting it might bring attention from his well-connected parents, and dealing with privileged people in power was not a battle Nancy wanted. Not reporting it, however, was against everything she stood for.

It was midnight, so she had some time to meet her self-imposed deadline of sunrise Thanksgiving morning. She closed her laptop, needing some time to figure it all out. A stillness had settled on Lina's house when Nancy opened the guest room door and stepped into the hallway. A warm slice of pie was what she needed to help her think better. In her fuzzy socks, she slid down the hallway across the hardwood floors. Before reaching the kitchen, she heard soft whispering and laughter. It was Lina and Noah.

"*Die Hard* will never get old," Lina said.

"I know, right?" Noah said. "This pie, though. Come here."

Lina giggled.

"How am I so lucky?"

"What do you mean?" Lina asked.

"To have you agree to be my wife. It's like I waited my entire life for you."

Tell him now, Lina.

"I haven't said 'I do' yet." There was a lightness to Lina's voice. Nancy wanted to yell: Tell him already. Tell him how you really feel. Stand up for yourself.

"Are you having cold feet?" Noah asked.

Lina laughed nervously, and it sounded like they kissed. "I'd be a fool for not marrying you."

Nancy sighed.

"I love you, Lina."

"I love you, Noah."

Nancy gritted her teeth so hard her jaw hurt. Hearing her best friend in the whole world shrink herself again turned Nancy's stomach.

She slid back to the guest room, furious and annoyed. Opening her laptop, Nancy had already composed the email in her head. She tapped the keys and sent it to her department head.

CHAPTER 21

The entire morning leading up to their late Thanksgiving lunch had felt off. Lina had made little to no eye contact with Nancy, and her replies to Nancy's questions had been single words: *yes, sure, gravy, thanks.* Lina had still worn the engagement ring, tucking her hand into her pocket or folding her arms across her chest when Nancy was nearby. Nancy had considered bringing it up to Noah to at least get the conversation started between him and Lina, but she was afraid it would come off as meddling. She'd at least been glad to have the kids to run interference. Their carefree banter, school updates, dating insights, and social media shares had made the day tolerable.

By the time they'd finished their feast, Nancy was bursting to leave. Shopping was the perfect distraction. She and the kids climbed into her Range Rover and jetted to the nearby mall. Being around Mimi and Danny filled her with such joy. It was like they were batteries and she was a run-down flashlight. Just being around them gave her energy and happiness. She hadn't a care in the world around the kids.

In the car, the topic was all about their mom and her impending marriage. Mimi was the one to bring it up first. "So what do you think about them getting married?" she asked.

Nancy peeked at Mimi in the passenger seat. "I think it's great, don't you? I mean, Noah is a good guy."

"He is, but what do you think about *Mom* getting married?" Danny said.

"What has she said about it?" Nancy said.

"C'mon, Auntie Nance. That's not an answer. That's what adults say when they're BS-ing." Mimi turned the music down. "I'm serious. Do you think Mom really wants to get married?"

"I don't think she does," Danny said, leaning up between the seats to participate in the conversation.

"Have you guys talked to her about your concerns?" Nancy didn't feel comfortable telling them how she really felt.

"I did when she first told me," Mimi said. "But she was all, 'Why wouldn't I get married to Noah?' and 'He's a wonderful person' and—"

"And 'I'd be out of my mind if I didn't marry him,'" Danny added.

"Yeah, what he said. It's like she can't be honest with herself." Mimi looked out the window. "I don't want her to turn back into who she used to be," she said softly.

"I get it, guys. I really do." Nancy tapped her steering wheel. "Here's a question: Do you want her to get married? Does that part bother you?"

"Not really." Danny used the front-seat headrests to pull himself up farther. "I mean, I like Noah. He's super cool and all. And he's good to Mom. It doesn't have anything to do with him."

"Yeah, he's not even a problem. It's her. Have you noticed whenever he brings it up, she gets quiet?" Mimi said.

"Or she changes the subject," Danny said.

"How about you two let her figure it out. It's a difficult thing what she's been through and what being engaged means now and all. Adults are weird like that." At the mall, Nancy parked at the very back of the packed parking lot. It was like everyone and their momma had decided to shop after eating.

"Hey, listen." Nancy turned so both kids could see her. "It's going to be wild inside. I need you guys to stay close. Pay attention and stay off your phones while we're in there. Okay?"

Agreeing, they all exited the car and headed to the mall. Inside was worse than expected. People packed every inch of space, and they had to move as one mass to get anywhere. It seemed busier, noisier, and hotter than last year.

The trio picked up sales on clothes, jewelry, bags. They waited in an obnoxiously long line at GameStop with Danny. He scored several of the games on his sales list but was out of luck with the sold-out gaming systems.

Each hour that passed, the bags grew heavier, their feet hurt more, and hunger revisited them. They shopped until the kids begged for a break. A break and food.

Nancy happily obliged, letting the kids drag her through throngs of people toward one of the restaurants in the mall. They knew better than to expect Nancy to eat anything from the food court. Danny took lead, pushing his way through the last crush of people. Mimi followed closely, reaching back for Nancy, who was just out of reach. In the chaos, their trio spread out, and Nancy got separated from the kids. Frantically, she pressed forward, scanning for Danny's tuft of dark, curly hair and Mimi's hot-pink hat.

Furiously, Nancy fought her way through the crowd to the kids, only to find them waiting for her at the restaurant. Only they weren't waiting alone. Mimi was talking in rapid fire to Dimple, Ashish's niece, while Danny was on his phone showing Ashish something. Why couldn't she escape the man already?

Mimi waved her over when she closed the space between them all.

"Hey, Dimple." Nancy smiled. "Hi, Ash."

Ashish had bags hanging from both arms. He shot her a half smile that looked more like a cry for help. "Hey, Nancy."

"How long have you guys been at it?" Nancy asked.

"Hours." His eyes went wide. "Hours, Nance. I don't think I can last much longer, but Dimple wants to go back to Sephora."

Nancy matched his grimace, noticing very large and very full Sephora bags in his collection. "Have you eaten? Or sat down?"

"She wouldn't let me. But now that she's distracted, I'm tempted to make a break for it."

"We're about to grab some food. Looks like the girls are deep into their conversation, so you may get a break." Nancy motioned to the kids. "Hey, guys. Did you reserve a table on the app?"

"I did when I texted Dimple to meet us," Mimi answered and checked her phone. "Actually, we're up next, so we should go in. Want to eat?" she asked Dimple.

"Um, yeah. Starving," Dimple said. "Is it okay, Chacha?" she asked her uncle.

Ashish nodded. "Thought you'd never stop. Yes. Yes, food. Yes, sitting. Yes, air."

Spending more time with Ashish was the last thing she wanted to do, but with their lives being so intertwined by mutual friends, it was bound to happen.

Once inside, they were ushered to their table. Suddenly Nancy didn't mind being around Ashish too much as long as she got to sit down. Her feet thanked her as she curled her toes in her sneakers. She was tempted to drop the kids off and head back to her house to soak until morning in her massive jetted bathtub.

"It's so busy in here," Ashish said once they were seated.

"Did you draw the short straw or something? How'd you get stuck on shopping duty?" Nancy asked.

"My sisters were supposed to meet me, but they both canceled, and Dimple really wanted to go shopping, especially after scoring so many deals when you took her last year." He grabbed a few of their bags to make more space. "I got these. My treat tonight."

"You don't have to do that," Nancy whispered.

"I know. It's okay. You look tired."

"So now you're insulting me?" she simpered, looking pleased with herself when he peeked back at her, blushing.

"I could eat everything on the menu right now," Mimi said.

Danny sat beside her, which left Nancy having to share a bench with Ashish.

"How was your Thanksgiving?" Nancy started.

"Parents are in India until the New Year. My sisters had Thanksgiving at their in-laws. Plan was for them to meet me here for dessert. Picked Dimple up around five-ish, and we've been shopping ever since."

"You were alone today?" Danny asked. "We had so much food."

"Yeah, you should've come over. Mom cooked like crazy." Mimi pointed at something on her phone screen and giggled along with Dimple.

"Were you at Lina's?" Ashish asked.

"Yeah. Since yesterday."

"Are you going to go see your parents?"

"This weekend."

"That's good. Let them know I submitted everything yesterday, but with the holiday and all . . ."

Nancy sighed. *Stupid fake holiday.* "Thank you, Ash. I'll let them know."

"I meant what I said the other day, you know." He gazed at her. "I'm here for you."

The way he said it made her all melty inside. His words were so sincere, and for an entire minute and a half, Nancy believed him fully. She wanted to believe him but knew better. He had told her he was there for her so many times during their frienifit period, but ultimately he'd failed when she couldn't make the commitment he'd wanted.

A few days after returning from Aruba, still on their vacation high, Ashish had gotten all serious one night while they'd been FaceTiming. He'd called himself her boyfriend and acted hurt when she'd corrected him. It'd been his line in the sand. Right then and there, he'd demanded to know what they'd been to each other. He'd wanted a relationship. A commitment. He'd wanted to make sure they'd been on the same page, working toward a future together, but all Nancy had been able to commit to was a solid friendship, good sex, and nightly phone calls. It hadn't been enough.

By the end of the call, Ashish had come to the conclusion that he needed to stop wasting his time trying to build something that would never happen. Nancy, not wanting to show how much he'd hurt her, had told him to go to hell before ending the call. She'd spent the next week trying to shake his words from her head with Tinder hookups, pints of Ben & Jerry's, and retail therapy. Nancy thought about their final conversation a few moments longer, keeping herself from rolling her eyes at his promise to be there for her. She half wondered if he'd meant he'd be there for her if she finally crossed that proverbial line in the sand to join him on his side.

Opening the menu, she asked the table, "What's good here?"

"The ribs are so good," Mimi said.

Ashish chuckled to himself, almost squirting water from his nose. Nancy was afraid to look, but when she did, his usual brown skin had a reddish hue to it. She joined in with his laugh, knowing exactly what he'd thought about just then.

"What's so funny?" Mimi asked.

"Yeah, what happened?" Danny asked, squinting at the pair, who were now in hysterics.

Nancy squealed. "Inside joke."

Ashish held his hands out to them. "You'd never believe it."

"Try me." Mimi crossed her arms.

"It's just when you said *ribs*. There was a time. It was so funny." Nancy couldn't stop laughing to tell the story of what'd happened.

Ashish composed himself enough to make coherent sentences. "So I have to preface this by saying we'd been busy all day and hadn't eaten anything since dinner the night before."

All the blood rushed to Nancy's face when she remembered *why* they hadn't eaten actual food for over twenty-four hours.

"We were invited to a cookout at my younger sister's house."

"She had these massive dogs. I think they're mastiffs or something like that. Think of a hundred pounds of fur and teeth," Nancy said.

"No." Ashish elbowed her playfully. "They're the sweetest things. She has three Saint Bernards. She fosters them sometimes."

"What happened?" Danny asked.

"Like I said before, we were starving and, well, you know how your aunt gets when she's beyond hangry."

The kids nodded dramatically.

"I'm not that bad," Nancy said.

"Sure." Ashish raised his brows at her. "So we went to the barbecue, and they were running behind. No food was done yet—"

"All they had were these small pickles and deviled eggs," Nancy interrupted.

"But we were too busy talking and hanging out with everyone there. Nance and my older sister had a bet going on when the food would actually be done, which made my other sister move even slower. It was funnier than it sounds now, but it wasn't until eight that night that the first few racks of ribs came off the grill."

"Mind you, we'd all been drinking hea-vi-ly." Nancy put her hands over her face.

"Only me and Nance were outside watching the food that'd just come off the grill. My brother-in-law ran inside to grab another plate and some foil. Nancy took that opening as her opportunity to grab a small rack." He laughed, holding his stomach.

Nancy pulled her sweater over her face, mortified at what had happened.

"She grabs this rack between her hands and is walking across the lawn to bring it to me." He sliced his hand out in front of him. "Then all of a sudden the dogs come out of nowhere, take the ribs, and haul ass." Ashish got all serious suddenly. "This woman, without thinking twice, kicks off her heels and takes off after the dogs. She tackled one of them and started wrestling the ribs from him. The dogs—they are really sweet dogs, like I said—they thought she was playing, and all three of them started licking and wrestling back."

"Auntie Nance, no!" Mimi said.

Nancy shook her head from under her sweater.

"When my sister called the dogs from her, there was barbecue sauce everywhere. Her dress was all messed up and her hair." He laughed. "Her hair had so much dog slobber in it."

"But I got that damn rib, didn't I?"

"No way," Danny said.

Nancy plucked the sweater from her face. "I sure as shit did. Got it from three ravenous beasts, but gave it back to them because *ew.*"

"What happened after that?" Mimi asked.

"After watching her completely unfettered and feral, I knew she was a keeper," Ashish said definitively.

What did he mean? A keeper? How easily he'd said it. "Ash, um, I think we'd better—" Her phone rang just then, and she answered it to keep from addressing his declaration.

"Hello?" Nancy covered one of her ears while holding her phone up to the other.

"Hank's in the hospital." The fear in Lucy's voice seeped through the phone and into Nancy's chest.

She reminded herself to breathe. "What happened?"

"Guards found him unresponsive in his cell earlier. I don't." She sniffled. "I don't know what happened."

"I'm on my way." She said it without thinking.

"Nancy?" Ashish asked.

She couldn't say it out loud. If she said it out loud, it would be real. She felt the table still around her.

"Auntie Nance?" Danny asked.

"Nance?" Ashish's hand warmed her back. "Is it Hank?"

"He's in the hospital." Nancy didn't realize she was trembling until he steadied her hand, taking it down from her ear. She nodded.

"I'll drive," Ashish said, fishing out cash from his wallet. "Guys, her dad is really sick. I'm going to have to take her to see him. Mimi, call your mom. Dimple, we're going to have to go. Danny, come and help me with these bags." Ashish called the waiter over. "We're going to have to head out. This should cover our time and drinks. Keep the rest." He motioned for the kids to follow him. "Mimi, you think you can take Dimple home and drive Nancy's car back to the house?"

"Yeah."

"We'll be fine, Chacha," Dimple said.

He searched Nancy's pockets for her keys and handed them to Mimi. "Let's go to my car first, then I'll give you guys a ride to hers."

It was like Nancy was watching everything in slow motion from a distance above. She knew she was walking but didn't feel her legs or even the feet that'd been aching moments earlier. She heard Ashish and the kids talking but couldn't really make out the words from the static in her head.

Was she going to lose her dad today?

CHAPTER 22

In her head, she knew the car was moving. She knew when it turned and when it stopped for gas. She even knew how long she'd been inside. What she didn't understand was why Ashish was driving. Why he'd been so quick to jump into action when she needed him most. Why he'd taken charge and made decisions when she couldn't.

She was there but she wasn't *there*. It was the strangest feeling, being in her body but not being present. It was like her world had suddenly been rocked. She'd thought she had months with her father. Months, at least.

Unresponsive.

The word described how she felt in that moment: unable to react, unable to process what was happening. It confused her even more because this wasn't her normal. She always knew what to do or how to respond. But not this time.

The roads to Waycross seemed emptier and darker than they'd ever been all the times she'd driven them. Ashish seemed unfazed. Focused. That was his normal, his status quo: levelheaded, rational, responsive. He was her opposite in every way. Their relationship never really made sense to her. But what made sense now?

When she closed her eyes, her father met her holding out his hands filled with all the time they'd missed. The first fifteen years of her life;

the last of his. And now, another two years she'd stolen from her dad. Her mind spiraled into all the what-ifs. What if she'd kept in touch with her mom? What if she'd played the game and kept her head down with Lucy? What if she'd ignored her boundaries and allowed her mom to continue to degrade her every single time they spoke? That would've been a small price for something as expensive as time. Time with her dad was all she wanted. She prayed for a few more days with him.

The phone rang in Ashish's car. Nancy pretended to be asleep.

"Hello?" he answered, using the hands-free feature.

"How is she?" It was Lina.

"Sleeping." He sighed heavily.

"That's probably for the best. What happened?"

"I'm not sure. I'm guessing something happened to her father. I didn't ask any questions but could see it in her face," Ashish said.

"I haven't heard her say anything about her parents in a hot minute. Is she back in touch with them?"

"Yeah. It's weird with her mom. I think she tolerates it for her dad. I wish there was something I could do for her."

"Is her dad still locked up?"

"Yeah. And he has cancer. I've been helping them request a compassionate release. Nancy didn't tell you about any of this?"

There was a pause. "No. No, she didn't tell me anything," Lina said softly. She knew it was petty, but a little part of Nancy wanted her friend to feel as neglected as she'd felt.

"Nance had a lot going on. Bet she was working on telling you. You know how hard it is for her to be all touchy-feely sometimes."

"I know, but . . ."

"I'll tell her to give you a call. That or I'll update you when we get there and get more information."

"M'kay. Hey, Mimi needs to practice driving to Athens for when she goes to UGA next year. We'll drop Nance's car off at her place tomorrow."

"Bet she'd appreciate that," Ashish said.

"Wish there was more I could do for her."

"Same here. She deserves so much more. Wish I could've seen that a few months ago." He cleared his throat.

"I'm sorry, Ash. You being there is plenty. Thank you for taking care of her. I'd better go."

"I'll keep you updated." He ended the call. The car fell back into silence for some time, and Nancy began to drift off.

"Told you I'm here for you, Nance," Ashish whispered softly, gently placing his hand on her thigh. It was a sweet, calming gesture that made Nancy feel unworthy. With all that was going on, he'd had to take care of her because she was too weak to process life on her own . . . just like Lucy had said.

~

Bright patches of lights grabbed Nancy from sleep. She woke, clenching the seat belt, expecting to face an oncoming car. Instead, she faced blinding floodlights emanating from the emergency room entrance at the hospital. Seeing the signs made it real to her. Tangible. This was where she'd lose her father.

After a quick text message to let Lucy know they'd arrived, Nancy prepared herself for the worst. The brisk night air was calming as she set her feet on the asphalt. Bracing herself with the car, she stretched, realizing it was the first time she'd really moved in hours. Ashish met her on the passenger side, his eyes heavy, but Nancy knew he'd never confess to being tired. She couldn't believe he'd driven her all the way there.

Ashish held out his hand for hers. "You ready?"

Nodding, she relented, easing her hand into his warm, firm grip.

He squeezed slightly. "Hey, I'm here for you."

There was something in that phrase that gave her a fresh outlook. For the first time in a long while, she didn't feel empty. She didn't feel alone. For just tonight, she'd allow herself to lean into it.

They started toward the large concrete-and-glass block of a building to the emergency room. Nancy's knees buckled.

"It'll be okay." Ashish held her tighter, supporting her.

"Over here." Lucy took one last drag from her cigarette before stamping it out in the pebbles near the entrance. "Took you long enough. I've been here all by myself, and they're not giving me any information."

"I'm sorry, Mom. How is he?"

"Just said they ain't giving me any information. It's been hours and nothing. I don't even know if he's still alive, for Christ's sake."

"You want to go ask about him, Nance?" Ashish said.

"Like they'll give you anything." Lucy waved her hand all around. "But go and see. I'll stay out here. Can't take the smell of that place."

"Okay. We'll be back." Standing on her own now, Nancy forced herself to go into the hospital and up to the information desk. "Hi." She used her professional voice and included a soft, kind smile. "I'm here to see Hank Jewel. I'm his daughter. I believe he was brought in by Ware State."

The young girl looked confused for a second, then tilted her head to Nancy. "The prison, right?"

"That's it. Where can I find him or talk to a nurse or doctor about him?"

"I think he's on the respiratory unit." She hummed a Christmas song, tapping keys on the keyboard. "Y'all have a good Thanksgiving?"

"I guess."

"Guess it's not a good Thanksgiving if you're here, right?" She gave them a kind but apologetic smile. "Looks like he's on the eighth floor, but they're not going to let you see him. You need to check in with the nurses' station on the floor first."

"Thank you." Nancy took a few steps back from the desk and into Ashish. His presence was more than comforting. It was needed.

"Should we tell your mom?" he asked.

"Not yet. I don't want her being all belligerent with the nurses before we find out what's up with Dad."

"Elevator's that way. You want any water or anything?" Ashish said, capturing her hand.

"I'm good, thank you." Nancy watched the buttons illuminate for each floor. It was almost like a countdown to dread, only with the numbers reversed:

1. Her stomach felt queasy.
2. She shifted her weight from one foot to the next.
3. The back of her neck felt hot.
4. She took a deep breath but still couldn't really get enough air into her lungs.
5. The elevator was going up, but she felt like it was spinning round and round.
6. She wiped her palms on her pants.
7. She couldn't catch her breath.
8. Her ears popped.

She swallowed hard, taking steps to follow Ashish out of the elevator. The floor was quiet. Too quiet. It smelled like bleach and sickness.

"There's the nurses' station. Want me to ask?" Ashish said.

"I'm okay," Nancy lied. She opened her mouth to ask about her dad, but fear clipped her tongue. How would she deal with any bad news? She opened her mouth again to speak, but the words refused to spill. If she didn't ask, she'd never know, and maybe that would be better than losing her father.

She couldn't do it. She couldn't bring herself to ask.

Ashish seemed to pick up on her hesitance and spoke up. "Hi, we're here for Hank Jewel."

"Jewel?" The nurse flicked through some notes. "I'm sorry, but visiting hours start again at ten a.m."

"I know, but we jumped in the car as soon as we found out something happened. Drove from Atlanta. Is there any way?"

"I'm afraid not."

"Can I at least know what happened to my dad?" Nancy asked. "Is he going to be okay?" she said in the smallest voice. She didn't realize she'd started crying until the nurse handed her a tissue.

"Hold on. Let me check his file, okay?" She sat in front of a screen, pressed a few keys. "Do you have any ID?"

Nancy fumbled in her purse for her license and handed it to the woman, Ashish kneading her shoulders the whole time.

"Jewel." She grunted, surprise in her eyes. "Oh yeah, from Ware State, right?"

They nodded.

"Oh, honey, it's pneumonia. Came in with a pulse ox in the low nineties. Gave him steroids and he's on oxygen. No vent or anything. He came to pretty quickly when they started his IV line, so—" Her thumb ran down the screen. "Yup, there's a note that he was severely dehydrated. That's probably why he fainted."

"Dehydration and pneumonia?" Ashish asked. "What is his prognosis?"

"He'll be here for a few days with the antibiotics in his drip, and I guess depending on the chest X-ray results in the morning."

The words made sense in her head. Pneumonia. Chest X-ray. Antibiotics. Dehydration. These were all things she could deal with. They were all treatable. That reassured her a little. Breathing deeply to keep her calm and focused on the problem at hand, Nancy asked, "I know it's late and it's beyond visiting hours, but is there any way, any possible way I can see my dad? All I need is five minutes. I just really need to know he's okay."

The nurse glanced down at her phone, then her watch. Pulling her lips to one side, she clicked a few things on the computer screen. "If you can promise to be in and out in five minutes."

"Yes! I mean, yes. Five minutes."

The nurse looked over her shoulder. "Come with me."

Nancy scurried after the tall woman, hearing her clogs squeak a rhythm against the tile floor. Two armed prison guards stood as they approached.

"Now you know that old man ain't going nowhere. Let them in for exactly five minutes, okay?" the nurse asked.

The bearded one took his hand off his holster. "You know the rules, Lizzy."

"And I know you're gonna want to stop by after your shift, Isaac. Five minutes."

"Why you always gotta do that, Lizzy?"

She went up to him and tenderly stroked his beard. "I like to keep it spicy. Five minutes and you better come over later. I made your favorite." She winked at Nancy conspiratorially.

"Miller, you're up for a break anyway. Bring me back a coffee." Isaac pointed at Nancy and Ashish. "Five minutes, you two. No touching. I'll be watching." He pushed open the door to Hank's room.

"Hey, Nancy Bear," Hank greeted her weakly. He moved to sit up, struggling against the handcuffs holding him to the bed.

"Dad!" Nancy rushed over to him and hugged him.

"It's okay, Isaac. She knows. She knows." Hank pried her arms from around his neck. "We're all good."

"You look like hell," Nancy said, noticing the dark bruise on his forehead and the patches and lines connected to various beeping machines.

"I've felt better," Hank said. "Good to see you again." He waved at Ashish, who was now at the foot of his bed. "This should make a pretty compelling argument in my case, no?"

"What did the doctors say?" Nancy asked, fussing over his blankets, pulling them over him, and tucking them in around him.

"They said I'm ready to run a triathlon." He banged his chest. "Lucy here still?"

"Yes. She's downstairs. We didn't know they were going to let us—"

"No bother. She was in here raising all sorts of hell earlier. Heard her all the way down the hall. It's good for her to have a cooling-off period, don'tcha think?"

Nancy could only imagine the words that flew out of her mom's mouth. She cringed, noting she'd have to bring a fruit basket or catered lunches or something for the hospital staff that had to deal with her.

"She'll be okay," Hank said. "How are you, Bear Bear? I'm worried about you."

"I'm fine. I'm good, really."

"I know that look," he said.

"I'm just worried about you, that's all," she confessed, pulling her sweater tighter around her.

"I made peace with my maker a long time ago. If it's my time, there's no stopping it." He stretched his hand out to hold hers, exhaling slightly when she wrapped both of hers around it. "What are you afraid of, Bear Bear?"

"I won't have anyone if you leave." It leaked from Nancy's mouth before she realized. Her greatest fear. Her deepest confession. It was all out, laid bare for the world to judge.

"Let me tell you a little secret," he whispered and motioned for her to come closer to him. "You're never going to be alone. Love never really goes away; you just have to look for it a little harder. Pay attention to the small things. Notice the life around you, because it's there. Little by little, you'll start seeing it. Maybe find it in a beautiful sunrise, or a simple flower after a rainstorm. I'll make sure you're surrounded by nothing but love."

She nodded but didn't believe him. It was a fact: when he passed, she'd have no one who really got her, especially now with her and Lina turning another season in their friendship. She felt emptier in that moment than ever before.

There was a sharp thump at the doorway. "Time's up."

That was it. She gently squeezed his cuffed hand. "We have to go, Dad."

"I know. I know." He blew her a kiss. "Let's not tell your mama about this, okay?"

Nancy started back to the door. "Okay."

"And Nancy," Hank called. "Bring my smile next time, okay?"

CHAPTER 23

"What happened?" Lucy stopped them as soon as they exited the elevator. "Did you talk to anyone? Did you see him? You guys were up there for so long."

"It's pneumonia and dehydration," Nancy said, no fight left in her voice.

"What about the cancer?"

"I didn't ask them about that. He fainted because he was dehydrated."

"Why didn't you ask them about the cancer? They could do something about it, you know? While he's here and all." Lucy's pupils claimed most of her hazel eyes, and she trembled.

"Are you okay?" Nancy reached for her, but Lucy swatted her hand away.

"Of course I'm not okay. My husband is dying, and you didn't do anything about it. You were too lazy to ask about his cancer. Bet you couldn't even talk to the nurses or anything." She spat. "Why did I even call you? Why do I keep relying on you when you're not worth the time?"

Ashish made a pocket of space between Nancy and Lucy. "Ms. Jewel, I assure you—"

"And YOU." She pointed her finger at him. "You didn't do shit. You probably ain't even a lawyer. Where'd you get your degree?"

"Mom, we are not doing that, do you hear me? I will not have you—"

"And I will not have you visiting Hank anymore. He is *my* husband. *Mine.*"

"Let's go, Ash." Nancy started walking away, holding Ashish's hand so tightly she shook.

"There you go running. Thinking you're so much better than everyone else with all your fancy degrees and your fancy clothes and your money. Know what? You can keep all of it. Don't send any more to your dad. Don't call me or even think about me anymore. I never even wanted to be *your mom.*"

"Glad to hear, because you've done a shit job," Nancy called over her shoulder.

"And you ain't shit either. That's why you're gonna die alone. No one wants you. I never wanted you, that's for damn sure."

Nancy's legs begged to run. Run fast and far away from her mother's words. The piercing, biting, hurtful things she'd said made her feel all broken and discombobulated. Outside, she sucked in the bitter air for dear life, hoping to wash the words from her head. But they stuck, clinging to every good thought, clouding her memories with their venom.

In the car, she rocked in the seat, whispering. "You're brave, brilliant, and badass. Boss up. You're brave, brilliant, and badass. Boss up. You're brave, brilliant, and badass. Boss up. You're brave, brilliant, and badass. Boss up." Her words were overshadowed by Lucy's: *That's why you're gonna die alone. No one wants you. I never wanted you, that's for damn sure.*

She was fully crying now. Right in front of Ashish. Her cool girl facade had come crashing down, and now he was seeing her for the hot mess she truly was. Her mother was right: she'd die all alone one day.

"Hey, Nance," Ashish said softly, pulling away from the hospital.

She stopped rocking.

"I can't make it back to Atlanta tonight, and I don't think you can, either, so I got us a room. Just one because"—he sighed heavily—"I . . . don't want you to be alone tonight. But it has a sofa bed, and I'll sleep there."

There was nothing to say. She had no words. She was an empty vessel painted to look like a functioning person—pretty clothes, pretty life, pretty face full of makeup.

Looking out her window, she followed the thin white line along the highway as it ran in front of the car in the dark. It reminded her of the many times she'd tried to make Lucy happy, make Lucy love her. Getting her mother to love her was like the car trying to catch up to the line; no matter how fast they went, the line would always be in front of them. It wasn't just impossible; it was futile.

Fact was, her mother would never love her the way she wanted. It didn't just hurt; Lucy's rejection and now confession had hollowed her out even more, leaving a void for her words to echo loudly.

"I'll be right back," Ashish said, turning into the local Walmart. "Do you want anything?"

"No." Nancy leaned her head on the cool window. She'd usually jump at a midnight Walmart trip, more to people watch than anything. Tonight, however, a Walmart run was the last thing she wanted. Too many people. Too many things. Already on edge, she'd have full sensory overload.

Watching passersby through the patch of fog on the window, where the warmth of her face met the chill in the air, was like looking at a poorly filmed show on a cheap TV. There was the older man in his scooter shopping cart who let his small three-legged dog perch in the basket. He slowly wheeled past Nancy without realizing she was there. Then a rail-thin woman with gangly arms and legs tromped by. Next up was a flock of teenagers, each of them sporting a letterman jacket and hope for a future. Nancy remembered how that felt. Hope for a better life. Hope for a better relationship with her mom. Hope for happiness. She should've guessed none of those things would come true when her mom had destroyed her very own letterman jacket.

When her phone rang with an unrecognized phone number, she hesitantly answered it. "Hello?"

"Um, hey, Nancy, it's Jeff."

Her brother was calling her? He'd had her phone number this whole time? "Jeff? What's going on?"

"Mom could really use your help right now," Jeff said.

"What? I was just with her."

"Got off the phone with her and she's really struggling with Dad being in the hospital."

"She just cussed me out and told me she never wanted me." It hurt hearing those words again.

"Don't make this about you, Nancy. Can you please just go and help Mom? Just be there for her?"

"Are you serious right now? I haven't heard from you in twenty years. Twenty freaking years and you come at me with this nonsense now all because Mom fed you some BS?" Nancy seethed.

"Stop making it about you. God, Mom's right."

"Then you come down here and help her. I'm done with this whole clown show." Nancy ended the call. The nerve of her brother. The absolute nerve of him to call with nonsense. What had Lucy told him? What had she been telling him this whole time for him to come at her so sideways? If he'd had her phone number, why hadn't he called her sooner?

Ashish hurried through the parking lot, several bags in his hands. He stuffed them in the trunk and started the car, rubbing his hands together in front of the heater to warm them. "The temp has dropped so quickly. Are you cold?" He felt her hands. "Oh, wow, Nancy, they're freezing." He turned the heat up higher. "I'm sorry for not leaving the car running. I don't know what I was thinking."

"It's okay." She figured her cold hands meant the ice from her heart had finally claimed every other part of her.

At the hotel, Nancy went through the motions: waiting in line while Ashish checked in, walking to the room, waiting for him to open the door, entering the room. He left to get some water bottles and the bags out of the car. She wanted nothing more than to crawl into the king-size bed, but she felt gross and sticky from being in the mall with the kids and from the visit to the hospital. All she wanted was a hot shower and sleep, but she remembered she didn't have any clothes. They'd left Atlanta so quickly.

Before she could decide her next steps, a slew of texts from Lucy flooded her phone:

Lucy: Don't come back to the hospital. I found someone who will help me.

Lucy: That's what you kids do, though. You make me have to find strangers to help because y'all don't care about me.

Lucy: Your brother does the same thing. He didn't even bother to show up for Thanksgiving. I'm gonna go back home to all the food I left out on the table.

Lucy: I know you saw these messages.

Lucy: I wish I would've put both of you up for adoption. Maybe then Hank wouldn't have made the bad decision and gotten arrested.

Lucy: You made my life miserable.

Nancy stood in the center of the room, thinking of a text message to reply to her mother. Ashish entered minutes later, shopping bags hanging from his wrists, water bottles tucked under his arms. He busied himself pulling out clothes and bags of snacks. "You probably want to shower and eat, so I picked you up a few things."

He held up a ham-and-cheese Lunchable and produced a small can of wine. "All the restaurants are closed. Charcuterie in a pinch. And there's some chips, cookies, a protein bar, even. I wasn't sure what you'd be in the mood for."

She looked over everything he'd done for her, knowing she could never repay him the way he wanted. "Thank you."

She went through the clothes, impressed at his selections. Plucking the flannel pajama dress, a pair of panties, deodorant—the deodorant she always used—and some fuzzy socks, she went to shower.

Her phone was dead by the time she entered the bathroom. It'd been hanging on to the last of its power since the mall. She was grateful for the silence. She shook her head, her fingers slick with shampoo, trying to once again dislodge her mother's insults.

With the water hotter than usual, Nancy's skin tingled and burned. Shaking, she forced herself to stay in the hot stream for something more to feel than sadness. When she looked down at her arms and legs, they were bright red with raised chicken skin.

Her skin was still red when she dressed. The soft flannel eased the burning. After piling her hair high on her head and wrapping it with a towel, she exited the bathroom, ready to sprawl out on the bed and sleep for a thousand years.

When she turned the corner, Ashish was sitting on the bed fast asleep, his head tilted to the side. He'd changed into a white shirt and a pair of flannel pajama pants that matched Nancy's pajamas. She couldn't help but smile. She also couldn't let him sleep on the hard and lumpy sleeper sofa.

She flicked off the TV, plugged in her phone, and turned off the lights. It was dark, but with light seeping in from the gaps in the curtains and under the door, she had enough visibility to navigate her way around the room.

Slipping into the bed, she nudged Ashish. "Why don't you lie down?"

He looked confused at first, then said, "I'm good. Didn't mean to fall asleep. I'll go make up the sofa bed." He moved to get up, but Nancy stopped him.

"Ash, it's okay. You're exhausted. Please just lie down. I don't . . . I don't want to be alone right now," she said a little louder than a whisper.

"Come here." He slid into the bed beside her, opened his arms.

She hesitated.

"It's okay, Nance. You can let your guard down. I'm not going to hurt you."

She turned to face him and nearly broke as he gazed at her. Gently, he caressed her cheek. There was tenderness in the way he traced the outline of her face and down the curve of her shoulder. Holding each other's eyes, they shared a breath, in and out, in and out. Breathing as one. They lay like that, holding each other without turning away, until they both drifted off to sleep.

CHAPTER 24

"Hey, Nancy. Can I talk to you for a moment?"

It was Monday afternoon, and Nancy was in the middle of her planning session. She'd just finished her last class of the day and was entering grades. The last thing she wanted to do was talk to Beckett about the email she'd sent over the Thanksgiving break.

"Sure." Nancy gritted her teeth, plastering on a fake smile. She and Ashish had taken their time driving back from Waycross the day before. It'd been a quiet drive, one they had both needed. When they'd arrived at Nancy's house, Nancy had been surprised by the flower arrangement and bottle of wine Lina had left in her kitchen along with a note inviting her to lunch on Tuesday. She'd been on pins and needles, anxious about their impending conversation, and threw herself into work. Taking a break now would let her mind wander to thoughts of her mom, her dad, Jeff, Ashish, Lina, and the larger implications of Lina's lunch invite. All she wanted was to submerge herself in numbers and words.

Beckett hesitated for a minute before entering Nancy's office, once again dapper in a navy pantsuit. "How was your holiday week?" they asked, adjusting their glasses high on their nose. They surveyed Nancy's office, strolling from her bookshelf to the small lounge area Nancy had set up when she had scored the large space. She'd prided herself on how well appointed her space had been. Glam industrial had been her goal, and with the gold and mirrored accents dotting her reclaimed wood and steel furnishings, she'd accomplished just that.

"Thanksgiving was the usual. Lots of eating and shopping." Nancy kept it vague, unsure of how she'd tell anyone about her father—out of embarrassment, she'd already told everyone her father had died many, many years earlier. "Looking good, by the way."

"Thanks," Beckett said, not quite making eye contact with Nancy as they fidgeted with their tie. Beckett plopped onto the small couch in the lounge area and patted the seat. "Let's talk."

Having enough of the dance, Nancy stood. "Is this about Jeremy Pressley's plagiarism?"

Beckett frowned. "Yes and no. I think it's best we talk it through."

Nancy perched on the sofa beside them. "Should I start?" She huffed. "Let me guess how this is going to go: Jeremy Pressley is from one of our most esteemed families. His parents are well-connected alumni who fund several major programs at the university."

"Nancy, it's worse than that." Beckett gave her a grave look. "Jeremy Pressley has brought allegations of sexual harassment and other improprieties with students against you."

Nancy leaped to her feet. "Are you serious? He's the one who harassed me on multiple occasions."

"He has proof."

"Beck, come on. You're not going to take this kid's side over mine? You've known me for years. Sure, I'm a flake, and I've gone through a lot of the staff here, but a kid? A kid like Jeremy? You know there are lines I will never cross."

"I know, Nancy. I believe you, but there are some pics of you guys at a bar. And he's produced some other photos of you with another student."

"What student? Who are we talking about?" Nancy seethed. This was not how her week was supposed to go. She was supposed to be mindlessly ignoring her problems, not having more shit shoveled into her wheelbarrow.

"Beck," Nancy started. "Beck, I can't go through this right now. My dad—" She choked up. "He has cancer and my mom is—"

Confusion flitted across Beckett's face. "But I thought—"

"I lied, okay? I lied because he's been in prison this whole time and it's embarrassing. It was embarrassing when I was a teenager, and it's humiliating now, and now I guess there goes my character statement because now I'm a liar." She hated being embarrassed by her dad and wished more than anything else she could shake the fear and rejection she'd felt at fifteen. She loved her dad and was so proud of the incredible man he was and how much he loved her.

"Hold on, Nance," Beckett said. "Your dad is alive and he's been in prison and now he has cancer?" Beckett pinched the bridge of their nose. "Why didn't you tell me? You know I'm here for you, Nancy."

"I know, I just. It's hard for me." *To let people in.* "I'm trying here. I'm really trying." Nancy heard the weakness in her voice; the desperation and fear, and it made her sick. *So weak.* She couldn't even fight for herself properly.

"Here's what I'm going to do." Beckett stood alongside Nancy. "The plagiarism checker doesn't lie. He's guilty of that. That's a fact. Of course, that makes his accusations more suspicious."

"Right? I mean, come on, already. Talk about deflecting."

"But I still have to go through my process. So, as much as I hate this, I think it would be best if you had your class submit their final online instead of any further in-person classes."

Nancy wasn't sure what hurt more: Beckett not fighting harder for her or Nancy not being able to interact with students anymore as if she were a predator. "That's complete bullshit and you know it."

"This will give both of us time, okay, Nancy? Go home. Give them a final so hard there aren't enough open books for them to use, watch a bunch of TV, and if all goes well, you'll be back in the classroom come January." Beckett scratched their neck. "It's the best I can do right now. You know my hands are tied, especially with someone like Jeremy Pressley and his family."

"Whatever." Nancy went to pack up her stuff, shoving folders and pens into her leather messenger bag a little too forcefully. She made a scene of doing so in hopes that Beckett would change their mind. She had no such luck.

She stomped from her office, through the hallways, down the stairs, across the grassy knoll, through some parking spaces, and to her car. *Furious* wasn't even the word she'd use.

On her way home, she had half a mind to find Jeremy Pressley and confront him about his allegations. Threaten him so good he'd recant everything and beg for her forgiveness. *And who was the other student?* she wondered, picking the polish from her nails. Her cuticles were all dry and cracked. She could go for a manicure. Anything to get her through this nonsense.

Taking all side roads and opting for the long way through the adjacent town, Nancy arrived back home an hour later, still seething. She couldn't wait to tell Ashish to see if he could provide any legal insight.

Storming through her front door, she said, "You wouldn't freaking believe what happened today."

Ashish met her in the kitchen, a hand towel thrown over a shoulder. Steam rose from several pans. She was overtaken by the succulent aroma of basmati, herbs, and spices. She suddenly forgot what she was about to say.

"No 'Honey, I'm home'?" Ashish smirked.

"Wasn't expecting this." Nancy shrugged off her bag and coat, kicked off her shoes.

"Felt guilty about crashing. This is my thank-you." He did a jazz hands gesture toward the stove.

"I asked you to stay, and you had to come back to Athens tomorrow anyway." Nancy pulled her hair up into a ponytail for something to do with her hands. She could almost get used to this. "Are you really going to entertain an offer from the school?"

"I don't know. I mean, it would come with a lot of benefits." The way he stared through her in that moment made her all warm inside. "I guess we'll see what happens. Ready to eat?"

"Didn't have an appetite until now."

Ashish looked concerned. "What happened?"

Nancy shook her head, not believing it herself. How would she even sound telling him about her accusation? "Maybe over dinner. We still have that wine Lina left?"

"If you're asking if I was day drinking alone, no. The wine is intact. Grab the glasses and I'll get the plates."

They gathered everything and met back up at the table, Ashish in his usual chair, Nancy in hers. It felt so oddly familiar and normal, Nancy wondered why she'd had such a difficult time wanting this between them. Pouring the wine, her mouth watered at the chicken covered in spices and herbs of all sorts. She could taste it without actually tasting it.

"How was your day, Nancy?" He laughed at the ridiculousness of it all. They'd done this dance already, and it had been an epic failure.

"Well, honey," Nancy simpered, sharing in the silliness, "my day was an absolute nightmare." She took a long drink of her wine.

Ashish joined in with her, emptying his glass. "Oh, I can't let you have all the fun."

She refilled their glasses and told him all about the accusation and Jeremy Pressley's plagiarism. By the time she'd gotten to the part about where she was asked to basically stay away from students until they figured out she was innocent, they were on their fourth glass.

"What proof did he offer?" Ashish asked.

"Beck mentioned photos and other students corroborating."

"Damn, Nance."

"Tell me about it. Just as you're about to join the UGA family, I'm going to be out of a job." She raised her glass. "Let me know if you need a room to rent."

"Wow, you'll make me pay rent? That's cold. No ex-boyfriend discount?"

"Technically, you were never *really* my boyfriend. Remember the whole 'no labels' thing?"

Ashish made a face, drank. "That's right. We were just us. Us, but together-ish, wasn't that how you put it?"

"It sounded good at the time."

"And now?" he asked, straight-faced.

"It sounds like a disaster waiting to happen, just like everything else in my life. Like, why am I even here?" She emptied her glass, poured another. They'd gone through two bottles so far.

"What do you mean?"

Nancy was on the precipice of a long, hard spiral down into the depths of her emptiness. Everything she held dear was leaving her, and now her job—the one thing she was good at—was on the chopping block as well. "My mom never wanted me, so why did she choose to keep me? She could've gotten rid of me or dropped me off at a fire station."

"Hey, don't say that." Ashish made his way around to her side of the table and knelt beside her. "Look at me." He had her turn her legs until she faced him. "I think your mom loves you. Deep down, she really does. I don't think she loves herself very much, and it's hard for her to see you so happy and successful."

"I'm not happy, Ash," Nancy confessed aloud for the first time ever in her life. She was amazed at how loose her lips could get with a healthy amount of wine. "I'm really not happy. I'm lonely and feel empty most days. All I want is for my mom to love me, and she'll never do that, so where does that leave me?"

"With acceptance."

"I don't think I can ever accept that."

"You might have to."

"It hurts too much. Why can't she just love me?" Hearing herself say it aloud made her feel lonelier. She looked up to find Ashish giving her one of his signature X-ray looks straight to her soul.

"Is that what you want?"

"I want to be loved."

He brought his face to hers so their mouths were a whisper apart. "That's all I've been trying to do."

She searched his eyes for the truth. It hit her like a Mack truck to her gut, furious and powerful, when she saw love there instead of lust. Fear shivered through her. Could she let him love her? Was she even lovable?

Her lips brushed his, tasting him, wanting to taste more. Needing a taste of his love, if only temporarily.

He stood, offered his hand. "Come with me."

Following behind him without a word or hesitation, Nancy went where he led. Once in her bedroom, he brought his head to hers once again. This time, he claimed her lips. Claimed her very being with a ferocity and passion she'd never felt from him before. It left her panting. Wanting. She hooked her arms around his neck and enjoyed exploring him again. The subtle things she'd never noticed in his kiss before. He lifted her shirt, his fingers grazing her breasts.

"I want you, Nancy. I've always just wanted you," he growled in her ear. "It's always been you." He helped her take his shirt off, pants off, boxers off, and stood before her bare. It was all he could give her in that moment: himself fully, wholly. "I love you."

Responding in kind, Nancy stepped back, showing herself to him for the first time ever. She'd had so many insecurities about her body that she'd always made sure to wear some lingerie or a sexy top or something, but had never shown herself to him. Never let him see her in her entirety.

Tonight, she bared it all for him.

CHAPTER 25

Nancy woke late the next morning. She couldn't remember the last time she'd slept in on a weekday. When she checked her phone, she clambered to her feet groggily and pleasantly sore in all the right places. Smiling, the memory of how she'd felt last night beneath Ashish's weight, his embrace, rushed into her head. She groaned, wanting seconds and thirds. Wanting to maybe, just maybe, try the whole commitment/relationship thing.

Slipping into her robe, she stretched, wondering where Ashish had gone. Panic stopped her midstretch when she smelled the familiar scent of pancakes. Pancakes after a night like the one they'd had meant one thing: commitment. It was so fast. Like, they'd *just* made up last night. She was hoping for a few weeks or months of a trial relationship before even daring to fully commit. No, she did not want pancakes and thought Ashish had understood her last night. She didn't mind giving it another go, but it would have to be on her timing. Why couldn't he understand that?

She stormed into the kitchen, some of her fire smoldering when Ashish turned and gave her one of his knowing smiles, like he just knew without a shadow of doubt that he'd destroyed her over and over last night. And he had every right to be proud, but he didn't have the right to now expect what she couldn't give him.

He came from around the counter and kissed her, tasting like sticky syrup. "Good morning, gorgeous."

A part of her was all giddy, but she had boundaries to instill. "Morning. When is your meeting?"

"In about an hour or so. I had some calls earlier and didn't want to wake you." He smirked. "But I don't think anyone could've woken you this morning." Tucking some hair behind her ear, he added, "I've never seen you resting so peacefully. How are you? Hungry?"

"I'm good." She made some space between them. "Guess I needed that sleep."

"You okay?"

"You made pancakes."

"And they're delicious."

She watched him flip steaming pancakes onto a plate and smear them with butter before drowning them in syrup, her stomach begging to be satiated while her heart searched for a reason to shut it all down.

He set the plate in front of her, pecked her on the forehead. "Hope you like them."

"Thanks." She'd really try this time, she convinced herself while cutting into the stack. The syrup dripped in a long rivulet from her fork back to the plate.

"What do you think?" He leaned against the counter.

"Good," she said, her mouth full. She could do this. She could have this normal life with him and be his girlfriend. She could wake up every morning to pancakes and go to sleep every night curled against his chest.

"So I was thinking I'd accept the position if they offer today."

"You can't do that. You can't move and leave your parents and sisters to be with me. I don't even know if I'll be here after this investigation. I could be teaching in England or something."

"Then I'll go to England with you." The sincerity in his gaze seared her from the inside out.

"I don't want that. I won't have that. I'm not more important than your family. And I'm not sure I want another relationship. I liked what we had. We were just us. Nancy and Ashish, and I thought we made it work. We had fun, you know?" Nancy said.

"We weren't just Nancy AND Ashish, we were together whether you want to face the facts or not. We were us, we, NancyAndAshish. And you are more than capable of love, and I'm more than capable of loving you."

"You don't even know me. You *just* learned about my horrible parents, and that was happenstance."

"Did I run?" He glared at her, daring her to say otherwise. "Am I hiding? Did I ghost you when I found out about something you consider to be your dirty secret? No. I don't have a problem with your parents. They're just that: *your* parents. You wouldn't be you without them. All the good. All the bad. I want to experience it all, Nancy."

Discomfort at his openness prickled her, but she tried her hardest to ignore it.

"I could put my place up as an Airbnb or a rental, since I'll probably be working at the university soon," Ashish said. "We could really give this a go, Nancy."

A thick chunk of pancake wedged in her throat, and she coughed heavily when she noticed his belongings strewn about her place like he'd already moved in. She choked down some coffee, feeling her heart pick up pace, focusing on how his messenger bag hung on the chair, then how his shoes lined up perfectly beside hers, and how he'd moved some of her dishes around to cook.

She felt herself slowly slide into a spiral, wondering if he'd want to start moving other things like her couch to make room for his. Or his gym equipment—would he suddenly want to take over her guest room with his excess stuff? How would her plants do if he shifted them from their perfect window spaces to accommodate for the plants she'd given him?

Would he try to slowly assimilate his things with hers, or would it be an all-at-once scenario?

She continued ruminating about the changes he'd make or how he'd add his stuff to her house or plans they would have on the weekends now that he'd be there and now that they were going to really work to make this thing happen.

Her vision reddened, and her eyes narrowed with each thought. Each theoretical *change* to her home. Her environment. *Her.* She placed her fork back on the plate and pushed it away from her, then rose, needing to feel the freedom of her own body.

"Hey, maybe this summer we can do a barbecue with both our families. I mean, I'd love for our parents to meet."

"Ashish, stop." She said it slowly, sounding out each word to keep from screaming like a banshee.

"What's going on, Nance?"

"I don't think I can do this."

Ashish sighed, looking up to the ceiling. "This again?"

"Moving *my* plants and replacing *my* couch and making plans for *my* parents." She pinched the bridge of her nose.

Confusion crinkled his brow. "Nance, I don't—"

"I can't do any of that. I can't give you what you want. I'm not that person. I might never be that person. I don't even think I know how to be that person." Nancy picked at the belt on her robe.

"Just say it: You're terrified of being in love. Terrified of someone, ME, loving you. You don't think you're lovable." He was firm but kind when he said it. "I love you, Nancy Jewel. I've loved you for years. When you finally said you'd go out with me, I couldn't believe it." He clasped his hands above his head. "I ruined that this summer. I was such an asshole, but I'm trying to make it right."

They were going in circles now, and she had to meet Lina in less than an hour. "Ashish, last night was incredible. I've never experienced anything like that in my life. I like you. I'm super attracted to you and you know this. But that is all I can give you right now. I'm not ready for the moving in and the changing around of my space." She looked at her feet. "I don't think I'll ever be ready."

Ashish considered it for some time, pulling his lips taut. "I'll, um . . . I'll be on my way, then. Think we crossed our signals, or something got lost in translation last night." He disappeared into the guest room. Moments later, as Nancy was tossing the pancakes in the garbage and cleaning the kitchen, he reappeared, bags in hand. "Before I go, I have to say this." He stood firmly. "I saw you this weekend." Holding up his hand to stop her from saying anything, he added, "I saw *you*. The real Nancy. The one who hides behind the brashness. The one who loves and wants to be loved. The one who can be vulnerable and who can trust someone. I saw *her*. I love you, Nancy, and I'll take all of you. I definitely will, but the real Nancy is ready to be loved."

With that, Ashish pecked her on her forehead and left, leaving a vacuum in his place. Nancy tried to wrap her head around everything he'd just said and came up wanting. At the end of it all, she wasn't the woman from last night.

She was just Nancy and she was unlovable.

CHAPTER 26

After stewing in the shower about whether or not she'd made the right decision with Ashish, then in the car over why she'd had sex with him despite her reservations, Nancy made it to the restaurant just in time to meet Lina for lunch. Her friend was waiting outside the entrance.

Lina waved her over. "Hey! How's it going?" They hugged, but it felt off.

"Hey," Nancy said, matching Lina's energy. "Do you have a table already?"

"Yeah. Just stepped outside for some air."

"You okay?"

"Mm-hmm." Lina shot her a curt smile.

After they'd found their seats and placed their orders, Nancy said, "Oh, thank you for the flowers. They're beautiful, and the wine was so good. Me and Ashish . . ." She didn't quite know what to tell her friend about the epic failure that was known as NancyAndAshish.

"Oh." Lina opened her napkin and smoothed it across her lap. "I'm glad you enjoyed it."

Nancy started: "I'm sorry I didn't tell you about my dad. There was so much going on, and then you got engaged and I didn't want to ruin your joy."

"Ohmigod, I'm so glad you said something. I was about to start. I'm so sorry, too, about the whole engagement thing and not being up front about how I felt."

They shared an exhale.

"How's your dad, Nance? Is there anything you need?"

"It's stage four lung cancer." Nancy said it slowly to hear herself say the words. To have them resonate in her reality. "He was hospitalized for pneumonia and dehydration, but I think he's going to be okay from that. It's just a matter of time now."

Lina hugged her friend. "I'm here. You know this, right?"

"I know. Thank you." Nancy inhaled deeply.

"That just reminded me of the time your dad kept trying to smell my hair." Lina laughed.

"Ohmigod, I haven't thought about that in ages." Nancy joined in on the laughter.

"It was what, your wedding, right? Keith. It was when you married Keith and we were all dressed up, taking the wedding party photos, and Hank kept inching closer to me," Lina said.

"Then you called him out and I was like, what the actual hell, Dad? I'm trying to smile for the camera and all you want to do is be creepy."

"It was sort of cute, though. He came up later and apologized and explained he wasn't trying to be creepy; he was trying to place where he'd smelled my perfume before because he wanted to buy some for your mom."

"I remember now. Mom kept saying how much she loved your perfume, and he was trying his hardest to figure the notes out." Nancy clapped her leg, giggling.

"That was hilarious and so cute at the same time."

"Didn't you give it to him or something?" Nancy asked.

"I sent a bottle to your mom, from him."

"That's right. She thought he'd bought it for her and bragged about it for weeks." Nancy smiled, her heart warm at the memory. Hank had always been so thoughtful and loving. The way he doted on Lucy was both sickening and admirable.

The laughter wiped all the awkwardness and unsaid animosities from between them. It made Nancy want to come clean about her drama with Ashish.

"So, um . . . Ashish and I." Nancy looked away.

"What happened with Ash?" Lina raised her brows.

"He's just been *there* for me. Like, he freaking picked up and drove hours so I could see my father. He met Lucy."

Lina grimaced. "You mean he *experienced* Lucy?"

"Yeah. She's definitely an experience." Nancy chuckled. "And he didn't judge me or ghost me afterward or anything. I thought we were on the same page again, but he had to go ruin it and want definitions and commitment and all."

Lina reached for her friend's hand. "Nancy, I love you. You are my sister by choice. Do you hear me?"

Nancy nodded.

"Ashish loves you. That man is crazy for you. What is so wrong with commitment?"

"I've been married three times already. Don't you think I'd get it right by now?"

"But those weren't real. This is real," Lina said dreamily.

"How do you know anything is real?"

"Can you imagine not having him in your life the next twenty years or longer?"

Nancy hadn't ever considered Ashish not being part of her life in some way or another. "But not love."

"What is so hard about believing someone loves you?"

"It just doesn't happen for me. I'm not like you. I don't fall in love and marry the first one who asks." Crap, she wanted to immediately take it back, but harsh words, once dropped, can never be put back in. "I didn't mean it like that."

"I think I know what you meant," Lina said.

"I'm serious, Leen. It wasn't like that."

"I would rather try and fail at love until I get it right than chase people away out of fear."

"I'm not afraid of being in a committed relationship. Just not the kind Ashish wants. That's not for me."

"Tinder hookups every other night are better?" Lina asked.

Nancy felt like they were in a boxing ring, throwing jabs here and there. She didn't like it, but she also didn't want to be pummeled against the ropes. "Tinder is better than settling just because someone asks me to marry them."

"I was expecting you to bring that up." Lina fished the ring from her purse and slid it on her finger. "I love Noah. Maybe I don't really want to marry him, but I'm not afraid to try. You always think I'm so stupid and emotional. Sometimes that's okay. It's a risk."

"But you don't want to get married. That should matter. You shouldn't settle with it just because you don't want to hurt Noah's feelings. It's cowardly."

"Cowardly? Cowardly is not being honest with yourself. Cowardly is not facing your mommy issues just like everyone else so you can finally live." Lina slammed her hand on the table. "I almost fucking died, Nancy. Don't I deserve some modicum of happiness, even if it doesn't last? I mean, if we divorce in two years, I can say I tried, right?"

"Trying is enough. Settling isn't enough. Yes, you almost died. I was right there by your hospital bed. I was wrecked. I didn't know how I would even function without you. I'd already lost you once and couldn't imagine it again."

"It happened to me, and now you're making it about you. Typical." Lina blew out, annoyed.

"That's not what I said. You're twisting my words; I don't even know why we're doing this. We're clearly at an impasse." She sort of meant it, but when she saw the hurt in Lina's face, she wanted to take it back.

"I agree. I think you liked being my friend more when I needed you. I always used to need you in college, then when I was married. Now you don't know how to respond when I don't need you. I'm not a charity case." Lina placed two twenties on the table, stood. "And you know what? I'm not the hot mess anymore."

Before Nancy could respond, Lina was making her way to the door.

"Do you want these to go?" the waiter asked, sliding two plates of food onto the table.

The smell and thought of eating just then turned Nancy's stomach. What had she done? Why hadn't she stopped Lina? "Um, yeah. Thanks," she said, knowing she had to make everything right. She called Lina.

"What is it?" Lina asked.

"I'm sorry. I didn't mean to—"

Lina sighed. "Look, Nancy, if you can't support me trying to be happy, then I don't think—"

"But I want you to be happy. I just want you to be honest with yourself. Deep down, you know you don't want to be married anytime soon."

"It's *my* decision. Mine. Not yours." Lina ended the call.

That was that.

Hurt and a little numb, Nancy found her way back to her car, the bag of to-go plates dangling from her wrist. She replayed the conversation, wondering where she'd gone wrong. Where they'd gone wrong, until it hit her: she'd lost Lina. That was Lina's final straw. Their season had come to a messy close, and Nancy wasn't quite sure they'd ever recover.

Without her job, Nancy had little left. It was like her very own twisted self-sabotage checklist of sorts:

1. Lose the rest of her self-respect by considering sleeping with Keith again. Check.
2. Lose big brother that she hadn't heard from in over twenty years, who decided to randomly call her one night. Check.
3. Lose best job ever. Check.
4. Lose the man she could actually see herself in a relationship with one day. Check. Ashish hadn't reached out with a call or text. He was done; this she knew.
5. Lose best friend. Check.

Nancy guessed they were now ex–best friends. She'd add Lina to her long list of exes: ex-husbands, ex-parents, ex-boyfriends, ex-frienifits, ex-hookups, ex-students, ex-jobs. The farther away she got from the restaurant, the louder her mother's words haunted her: *So weak. That's why you're gonna die alone. No one wants you. I never wanted you, that's for damn sure.*

The guard gate was all decorated for Christmas by the time Nancy returned to her neighborhood. Festive garland swooped high and low, dotted with bright-red bows and oversize ornaments. Massive nutcrackers stood at attention, flanking each column, their steely eyes judging Nancy. Instead of presents and cookies, she had ghosts of her failures. One after the other, reminding her of every mistake, every missed opportunity, every time she'd sabotaged herself thinking she didn't deserve happiness.

Her mind spiraled down, down, down into the abyss of self-loathing. She'd never felt emptier. Hollowed. A shell of a person. Her heartbeat picked up pace as she pulled to a stop to greet Tony. She couldn't catch her breath, no matter how hard she tried. Gasping for air, she gripped the steering wheel, her legs trembling.

"You okay, Nance?" Tony asked, his hand hovering over the entry button.

Clenching her chest, she felt like her heart was trying to claw its way out of her rib cage. *A heart attack?* Her head felt like it was about to explode. She braced herself against her seat as the world spun around her and darkened. All she could think of was how her mother's prophecy was fulfilled. She was about to die alone.

When Nancy came to, she was surrounded by EMTs, being wheeled in an ambulance. The blood pressure cuff kept squeezing and releasing her arm. They rushed her to the emergency room, started a line, and dotted her chest with sticky leads. Doctors and nurses tossed around words like *chest X-ray* and *blood work*. Nancy's head felt too fuzzy and her body too foreign to process any of it.

After some time and some meds, Nancy's heartbeat stabilized and her breathing slowed. Shivering on the cold, sterile emergency room gurney, Nancy turned to see a young woman enter her room.

"I'm Delilah," the woman said, opening her tablet. "I'm going to need a little bit of personal information from you."

Nancy's throat was dry, and she felt the seed of a massive migraine sprouting. Talking was the last thing she wanted to do just then.

Delilah rattled off some basic questions: Nancy's legal name, insurance company, address, home phone. "Now, for your emergency contact," Delilah said pointedly, like it was a normal question because *everyone* had someone they could call in case of emergencies.

Nancy froze, suddenly reminded of how truly lonely she was. She rolled back over in her hospital bed, pulling the covers up over her shoulders, and whispered, "I don't have one."

CHAPTER 27

By the time she was released from the ER, her hands and arms were mottled with purplish-blue bruises from the nurses having to try multiple times to insert the line for an IV. Her eyes were bloodshot with dark, heavy bags beneath them. Turned out she'd just had a severe panic attack and would live. She'd live longer if she started therapy and some antianxiety meds.

Instead of sulking at home, Nancy drenched her plants, packed a bag, and hit the road. She hoped that seeing her father would be a bright light in her life. *At the very least, sulking in a hotel room will be better than sulking at my house,* she thought.

The first few visits with her dad had been short check-ins, but today Nancy found herself excited to spend some time with him. Still recovering in the hospital, Hank perked up when he saw Nancy. He struggled to sit up until he was wheezing and out of breath. Nancy ignored the voice in her head that reminded her he was on borrowed time. Instead, she cut across his room and opened the blinds to let the sunlight in.

"Where's my smile?" Hank asked, squinting against the neat rows of afternoon sunlight bathing his face.

Steeling herself, Nancy gave him one of her best smiles. "How are you today?"

"Didn't Isaac out there tell you? I'm getting discharged soon. Yes sir-ree, I am." A mischievous grin crinkled the corners of his eyes and scrunched his bulbous nose. "Hearsay, I'm registered for the Peachtree Road Race this year. Twenty-six miles don't have nothing on me."

"Dad, I'm sure you're going to win. Guess I should put some money down on you."

"I'm a shoo-in." He stilled as his blood pressure cuff buzzed, then slowly inflated. It was one of the various machines and lines attached to him in one way or another. There were the black stickers dotting his chest to monitor his heart; the thin plastic oxygen tube wrapped across his face, squishing his wrinkles; the IV lines pumping him with saline solution and meds; and the bright-orange hospital bracelet with his name and the words WARE STATE PRISON.

Nancy eyed the lunch tray beside his bed. It was untouched. "Hey, why haven't you eaten?"

"Watching my girly figure." A cough tore through his chest, wringing him out like a wet rag. His arms flopped to his sides, and he blinked slowly as though he was forcing himself to stay awake to be with Nancy. Her heart wanted to reach out to him. To hold him and hug him and let him know it was all going to be okay . . . but it wasn't going to be okay. Not for him. Not for her.

She carried on, pretending to be stronger than she felt, and lifted the hard plastic dome covering his plate. "*Mmm.* This chicken looks pretty good," she lied. The chicken looked as tasteless as the side of a box, and the mashed potatoes puddled in a sad blob beside some over-cooked green beans. Nancy opted for the Jell-O instead. "Blue Jell-O is the best flavor. You're so lucky."

"You can eat it."

"Dad, you gotta eat something. You have to keep up your strength."

He pounded his chest. "Fit as a fiddle." He narrowed his eyes and motioned for Nancy to come closer. "Now, if you can smuggle in some of your mama's chicken and dumplings, I promise you I'll eat the entire pot."

"I'll see what I can do." Nancy couldn't help herself. She knew the "no physical contact" rule still applied, and Isaac was mindfully watching them. Being this close to her dad, she couldn't help but lean in to gently hug him and peck his forehead. "I love you, Dad."

His now cloudy blue eyes filled to the brim. "Love you, Bear Bear."

"Come on, Ms. Jewel," Isaac called from the doorway. "You know the rules." She'd visited enough since Hank had been hospitalized that she knew all the guards and nurses.

"I know, I know. I'm sorry," Nancy said.

"I'm not," Hank added and coughed so hard and so long he hardly had enough energy to keep his hand up to his mouth. When he was done, his eyes slowly closed. His breathing found a decent pattern until he was fast asleep.

Nancy studied him, whispers of the times they'd spent together playing in her mind, until the bright sunlight faded as the sun set. It was like laughter had permanently etched itself into his face through deep crinkles and sharp creases. Even fast asleep, the corners of his mouth turned upward. It brought a small smile to her own face and the memory of the first time she had called him "Dad."

It had been during their epic failure of a cross-country road trip. Sixteen-year-old Nancy had freaked out for an entire week after losing her virginity, thinking she'd certainly either:

1. caught a sexually transmitted disease and was now going to slowly die, or
2. was pregnant.

Every little pain, cramp, itch, or moment of car sickness had been a sure sign of some sort of consequence from teen sex. Sex ed had failed her. She'd lost sleep as they camped at night and had been on the verge of tears throughout the day when they'd been traveling or sightseeing. By the eighth day after her deflowering, Nancy had been a nervous mess.

The family had been in the hot station wagon the majority of the day. Lucy had planned to get to her friend's house by nightfall, and they'd been running behind schedule because Hank and Jeff had gone on a nature trip at the campsite that morning. Lucy had been so pissed at them for messing up the day she'd planned. She'd snapped and cussed at everyone, and by sunset she'd refused to make any more pit stops. As life would have it, Nancy's bladder had been ready to explode. Nancy had been sure it was a sure sign of pregnancy—weak bladder, constant need to pee.

Her legs had bounced in the back seat when she'd initially asked to please stop.

Lucy had rolled her eyes, glancing back at Nancy in the rearview mirror. "No. You can hold it. We only have thirty-five more minutes."

Thirty-five minutes and Nancy had been sure she'd be sitting in a puddle. She'd crossed her legs and breathed slowly, but her bladder had had other plans. "Mom, please? I really have to go," Nancy had said, nearly in tears. The bumpy road hadn't helped either.

"No. I'm not stopping."

Jeff had elbowed Nancy to get her attention. He'd had a red Solo cup in one hand and poured water into it from another cup. Droplets had sprayed Nancy's leg.

She'd struck the back of the passenger seat, angry and annoyed. "But I'm about to pee," Nancy had pleaded, pain in her abdomen.

"Damn it, Nancy, I said no." Lucy had swatted her hand toward the back seat, clipping Nancy's calf with a thwap. Jeff had laughed.

It stung. "Moooom." Nancy had squirmed, crying.

"Nancy Melissa Jewel, you're gonna pick a switch if I have to stop."

"Honey, just pull over. There's a station at the next exit," Hank had intervened.

"We wouldn't have this problem if you listened to me this morning." Lucy had scoffed.

Nancy had bawled for her mother to let her pee, watching the exit rapidly approach. "MOM!" She'd felt a little pee escape. A few more minutes and it would've been over for her. For the seat.

"I swear I'm gonna—"

"Lucy, pull over." Hank's voice had boomed in the car. "Now!"

Lucy had hesitated momentarily, then jerked the car toward the exit. She'd screeched to a stop, jolting everyone forward. "You happy?"

Nancy hadn't waited. She'd darted into the gas station for the bathroom, relief unwinding her when she went. She must've sat on that toilet for five long minutes. When she'd gone to wipe, she'd noticed crimson blotches in her panties. She hadn't been pregnant! Relieved both emotionally and physically, Nancy had wadded some toilet paper, stuffed her panties, and washed her hands, splashing her face.

She'd skipped all the way to the car. The evening glow had seemed brighter. Their car had looked cleaner. Her family, even, hadn't looked so miserable from the distance. Her mom had been off in the nearby brush, looking for a switch to punish Nancy, but even that hadn't been able to steal her joy.

Jeff had beaten Nancy back to the car by the time Nancy had opened her door.

"Hey, Bear Bear," Hank had called from behind her. He'd picked up his pace to close the space. "You okay?"

Nancy had nodded, smiling. "Thank you."

"I think everyone needed to go. You should've heard Jeff. Didn't think he'd ever stop." He'd chuckled.

"But, Mom—"

Lucy had approached them, a thin branch from the nearby scrub bush in her hand. The leaves had been picked off. It'd made a swishing sound as it cut through the air when Lucy had waved it. "Get over here, Nancy."

Hank had drawn up his height and put his hand out, stopping Nancy. "She had to go to the bathroom, for crying out loud, Lucy. Put that thing down."

"She heard what I said."

Hank had stepped in front of Nancy. "I had to pee too. So did Jeff. You gonna whip all of us?"

Nancy hadn't believed her ears. The rage behind Lucy's eyes had terrified her. She'd shrunk behind her father, stepping into his shadow.

"Actually, I'll take it for both of them, if it's so important to you," Hank had said.

They'd had a silent, tense standoff for some time until Lucy threw the switch. Hank had waited until Lucy had retreated to the driver's side, then turned around to Nancy and winked at her.

Relieved for the third time in ten minutes, Nancy had thrown her arms around Hank's waist and said, "Thank you, Dad."

"Thank you, Dad," Nancy now whispered in the stillness of Hank's hospital room. She wanted to thank him for that day, for so many more days they'd spent together, for being her dad.

Hank slept through the parade of nurses, hospital techs, and doctors during their evening rounds. Each visit seemed to take more out of him. She knew he'd eventually have nothing left. Nancy dipped into the hallway, gripping her phone. With a silent prayer for understanding, she called Jeff. He answered after a few rings.

"It's Nancy. Don't hang up," she said quickly, second-guessing her decision now.

There was no response.

"Listen, Jeff, I don't want to fight. Dad isn't doing well."

"I know. Mom told me," he said, a baby crying in the background.

"Is there any way you can make it down here this week?"

"This week isn't good."

"I don't know if he has another week in him, Jeff."

"I . . . it's, um. It's hard traveling with all the kids," Jeff said, his voice breaking.

"Oh. Yeah, I heard I have quite a few nieces and nephews."

"Yeah."

"So can you just fly down for a few days? Would that be an option?"

"I can't leave Amy with all the kids by herself," Jeff said. "Hey, Hank, stop messing with your sister. And pick that cup up before I come over there. Mel, TV off. Homework now."

Hank? Mel? Nancy wondered what they were like. "I'm just worried you won't be able to see him before . . ." She couldn't finish the sentence. She wasn't ready to face the finality.

"I can't just pick up and travel whenever I want, you know? Me and Amy both have jobs, and the kids are in school, and Christmas is in a few weeks."

"How about I cover your flights, car, hotel? For all of you?"

"I'm not taking your money, Nancy."

"C'mon, Jeff. It's okay."

"For you, maybe, but I don't want you throwing it up in my face down the road," he said.

"Have I ever done that? I would never do that to you."

"Look. I'm not taking your money. I made my peace with Pops a while ago. Mel, I said homework. Don't do that. No—" There was a loud crash on his end. "I've got to go. Thanks, but no thanks." He ended the call.

Nancy wanted to kick herself, wondering how she could convince him of the urgency. There was only one way to get Jeff to come down there immediately. With a deep exhale, Nancy called her mother.

"Is it Hank? I'll be up there in an hour," Lucy said frantically.

"Mom, I need you to listen and don't ask any questions, okay?" Nancy pinched the bridge of her nose, praying that her mom would just listen and not fight her today.

CHAPTER 28

Hope wasn't something Nancy allowed herself to do very often. Hope was usually a passing thought or a wish-upon-a-star type thing. But today Nancy hoped more than ever to see her brother in her dad's hospital room. She was almost giddy with anticipation as the elevator climbed the eight floors. Bouncing down the hallway, Nancy allowed herself to imagine how she'd clear the air with Jeff. How they would start over and keep in touch. How she'd dote on his kids . . . her nieces and nephews.

She had to stop herself from sprinting the rest of the way down the hall when she heard the din of laughter and children's voices rising from her dad's room. Desperate was not how she wanted to come across. Speeding up her pace, she froze in the doorway, not believing her eyes. Hank was sitting up in a nearby chair, clapping and laughing, his cheeks rosy, as a little girl twirled round and round in the center of the room. Nancy counted five kids total, including a baby in Jeff's arms. Jeff was taller than she remembered. He had on a flannel shirt and jeans. He looked freshly groomed—hair trimmed and clean shaved, a far cry from the scruffy stoner she remembered.

"Ah!" Hank sat a little taller. "She's here." He motioned for Nancy to enter.

Nancy felt a little weird having everyone stop and stare at her. While the kids looked at her with curiosity, the adults, save Hank, glared at her. She stuffed her hands into her jean pockets and rocked on her heels once inside. "Morning," she said to Lucy. "Good to see you, Jeff. Hi, Amy. Wow, the kids are beautiful."

Jeff mumbled a thanks.

She pushed through the awkwardness and quietness in the room. "Hi." She waved at the three toddlers around Amy's legs. Isaac was nowhere in sight to stop her, so she closed the space to her father and leaned in for a hug. His embrace was solid, and she wanted to stay there for some time. She wondered how he had recovered so quickly. Where had his strength come from?

Hank patted her back. "It's so good to see you, Bear Bear."

"You look good. Did you eat?" Nancy looked around for a space to claim.

"Lucy was just about to fix me a bowl of chicken and dumplings."

Nancy recognized the smell just then. It smelled like plenty and steaming bowls of joy. It smelled like a full belly and warm bed. It smelled like childhood . . . it smelled like home. Her mouth watered. "Hey, Mom, you need any help?" she asked, watching Lucy fuss with an old Tupperware container. Amy unpacked some Styrofoam bowls and plastic forks.

"Think we got it. Was up early this morning just to make this," Lucy said, spooning a heaping serving into a bowl.

"There's the good stuff," Hank said. A cough rattled in his chest. He closed his eyes, wincing against the pain. Jeff offered him a drink from a nearby plastic water bottle.

"Here you go, Hank." Amy offered him a bowl while Lucy filled more bowls and handed them out to the kids.

Nancy watched in amazement as Amy and Jeff worked in tandem, pulling out a blanket and placing it on the floor in a corner of the room. They herded the kids to sit "crisscross, applesauce" with their bowls.

Each child politely accepted, followed by, "Thank you."

Jeff buckled the baby into the stroller and accepted his own bowl from Lucy with his own, "Thanks, Mama."

"You eat yet, Nancy?" Lucy asked, then closed the container without fixing a bowl for her. "You probably did. Or you probably don't eat lunch or something. Am I right?"

Nancy had forgotten to barricade her heart before leaving her hotel room. She ignored Lucy's dig. "Actually, I'd love a bowl. It smells wonderful."

Lucy eyed her for a moment.

"Luce, fix the girl some food. You know she wants some. Hell, every doctor, nurse, guard in this place will want some as soon as they smell this room," Hank said, scooping food into his mouth with a contented smile.

"Come on and get some, then," Lucy said to Nancy, opening the container. Nancy crossed the room and made her bowl, making sure to take only a bit since there was only a serving or two left.

"Forgot you eat like a bird." Lucy tsked. "Gotta keep fit for single life."

"And I'm watching my girly figure too." Hank put his bowl down. He'd had only a few bites and looked like he was struggling to catch his breath.

"Where's your oxygen, Dad?" Nancy asked, scanning the bed for his tubing. Amy beat her to it, pulled it around Hank's head and over his ears. She watched as his breathing leveled, noticing how drastically his chest quickly rose and fell. "You okay?"

Lucy dropped her spoon into her bowl. "Of course he's not okay. He's still a prisoner. We still had to beg Isaac to let us all in here at the same time for at least once today. He's still struggling, Nancy. Open your eyes."

"I know, Mom." Nancy couldn't bring herself to fight with the woman.

"And all you're doing is having a pity party and begging for your brother and his family to come down instead of getting that Indian fella to get Hank out and at home. This should've been at home, not here. Not at Ware either."

Gritting her teeth to keep from getting angry, Nancy said, "Ashish has already submitted the paperwork. There was just one major holiday, and we're approaching another one with Christmas. There's nothing else to be done."

"I'm sure that's what he told you to get into your pants."

"Lucy, that is enough." A violent cough shook him to the bones, leaving him gasping and trembling.

"See what you did?" Lucy cried. "You see? We were just fine without you."

Tears knocked the backs of Nancy's eyes. She bit the insides of her cheeks. There was no way she'd cry in front of her mother. In front of Jeff. She zeroed in on Hank, wishing he could stand so she could hide in his shadow again.

"Luce, I'm warning you," Hank rasped weakly.

"Hey, Dad, it's okay." Nancy put her bowl down on the counter. "Let me help you get back in bed, yeah?"

He nodded slowly and allowed Nancy to bear some of his weight until he stood. Hunched over and thinner than he'd been yesterday, Hank's back was pocked with large brown spots. His chest sounded like crinkling plastic when he breathed too deeply. Nancy held herself together as best as she could, her jaw sore from clenching it so hard. When he took his first step toward the bed, Nancy grasped the back of his hospital gown, closing it, but also using it to steady him. Jeff stepped in on the other side, draping Hank's arm around his shoulders. Together the three of them took slow, small steps, dragging the IV along with them until Hank stood near his bed.

He paused, tears streaking his cheeks. "Feels good to have the whole family together again." He looked from Nancy on one side to Jeff on the other side of him. "I love you both, you hear me?"

"We know, Dad," Jeff sniffled.

Hank's arms tightened around them. "Remember what I said about love, okay?" He dipped his head from one side to the next, pecking each on the forehead before slumping into the bed.

Without communicating, Nancy moved to one side of the bed to grab Hank's legs while Jeff stayed on the opposite side, helping Hank scoot backward and turn. They worked together in small motions between Hank's coughing spurts, until Hank was comfortably lying on his back. Amy joined in, bringing his sheets and blankets to his chest. By the time Hank's blood pressure cuff began to inflate, his blinking slowed.

Nancy stroked his thinning silver hair, listening to the rattling in his chest as he settled into sleep. She wished for more time. One more day. One more week. One more month. When she looked around the room for a little comfort, she found none. Lucy was fussing over the kids, telling them to finish their bowls. Jeff's face was buried in Amy's hair. She patted his back as he sobbed.

That was how it would be going forward. Nancy had no one to pat her back. No shoulder to cry on. No mother or brother to console her. She took that as her cue to leave and slipped out into the hallway and down the elevator to her car.

~

The call came later that night, finding Nancy alone in her hotel room. The TV was on, more for light and noise than anything. When she saw her mother's phone number so late, she automatically knew.

"He's gone," Lucy said, offering nothing else. No condolences. No comfort.

"Okay," Nancy replied. But she didn't cry. She couldn't muster any tears. She felt . . . relieved and grateful her father was no longer suffering. Despite missing him like missing a piece of her heart, she knew he had been ready to let go.

"Not having a funeral or anything. He's being cremated," Lucy said.

They both sat in the silence between them.

"I'm probably going to move to Virginia in a bit to help Amy and Jeff with the kids."

That was expected. Being with the kids would give Lucy something to do. Someone to fuss over. Make her feel needed. "That's good. They're cute kids."

"I'll have to talk it over with Jeff, but maybe"—Lucy exhaled and Nancy could almost smell the cigarette her mom was working on—"maybe you can come up for Easter or something. I mean, if you're not too busy."

Nancy gawked at her phone. Had her mother just invited her to Virginia for Easter? Easter with Jeff and his family? "I'll add it to my calendar."

"You probably don't even have the time," Lucy said with an edge. "Guess we'll see."

To her surprise, Nancy wasn't as distraught as she had expected . . . as she'd anticipated all this time. She chewed it over a minute, her heart both missing her dad and grateful for having known him. If anyone had ever loved her, Hank had. It was as though a light had switched on in her mind, illuminating the truth and destroying all her mother's words: she *was* lovable. This time, Nancy would not allow her mother to take her power. Mentally and emotionally, Nancy carefully constructed the boundaries in which her mother would reside going forward if they were to have any relationship. Visiting her mom and brother in Virginia for Easter might be a good idea, but it also might come at the cost of herself. Either way, it would be her decision. Her power. The thought brought peace and calm to her silence. She exhaled and said, "Yeah. I guess we'll see."

CHAPTER 29

Not quite wanting to head home, Nancy found herself on the road, aimlessly driving from one town to the next. She traced the Georgia and South Carolina coastline from Savannah to Charleston to Myrtle Beach, staying wherever she could find a room, anywhere from one night to four, depending on how she felt. For the first time in her life, she sat in her loneliness. In her stillness and silence. There was no music beating in her car, no audiobooks or self-help podcasts to pull her out of whatever she was experiencing, and no one to call. She was alone and adrift like a leaf in the wind.

It had started the day after Hank had passed when his words came back to her: *Love never really goes away. You just have to look harder for it.* Instead of making a right out of the hotel parking lot, she had made a left to chase after the most beautiful sunset she'd seen. It had been as if its burnt-orange rays had reached out for her to warm her face and dry her tears. Before she realized, night had claimed the sky and the road she'd been on was taking her to Savannah. The next day in Savannah, she caught another beautiful sunset. On the pier, in the frosty December air, she had wrapped herself in a hotel blanket to watch the sun make its final trek across the sky and dip into the ocean.

She had felt her father in that sunset. She had felt him in strangers' laughter. In the smell of the food wafting out of the restaurants lining

River Street. In the beauty all around her, and she chased after it, not wanting to let him go. Not ready to let him go.

It was a few days before Christmas, and Nancy was holed up in some small coastal town just across the North Carolina–South Carolina border. She had been on the road for a couple of weeks so far but wasn't quite ready to go home. Or at least she wasn't quite ready to face what might be waiting for her at home: dead plants, rotten food in the fridge, no job, no friends . . . she rolled over in her bed, doom scrolling through everyone's holiday photos. There were the Christmas-decorations photos, the family-stockings photos, people-playing-in-snow photos, the smug "look at me I'm on a beach while you're freezing" photos, and the food porn. Nancy balked at the people getting engaged over the holiday season like they couldn't pick a random day to remember. She wished in that moment she could call Lina and have her share in her jesting at the tackiness of it all. But she was sure Lina didn't want to talk to her, not to mention Lina was also most likely busy with her engagement-party planning.

The thought of showing up at Lina's engagement party flitted across Nancy's mind. She shook it off, not wanting to deal with another rejection. Her phone rang just then. It wasn't like she had anything else to do, so she answered it.

"Yeah?" Nancy said.

"Holidays suck, am I right?" It was Beckett. "I'm so over it. I've gained, like, ten pounds in the last month. I swear I will scream if I see another cake."

"I'm sending you cake right now, Beck."

"You know what? I had news, but I'll wait," they said.

"What is it, Beckett? You're interrupting my pity party."

Beckett giggled. "Then this is going to be so worth it. Hell, I should stop by."

"I'm not even home. Do, please, stop by. Clean up my place and water my plants while you're at it," Nancy deadpanned.

"Where are you?" Beckett asked.

"Somewhere in North Carolina." Nancy left it at that and Beckett didn't press.

"You're not fun anymore, Nance," they said.

"What do you want, Beckett?"

"We got Jeremy to recant everything."

Nancy shot up in her bed a little too quickly and steadied herself with the headboard when she sat. "What happened?"

"A student came forward. Funny, though, it was the same student Jeremy alleged improprieties with. She brought her dad and visited my office last week. She corroborated everything you said and even gave us a little more than we needed. Turns out she had recorded a disturbing incident in which Mr. Pressley had harassed you. I was quite uncomfortable watching it myself."

"No way."

"It's a Christmas miracle." They laughed. "We couldn't expel Mr. Pressley because of his connections, but he failed your class, and that's staying on his permanent record. He also has to go before the disciplinary board for harassing you."

Vindication swelled in Nancy's chest like the rising sun, bold and bright. "I'm back to teaching next semester, right?"

"Bet your ass. Plus, you're tenured, and that would've been more paperwork than I ever want to bother with."

"I'm taking you for a drink when school starts."

"Only after work. We can't do lunchtime margaritas again. I haven't lived that down yet."

Nancy smirked, hoping her guess was correct. "Hey, Beck, who was the student who came forward?"

"I'm not at liberty to say, but they had to drop your class because there was some questionable behavior on your part. I mean, I get what happened, but still. You're the professor."

Nancy scurried to find her laptop in the heap of clothes on the nearby chair. She opened it and logged in, guessing who the student may have been. "Thank you, Beckett."

"Didn't I tell you to trust me?" they said, a little too sure of themself.

"No, you never said that. You said you'd figure something out."

"Same thing. Hey, gotta run. Have a good holiday."

Nancy scrolled through her roster to find Elysse Mason listed as having dropped her class. *Elysse?* A smile played on her lips. Elysse had stood up for her when she needed it most. Nancy couldn't believe it. Someone had had her back?

Her phone vibrated with a text from Mimi.

Mimi: Merry Christmas, Auntie Nance! We miss you and love you. What did you think about your gift?

Nancy: Thank you, sweetheart. What gift?

Mimi: Forgot you never check your mail. Go check your mail.

Nancy: That's so sweet. Thank you! Can't wait to open it.

Between all the beautiful sunsets, Elysse's kindness, and now Mimi's gift, Nancy wondered if it was all part of the love Hank had told her to keep an eye out for. She wasn't quite sure how, but she felt a warmth, like a hug, surrounding her. "I love you, too, Dad," she whispered and figured it was time for her to head back home.

∽

After seven hours of driving, the guard gate's festive lights were like a lighthouse beacon, welcoming her home in the dark night. Exhausted, Nancy slowed to a stop to greet Tony.

"You're okay!" Tony came out of the small guard station, puffs of air fogging in front of him. "I didn't know what happened to you. You were taken to the ER one minute and then gone."

Tony was worried? Nancy couldn't believe it.

"I'm okay. Had a panic attack, then went to spend time with family. Guess I have a certain flair for the dramatic."

"I was worried about you. Swapped a few shifts so I could be here."

Nancy was taken aback. She hadn't expected Tony to have cared about her. "Wow, Tony. Thanks for caring."

His brows pinched with concern. "Are you okay, though?"

"I am." She sighed. "I'm going to be okay." And for the first time ever, she actually believed it.

"Oh, I've got some packages and stuff for you. You haven't been home, so they've piled up." Tony checked something on his pad. "Pop the trunk and I'll help you."

"Huh, um, okay?"

She still didn't understand. Who would've sent her anything besides Mimi? She hadn't even expected anything from Mimi; that'd been totally random in itself. But she obliged, opening the trunk.

Tony loaded the trunk of her car with box after box and a stack of envelopes. She felt like a kid at Christmas. She giggled. "It's a Christmas miracle," she said to herself, feeling totally silly and still excited to go through the mail, hoping it wasn't all junk mail.

It took several trips from her car to her house to empty her trunk. The packages, letters, and large envelopes stacked high enough in the living room to put her wilted and drooping monstera to shame. She sorted through the large boxes first, not recognizing the sender until she located Mimi's package. It was a small box with cute scribbles around it. Inside was a Tiffany box that held a picture frame.

Nancy choked up, recognizing the photo of her and the kids hanging out at the pool over the summer. They'd decided to splash Nancy, but Nancy had a water blaster hidden in her layers of towels, so before they had managed to spray her, she nailed both of them. Lina had captured the moment they all collapsed into a lounger together. Danny was hanging on one side of her, Mimi on the next, and they all had these wide, bright smiles. It was a beautiful photo. Nancy stood, marched over to her bookshelf, and proudly displayed her framed photo. Her first photo. She belonged in her house. In her life.

She wondered what the other boxes contained, rising from the floor. Nancy was finally ready to tackle the pile of boxes crowding her monstera. A few of them were online purchases. One was from her department head and the university. One was from Lucy. And the largest one was from Lina. Nancy ripped into the box from her mom first to find stacks of photos from her childhood with a hand-scribbled note containing Jeff's home address. Nancy figured it was her mother's way of clearing the air between them. With Hank gone, they had to figure out a new normal.

Nancy wanted to read into it, but decided against it. Her nerves were too on edge over Lina's box. She shook it, wondering if it would be Nancy's leftover box, like the one she'd had tucked in the bottom of a closet for Ashish. Would she open the box to find items she'd left at Lina's throughout the years, signifying a definite end to their relationship?

Terrified, she sliced open the packing tape and peeled back the folds of the box. Inside was a note tucked into a ribbon wrapped around what looked like a dress. The note read:

Nancy,

My sister has to be my maid of honor whether we're speaking or not. Say you'll be beside me because I need you and I'm sorry.

Lina

Nancy was a hot ball of emotions with that one. Of freaking course she'd be Lina's maid of honor. She pulled out the dress and held it up to her, imagining how it would look with a few adjustments.

There were Christmas cards of all sorts, but the one that stood out to her most was the one from Elysse. It was a photo of her and Elijah smiling in front of a lit Christmas tree.

Professor Jewel,

I will never be able to repay your kindness, although I tried. Family isn't always the people you are related to—you've shown me that and I am forever grateful. See you in summer session!

Elysse and Elijah

If Nancy's heart wasn't already full enough, it was bursting at the seams after reading Elysse's card. Her card wasn't the only one. There were at least ten more from current and former students that the university had forwarded, thanking her in some form or another. Letting her know they appreciated her.

After sifting through the cards and boxes, Nancy turned her attention to a letter. Her heart melted when she recognized her father's handwriting. She could barely contain the excitement and longing as her fingers grazed his careful pencil lines. After reading Hank's letter, she held it to her chest, feeling his love surround her once again.

Nancy Bear,

There's so much I want to say and so much I want to apologize for, but I'm afraid we don't have the time. You and your brother are the best things that have ever happened to me. You two are the best part of me.

I need you to know how special you are. Your smile is a balm to my soul. That day after you ran away and I found you at Winn-Dixie so many years ago was the day I felt reborn. I thought, maybe she'll stay next time and we'll work it out together. You gave me a second chance to be a father, and I tried my very best by you.

I'm giving you a second chance right now. A second chance to know, without a shadow of doubt, that you are loved. You are loved more than you realize. By me, your mama, Jeff, your friends, and by that Ashish guy. I saw it in his eyes.

When you first came to visit me, I knew everything was going to be okay. I made my peace that day in the prison. I want to give you the opportunity to make your own peace with the demons you're fighting. I'll take care of your mama for you and everything will be all right.

Look for my love. It's there, even when I'm gone.

I love you, Bear.

CHAPTER 30

The night had a chill in the air that felt good across her skin as she crossed the street to the hotel. She'd missed the valet and had to pray for a space. After circling the block and packed parking deck for an ungodly amount of time, she eventually opted to use the valet at the restaurant two blocks down. Walking the two blocks in four-inch heels wasn't the most ideal decision, and she'd definitely pay for it once she slipped off her shoes, but she was already late, and circling the block for the rest of the night was not an option.

New Year's Eve in Midtown Atlanta was the busiest she'd ever seen the streets at night. It rivaled nights during football games, soccer games, shows, everything. Every restaurant, hotel, club was packed to overflow that spilled out onto the streets. She knew she'd made the right choice.

Once she entered the hotel, she checked in with the concierge for entrance into the private party in the penthouse. The concierge checked her name off the list and began escorting her through the lobby, past the elevators, and over to a set of keyed elevators that went directly to the top floor.

Nancy marveled at the luxury of it all and mentally high-fived Lina. She could do a whole lot worse than Noah, that was for sure. When the elevator doors split open, Nancy's mouth almost hit the floor. The dark room was covered in flowers. Roses in every color poured from elaborate vases and pieces of artwork. Each surface had some sort of rose bouquet on it, begging to be photographed.

Nancy scanned the room and found Mimi and her gaggle of friends in a corner picking at the shrimp. The girls were beautiful, their sparkly dresses matching the chic decor. Danny found Nancy first, two glasses of berry-colored liquid in his hands.

"Hey, Auntie Nance. You look good," he said.

"Thank you. And you don't look too bad yourself. Where are your friends?"

A blush washed across his face. "I only brought one."

"That kind of friend, okay." Nancy fist-bumped him. "Am I going to get an intro?"

"He's over there. I was bringing him a drink." Danny shrugged with the glasses. Nancy followed his gaze over to a tallish boy with a smattering of freckles and wild, curly hair. He looked uncomfortable in his suit but grinned when he noticed Danny motioning toward him.

"Cute-ie. I won't keep you. Before you go, where's your mom?"

"Not sure. I'll see you later." Danny hurried off to his date.

Nancy walked from one side of the room to the next without spotting Lina. She did, however, catch a glimpse of Ashish before ducking behind an obnoxiously large flower display. Her heart hurt when she recognized the girl he was with. She was the same one he'd gone to brunch with after he and Nancy had broken up. *Guess he's moved on.* She felt defeated.

But tonight wasn't about her; it was about Lina, and she needed to find her friend. Somehow she knew Lina must be in the bathroom hiding from all the people. People just weren't her thing.

Nancy checked all the bathrooms on the floor and came up empty. She searched closets, bedrooms, everything and could not find Lina. Taking the elevator back down to the lobby, she asked the concierge about her friend.

"Glad someone finally came looking for her." He glanced over his shoulder. "Follow me." He led her through a maze of hallways to a powder room at the very back of the hotel. "It's for VIPs that don't want to be seen."

"Gotcha, thanks." Nancy waited for him to push the door open, then rushed over to her friend, who was now sitting on the floor with her legs pulled up to her chest. "I'm here, Lina. It's going to be okay."

Tears had carved strange lines through Lina's makeup. "I can't do it. I can't go out there and announce to the world we're getting married when I don't want to get married."

"Honey, why didn't you talk to Noah?"

"Don't start, Nance." Lina rolled her eyes. "I didn't talk to him because I'm a coward. I'm scared he's not going to like what I have to say and he's going to break up with me."

Nancy stroked Lina's hair and held her close. "You, of all people, are not a coward. Sometimes I wish I had just a drop of your strength."

"You're just saying that because it's in the best friend's handbook."

They sat there for a moment, Nancy holding Lina, Lina reaching back for her friend. Lina had taken the first step by reaching out to Nancy with the invite. It was now Nancy's turn to fully heal their rift. "I owe you an apology, Lina," Nancy started. "I think you were right about me wanting you to need me and wanting a relationship where I'm the one doing the rescuing." It hurt to admit but also relieved her to say it. "I think that's just how I've always dealt with people so I don't get hurt when I need anything or when I'm the weak person."

"Nance—"

"Hold on. I lost my dad a few weeks ago and thought I would be alone, but I'm not alone. I'll never be alone because I have you and the kids and my work friends, and I have people in my life who genuinely care about me."

"Told you you're my sister. Blood doesn't make people family. Choice does. We chose to be sisters over drunk gummy bears, and I'm so glad we did." Lina sniffled.

"We did, didn't we?" Nancy chuckled. "You are strong, Lina. You are not a coward. You have the right to make whatever decision you want."

"You don't think he'll leave me?"

"If he does, you'll survive. You've been through a whole hell of a lot worse. Give me your phone?"

"Why?"

"Lina."

Lina handed over her phone. Nancy held it up to her friend's face to unlock it and dialed Noah.

"Hey, where are you?" Noah said.

"It's Nancy. I need you to come downstairs and have the concierge bring you to us. Don't ask any questions, Noah."

"I'm on my way."

"Gummy Bear," Nancy said after handing Lina back her phone.

Lina raised her head. "What is it?"

"I have a confession."

"Then Gummy Bear, bitch."

"I love Ashish." Nancy felt so free hearing herself say those words out loud.

Lina's eyes went wide. "Everyone knows, but I'm glad you finally do."

"But he's here with someone."

Lina laughed, shaking her head. "That's his coworker. I actually invited her because she helped him with my case. She's pretty cool and totally married."

"But they were together that day at the brunch place."

"Her husband was there too. You ran out of the place so quickly, you dork."

Nancy pulled her lips to the side. "So what would Lina do in my situation?"

"I'd tell him. I'd probably do something hella stupid and embarrass myself, but I'd tell him."

"Tell him what?" Noah asked from the doorway. He looked every way like a movie star in his jacket and tie.

"I'm going to give you guys some time to talk." Nancy patted Lina's shoulder. "You can do this." She ran out the door and found the concierge. "Hey, I need you to help me do something super fast."

Twenty minutes later, the concierge handed her a rather large mail envelope. Nancy tried not to drop it when she helped clean Lina's face. Somehow it was too important for Nancy to put down anywhere. She had a plan, and she had to go through with it.

After getting Lina back together, Nancy, along with Lina and Noah, entered the penthouse to applause. Nancy felt like such a third wheel. Carefully, she tucked the envelope under her arm and slid away from them. Noah held up his hands for everyone's attention.

"I want to first thank each and every one of you for coming out tonight. It truly does mean the world to both Lina and me." He threaded his fingers through Lina's. "Tonight we are here to announce something very special."

Disappointment clouded Nancy's thoughts, but she'd try to support her friend no matter her choice.

Lina inhaled deeply, looked over at Noah. He nodded, giving her hand a firm squeeze. "Tonight is supposed to be the night we announce our engagement, but to be honest, that's a step I'm not ready to fully take. Instead, we're announcing our promise to each other." She turned to him. "Our promise that once both of us are ready for that step, we'll take it together. I love you, Noah."

"I love you, Lina."

The crowd erupted in *"awwwww"* when they kissed. Pride swelled in Nancy's chest at the fact that Lina had stood up for herself again. Nancy laughed to herself, knowing Lina would say something like, *We're totally adulting*. Nancy couldn't wait another day to tell Ashish how she felt. It had to be tonight or bust. Knowing it was her turn to take a stand, Nancy scanned the room for Ashish. Nerves bubbled in her gut when she finally spotted him. But something was wrong, because he was waving goodbye at Danny and stepping onto the elevator.

She tried his cell, but it went straight to voice mail. The room felt loud and boisterous all of a sudden. Nancy's pulse beat in her ears, and her hands were so sweaty she almost dropped the envelope.

Lina seemed to have noticed Nancy's change and hurried over to her. "Are you okay?"

"He's gone. He already left," Nancy said.

"When?"

"He just stepped in the elevator." Nancy felt defeated. Sure, she could talk to him tomorrow, but who knew what tomorrow would hold? Would she even have the nerve to say anything to him another day? No. She had to do it tonight.

Lina called Noah over and told him what had happened. Noah snapped into action, getting the attention of a nearby waiter.

"We have the staff elevator in the back," the waiter said, then pulled out his walkie-talkie. "Better yet"—he held up a finger for them to hold on—"Anna. Hey, Anna, you there?"

"I am. What do you guys need?" Anna asked.

"I need you to stop the guy coming down the penthouse elevator."

"Why?"

"I'll explain it later. Just stop him. Make up an excuse. We're coming down right now." The waiter motioned for the three of them to follow him. They sliced through guests and crashed through the kitchen door. Once on the elevator, Nancy put her hands on her thighs and took in deep breaths. It was so surreal and nerve-racking, having people help her. Having to rely on other people to help her get to her goal. Having to trust people with her heart. She calmed some when she felt Lina's hand softly patting her back. She felt her eyes well when it dawned on her that she, in fact, had someone to pat her back when she needed it.

Nancy froze when the elevator opened. She couldn't do it. She couldn't take such a huge risk. Lina's hand was on her back again.

Her friend leaned over and said, "You can do this. I love you, Nance."

That did it. Her friend's words reminded Nancy of Hank and his unflinching love for her and confidence in her. Nancy straightened, took one step, then another, until she was out of the elevator and on her way to the lobby, where hotel employees were stalling Ashish.

Her heart awakened when she saw him standing off to the side, his arms folded across his chest. "Ashish." Nancy looked into his eyes and knew she'd made the right decision.

His face brightened.

She closed the space between them and tightened her grip on the envelope. She'd convinced the concierge to "borrow" a silver picture frame from the manager's desk and print out the photo she and Ashish had taken in Aruba. It had fit perfectly and looked like the frame had been made to show the beautiful couple. Nancy could imagine it on her bookshelf. In her house.

"Didn't see you earlier," Ashish said, unfolding his arms. He raked a hand through his thick hair. "You look great."

Before Nancy could lose her nerve, she pulled out the framed photo and handed it to him. His eyes widened with recognition at the photo of them.

"Before you say anything," Nancy said, "I want you to have this. I want us to have a life together. I . . . I can't see myself without you."

"What do you mean, Nance?"

"I want you to move to Athens. I want you to rent a room from me." She laughed at their inside joke. "I'll move some plants around, and your couch is way better than mine. I want you to be"—she inhaled—"to be my boyfriend, Ashish."

His eyebrow ticked up. "Titles?"

"Titles."

"Love?"

"I love you, Ashish."

Without hesitation, Ashish brought his mouth to hers.

"And I love you, Nancy. You are lovable."

Nancy looked around at Lina, Noah, and Ashish, and in the warmth of their smiles, she felt her father's presence. What popped into her head still surprised her, and though her natural instinct was to shove it back down, she knew it was the truth, so she said it out loud to give it even more power: "I know."

EPILOGUE

"Did you put everything in the car?" Lina asked Nancy for the eighth time that morning, a veritable hot mess to Nancy's smoldering dumpster fire.

"I did. No, actually Ashish did." Nancy turned her back to Lina. "Can you zip this up? I can't reach." Nancy flinched at Lina's cold fingers on her back as she pulled the zipper. "And Noah already dropped her off, right?"

"Earlier this morning." Lina nodded. "How's my hair? Is it too fluffy?"

Nancy stopped fidgeting with her dress and looked at her friend in the bathroom mirror. "Leen," Nancy called to get her attention. When Lina met Nancy's eyes in the mirror, they were as red and puffy as her own. "She did it," Nancy said.

Lina smiled knowingly. "She did, didn't she?"

"I'm so freaking proud of her I couldn't sleep last night," Nancy confessed.

"Same. I heard her come in super late and crawled into her bed to hold her. We stayed up almost all night just laughing and talking." Lina turned to look at Nancy directly now, taking her hands and holding them. "Mimi wouldn't have graduated without you. You know this, right? Our girl is a college graduate!" Lina squealed.

"She really is, isn't she?" Tears pricked the backs of Nancy's eyes as she thought about all the times she had managed to be there for Mimi throughout her college journey: the late-night texts filled with self-doubt and impostor syndrome, the emergency calls when she'd drunk a little too heavily and couldn't find her friends, the heartbreaks Nancy would mend with Ben & Jerry's, the assignment reminders, the weekends in Nancy's guest room when she needed space from campus, and the random pop-in dinners. Pride swelled in her chest when Nancy considered how far Mimi had come over the last four and a half years.

"Thank you for everything, Nance," Lina said.

"Anytime." They both took in the moment, inhaling deeply.

There was a knock at the bathroom door. "Hey, ladies, we're going to be late if we don't leave in the next few minutes," Ashish called.

"We'd better get going." Nancy gave Lina's hand a squeeze.

Lina wiped her eyes, then opened the bathroom door.

Ashish smiled, a mimosa in each hand. He wore a fitted dark-gray suit that highlighted the silver flecks in his hair and in his goatee. "A little precelebrating doesn't hurt."

"Wow, thanks, Ash." Lina accepted her glass and took a sip. "I'm going to go find Danny. He's always so late."

"Meet you in the car?" Nancy asked.

Lina nodded.

"And for *my wife*." He offered the glass to Nancy, then pulled it away, lifting his eyebrows ever so slightly until she kissed him.

"Thank you, *husband*." Blushing, Nancy sipped her mimosa, making sure to hold her glass in her left hand to show off her ring. Several carats in a platinum setting, it brought the cheesiest grin to her lips every time she looked at it. Marrying Ashish had never been planned. After three years of living together, he'd asked, and to her surprise, she'd accepted with the caveat that they'd probably never actually marry.

On a whim a month ago, while in Vegas, they'd eloped. Their ceremony had been intimate—just them, the officiant during sunset . . . and her dad. She'd felt him in the warm sunlight as it kissed the mountains, then dipped into the horizon. It had been as if he'd given her away himself. Ashish had picked up on her change and held her close while reciting his vows to her. She'd had no regrets.

"Have I told you what a stunning wife you make?" Ashish said, gently brushing a finger across her cheek.

"I guess you clean up okay-ish for someone's husband." Nancy stuck out her tongue. They kissed again, this time she half considered exactly how long they had left. Like, could they have time for a quickie before Mimi actually took the stage?

"Nance, where do you want the caterer to set up?" Lina called from another room.

"I love you. Go handle that. I'll see you in the car." Ashish waited for Nancy to drink another few sips, then took her glass.

"I love you more, Ash." Nancy kissed his cheek before heading to the kitchen to manage everything for the epic graduation party she'd planned. In the kitchen, she showed the caterer where to stage and how to access the grill. She pointed out the tables and chairs to set out in the backyard and where to put the bar. She even double-checked the obnoxious cake she'd had made just for Mimi.

Once satisfied that everything would be perfect by the time they returned, Nancy met Ashish in the garage. He held her hand and led her to the limousine waiting on the curb. Inside, Lina and Noah were snuggled and laughing at something on his phone. Lina winked at Nancy as she slid into the seat.

"How's married life, man?" Noah asked Ashish once the limo started moving.

"I'm still paying rent for a room, if that's any indication," Ashish said.

Nancy elbowed him. "Just a room? I thought you were paying the mortgage now."

Ashish feigned being hurt. "If that's what my wife wants."

Nancy eased back into her seat. "I could get used to this. You sure you're not changing your mind, Lina?"

Lina looked at her own ring, then at Noah. "I think we're good."

"Marry the man, already," Danny said and everyone laughed.

"Maybe."

Noah kissed her hand. "I'll take a maybe."

"Not happening." Nancy swatted Danny's hand as he reached for one of the mini bottles. "You're not twenty-one yet, bro."

"But we're in a limo," Danny said.

"Twenty-one." Nancy raised an eyebrow, daring him to try again. Instead he sat back, falling into a conversation with his boyfriend.

A text sounded on Nancy's phone. She opened it, glad to see it was from Jeff.

Jeff: We're running late.

Nancy: Mom?

Jeff: She's still mad you eloped.

Nancy: Let her stay mad. Why don't you leave the kids with her and come. You and Amy need a night out anyway.

Jeff: Amy says it's a deal.

Jeff: We'll meet up at your house later. Need me to pick anything up?

Nancy: Nope. Everything's taken care of.

Jeff: Mom's grumbling, but she's fine with the kids. They'll keep her good and busy.

Nancy: Ha. I bet. As long as tomorrow is my day.

Jeff: I thought you claimed the whole weekend.

Nancy: You know I did. We'll talk about it tonight. You guys be safe.

Jeff: See you in a bit.

Leaning back into Ashish's embrace, Nancy glanced down at her phone, then around the limo, feeling so much love she felt full. She'd been treated to a buffet and still wanted more. Love—that had been Hank's purpose. To show Nancy love and to have her feel it even when he was gone. She was loved. She was capable of loving. She was lovable.

ACKNOWLEDGMENTS

If you find yourself in the pages of this novel, please know you are loved.

Having a narcissistic parent has the ability to keep you from living your truth. I'm here to tell you to live that truth. Set those boundaries. Love yourself. You will never be able to fix them, but you can fix yourself by living the life you were meant to live.

When my debut, *Paper Doll Lina*, came out, I was overwhelmed by all the support I received. From the kind words, reviews, direct messages, and emails, readers shared their own stories of survival and overcoming. For that, I will forever be grateful.

You are seen and heard, and I am right here cheering you on as you make the difficult decisions.

To my editor, Alicia, your patience and encouragement when I lost my sister is something I'll never forget. Your keen eye breathes life into my drafts, and for that, thank you.

To the entire Lake Union team, you all are so very talented and passionate, and I thank you for your efforts.

Kat, my brilliant agent, I can never thank you enough. You continue to make my dreams come true, and I look forward to sending you all the books.

My writing family and community, I would be nowhere without you. I'm so thankful I found you so many years ago.

To my parents, my sisters, my friends, thank you for understanding the missed phone calls, the three-days-later text-message responses, the memes, GIFs, and TikToks sent for sanity, and my hectic work schedule.

To my children, Charlie and Hannah, you guys are truly the very best kids any parent could ask for. Your resilience, kindness, and love continually feed my creativity and keep me striving to be a better mom every single day.

And finally, Jae, from 1997 to now, I imagine the different lives we've lived both together and apart throughout eternity, and each one brings me back to you. Thank you for loving me and for our life together.

ABOUT THE AUTHOR

Photo © 2020 Ron Querido

After finding her way to Atlanta, Georgia, by way of Hawaii, the US Virgin Islands, Miami, and South Carolina, Robyn Lucas developed a successful career in communications and marketing. Her background came in handy when her teenagers created an award-winning mental health app. But living the fabulous life is tough, so Robyn grounds herself with piles of laundry, managing busy teenpreneurs, and writing women's fiction because it's cheaper than therapy. When Robyn is not writing (using a spreadsheet filled with plot bunnies for countless novels), she enjoys traveling, spending time with her teens, marathoning (TV shows, not running), reading, and snuggling with her dog, Trooper. She is also the author of *Paper Doll Lina*. For more information, visit www.robynlucas.com.